Pirate's Parole

Andy Neville

Written & Published by **Andy Neville**

Cover Illustration by **Elizabeth Peiró**
Back Cover Photograph by **Faisal Waheed**

www.andynevilleauthor.com

It's more fun to be a pirate than to join the navy.

—STEVE JOBS

Content Warnings:

To avoid spoilers, relevant content warnings are listed at the back of this book. Skip ahead to Page 315 to view these if you are sensitive to some themes.

Pirate's Parole

THE ISLAND

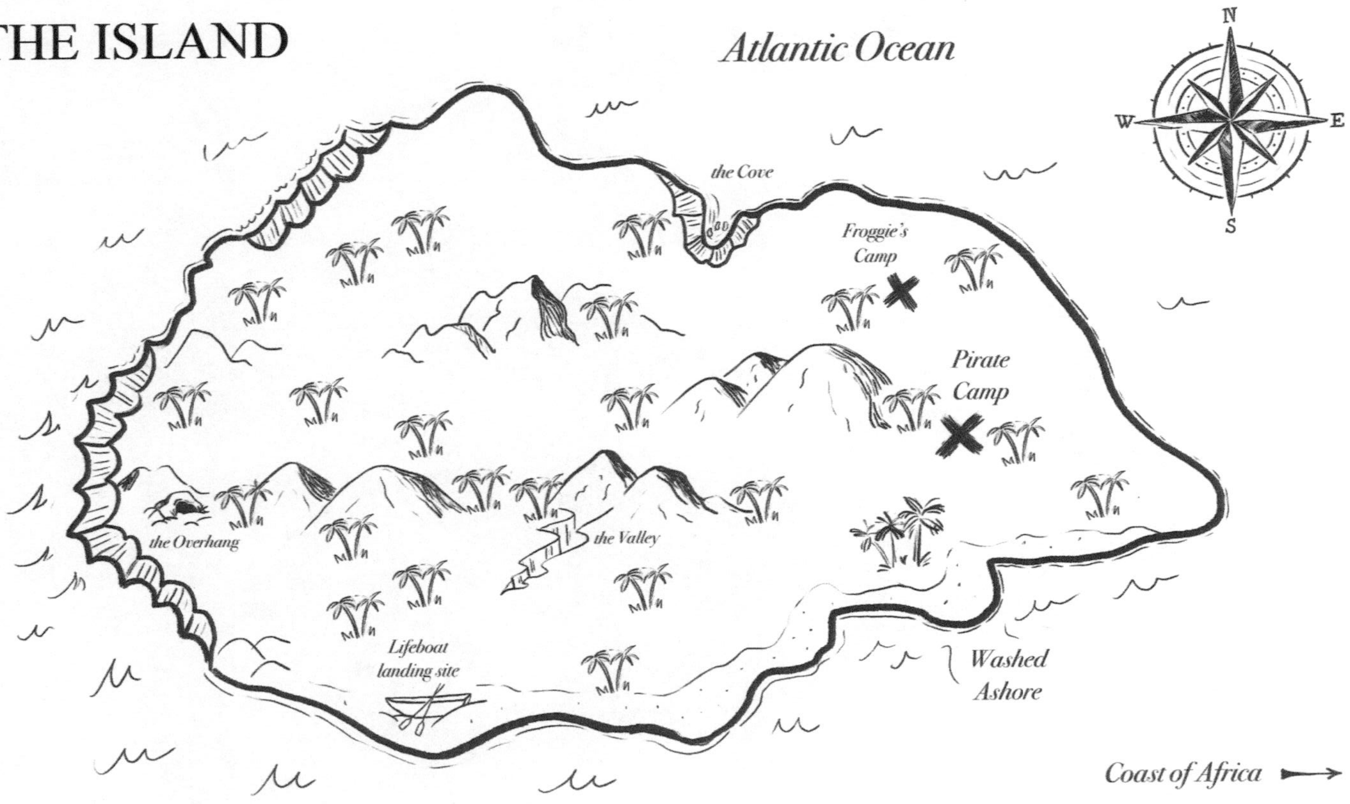
Atlantic Ocean
N
W
E
S
the Cove
Froggie's Camp
Pirate Camp
the Overhang
the Valley
Lifeboat landing site
Washed Ashore
Coast of Africa

$$— 1 —$$

Bodies littered the deck. Some were peppered with musket shot, others had swords still stuck between their ribs. The enemy dead were easily distinguishable by their meagerness; they wore only filthy shirts and breeches under poorly-patched coats. Some still had their hats, but very few of them had boots. Here and there the bodies of navy men stood out among them, in their bloodstained blue coats or white shirts, some of these still loose from frantic dressing in the dark. Around the piled dead, the deck ran thick with the blood of friend and foe alike, puddling together.

Admiral Wickerham was furious. On the deck below, his men hurried to gather the prisoners aside, keeping them pinned to the forward rail with pistols and swords as the admiral paced up and down the quarterdeck beside the body of Masterman, his first lieutenant, who had been killed in the first pass. The pirates' wallowing frigate had fired a canvas bag filled with lead shot, nails, spikes and glass in place of a cannonball, spraying the deck where the morning watch had only just seen their approach. Too late to even shout a warning. Without lights, the small, ungainly ship had managed to come up on the HMS *Courage* during the night. The ensuing battle had lasted so long that the sun had long-since risen.

Lieutenant Masterman's face had been covered carefully with a piece of sailcloth. The deck underneath his body was black with blood that had burst from a thousand simultaneous wounds when the ball hit directly where he stood. He had died instantly, the only small mercy that had been allowed him.

"Thomas!" Wickerham snapped, coming to a sudden halt. He had a deep gash to the side of his head; the surgeon had tried to treat him on deck and had been refused. A rising breeze whipped at the hem of his coat where there was a long tear; someone had tried to stab him in the back, but the sword had caught in the heavy fabric and sliced it almost in half when the admiral spun around and slit the man's throat.

Wickerham was in his late fifties, quite old now for the sea-faring life, but he was still as quick and robust as he had been as a young captain. He wouldn't give mind to anyone who suggested that he should retire gracefully to the country. It was said with pride by his men that salt water ran in his veins. It was even rumoured among them that Wickerham, decorated hero of the Battle of St Laurence, could swim like a fish — a skill that not many officers could boast. Despite his injury he stood tall and resolute; the very image of a King's man.

As Lieutenant Thomas approached the stair, he noted the very deep shade of red that coloured his captain's ruddy face, so deep in places it was almost purple. He'd never seen the man so angry, and it was enough to make his stomach twist with nerves. "Yes sir?" he panted, the heel of his boot skidding in a pool of blood and seawater as he came up the last step to Wickerham's side.

"Tell Harris I want their leader here immediately," the admiral said stiffly, turning his face towards the sea and into the breeze, perhaps hoping for some relief from the overpowering stench of death around them.

"Ah… the captain is dead, sir," Thomas pointed out, his gaze darting momentarily to where an unremarkable man lay in a sad heap with a surprised look on his face and a red hole in his throat. His hair was thin and balding, and beside him on a river of blood floated a ridiculous feathered hat, drifting in the breeze.

"I am aware of that, Lieutenant. I killed him myself," Wickerham replied. "Have Harris fetch whoever claims the command and bring him to me. Then have the blasted cowards lined up there. Go on, man," he added, his voice sharp with impatience.

Thomas nodded and hurried away, doing his best to keep his feet steady on the perilously glistening boards of the deck. His stomach roiled at the sight, the blood an inch thick in places. Having been at sea since the age of twelve, he had seen and fought in many battles, but none like this.

As the deckhands began to clear away the dead, he thought that he couldn't quite agree with the admiral's assessment that the pirates were cowards. For any frigate, let alone one in such poor condition, to attack a second-rate ship of the line was unheard of. The pirates' only advantage had been the element of surprise. In the end, the *Courage* had managed to bring her guns around to bear, and blasted aside most of the frigate's hull. The pirates, those who could jump the gap, had boarded just in time, though for most of them it had only been a temporary safety.

Looking over the starboard rail, Thomas could see the ugly

black sow of a ship sinking slowly in the distance. *And good rid-dance*, he thought, darkly. Until today he had never even seen a real pirate, but he still held the same righteous disdain for the men who turned seas to blood in their endless appetite for plunder as did any man who ever met with them. For the most part these men — and even the odd woman thrust into the life by birth or sin — had been eradicated over the last century, their numbers dwindling until only a few unhappy bands of brigands remained, keeping mainly to the strands of coastline they could reasonably control. Others went into slave-trading, an easier and legal — if no more moral — means of making a fortune out of human suffer-ing. Most crews, seeing a ship of the Royal Navy anywhere on the horizon, would make sail immediately and head in the opposite direction. It was impossible to say why this one had done such a foolhardy thing as to sail directly into the mouths of ninety guns.

Thomas found his superior, Second Lieutenant Fredrick Harris, directing the men who were standing guard over the pitiful remainder of the pirate crew. Harris had been second lieutenant, and would now have to take over Masterman's duties, which meant that Thomas would be doing Harris' work as well as his own unless Wickerham saw fit to promote an acting lieutenant from among the other officers. "Harris!" Thomas called out as he approached.

"Keep them steady, Gower," Harris instructed the stocky mid-shipman, who had a pistol in one hand and a sword in the other, both of them trained on the ragged men who stood in a disorgan-ised huddle against the rail. Harris turned to Thomas, his long fair hair coming out of its neat queue and stained brown with blood and filth in great disparity to his usually spotless appearance. "I hope you're here to tell me the admiral wants them all shot," he said, in a tone not at all confidential.

"Sorry sir." Thomas' lips twitched. He kept his eyes averted from the prisoners, not wanting to inadvertently meet any of their eyes. "He wants whomever is willing to speak for them, and to have them line up below the poop deck."

"Going to make a speech," someone muttered from behind them. "We ought to feed to them to the sharks." Thomas looked around, eyes narrowed, but over half the sailors were engaged in separating the dead with their heads down; it was impossible to tell who had spoken. Only one of the seamen met his eyes: a burly, dark-haired man with a blue tattoo curling out the collar of his loose shirt. Thomas found himself smiling with relief; Bill Blake had survived, then. The man acknowledged him with a careful nod before bowing back to his own work.

"That'll be quite enough of that, thank you," Harris said sharply, to all who could hear. "Any more mutinous remarks and those responsible shall be spending the rest of the voyage in the brig… where there will be very little room, I imagine," he added, with heavy distaste. He turned back to the group of pirates. "Who among you has seniority?" he demanded.

There was silence from the ragged band, other than some resentful muttering and groans of the wounded from somewhere in their midst. "Speak up," Harris snapped impatiently. "Who was second in command? Have you a mate? A boatswain?"

"You killed them!" one of the pirates piped up in a reedy voice from the middle of the ragged group.

Harris' jaw clenched. "A sailing master, then."

"*We* killed him," sniggered another voice. "Smarmy French bastard, couldn' unnerstand a word 'e was sayin'." A murmur of amused agreement went through the ranks.

As he turned to look properly at what was left of the pirate band, Thomas realised his brow was set in a deep frown; he tried to relax his face, not wanting to give away his discomfort. Looking at them closely for the first time in the light of day, he could see old wounds on many of them. Some had scars around their wrists and bare ankles — former slaves, perhaps, or jailbirds. They had mostly rotting, yellowing teeth and hair matted with neglect, the fair ones made ruddy and skin cracked with sun and sea exposure. Several had fresh wounds they had bound inexpertly with what scraps of material they could tear from their own clothing; some being kept standing by their fellows. It was truly pitiful, and yet, with most of their crew slaughtered, and facing execution themselves, none of these men cared enough to show any fear.

"Shall I tell the admiral they won't comply?" Thomas asked Harris, keeping his voice low.

"No." Harris, white with fury under his dirt, put a hand to his sword hilt. "One of you will step forward," he demanded of the pirates. "Or I choose a man myself, and then another, and each man will be flogged to within an inch of his life until someone takes command."

Thomas did his best not to show his real disgust. He understood that the pirates' sense of honour — or lack thereof — was shocking, but the proposed punishment was a sickening suggestion, after so much blood and carnage that day already. He had no doubt that Harris would go through with it, either; the tall man was an officer and a gentleman in his manner and appearance, but he had demonstrated from time to time a tendency to meanness that most often had its effect on the sailors of lower rank who could do little to protest their treatment. His temper also had a tendency to get the better of him, an unfortunate failing that was prevalent among too many officers.

Fortunately, the threat seemed to have already carried out its intended purpose. There was a low, urgent murmuring among the pirates, and finally a man pushed his way through to the front, the others parting to let him through. He had a thin, almost gaunt face, with hollow cheeks and black eyes. One of his hands, the right, was red to the wrist with blood, as though he had had it around the hilt of a knife buried into flesh. He was one of the better dressed of the pirates, with black boots over his trousers and a loose-hanging brown coat. "Osham Briggs, if y'please," he announced himself, sneering. His accent was English, but only in the sense that it was not French, or German. It was thicker with sea brogue than any Thomas had ever heard in his seven years at sea, almost incomprehensible. "I'll be cap'n o' this sorry lot, if ye insist," he drawled.

"We do," Harris said flatly. "Come with us, *Mister* Briggs." He spat, rather than said the word *mister*, giving it all the contempt he clearly felt it deserved. "Gower, have the rest of them lined up along the quarterdeck, if you please."

"Yes sir." Gower nodded, as his hands were too occupied with sword and pistol to salute.

Harris had Briggs walk ahead of him at sword-point. Thomas

could not do anything to help but keep watch, as his sword had been mislaid somewhere in the chaos of the battle. He would have to find it later; it had been a present from his parents which he should hate to lose.

"Do you think the admiral *will* have them shot?" he asked Harris in an undertone as they stepped around the remaining bodies and debris still littering the deck. "Surely we can't hold all of them."

"You know the admiral," Harris replied, in a tone that suggested he was trying not to sound critical. "He's a god-fearing man. Even murderous pirates cannot be executed without a trial. He will insist on taking them all back to England, for all they'll make a mockery of our supply. We shall have to put in again and add a week to our course. A shame we had to sink their ship," he added, wistfully. "We could have kept them aboard there, at least, then we wouldn't have to smell them for the next four months."

"I'd like to see what the admiralty board would have to say about taking a pirate's ship as prize," Thomas said, with thick irony. "Besides, with poor Masterman dead, *you* should have been put in command of it. I wouldn't wish that privilege on any man, from what we saw of her before she went down."

"Ha!" their captive interrupted, drawing the attention of everyone around them. "Ye're right there — what a pile' o' seagull shit!"

"Shut your mouth, Briggs, unless you want to be flogged after all," Harris hissed.

Together they marched him up to the quarterdeck. Briggs began to hum, softly at first and then louder, as though deliberately testing the edges of Harris' patience. When Thomas saw Harris' hand tighten on his sword hilt, he leaned towards him and spoke quietly. "Sir, he's only trying to goad you."

"The man is mad," was all Harris replied. "They're all mad."

They stood to either side of Briggs as they reached the stairs, unwilling to allow him to approach their captain with nothing to hold him back. "Ought we have brought irons?" Thomas asked, but there was no time for Harris to reply; Wickerham was already coming away from his conversation with Smythe, the surgeon, and coming toward them. They saluted in unison.

"Captain," Lieutenant Harris said formally. "This man is named Osham Briggs. He seems to have no rank among the crew, but he has named himself their leader nevertheless. Stand up!" he snapped, holding the blade of his sword across Briggs like a golden rope between him and the admiral. Briggs curled back his bony shoulders, looking up at Wickerham through smoke-reddened eyes.

"Sir, I am George Wickerham," the admiral introduced himself. To an untrained ear he sounded calm, but all aboard who had served a year with him or more knew well to fear that tone of voice. "Captain of this ship and Admiral of His Majesty's Navy. I will not hold you yourself personally accountable for what transpired here today. I should hope that, our situations being re-versed," — Thomas thought he heard Harris actually grind his teeth at the suggestion — "that my men would not be held to account for obeying *my* orders. I am prepared to grant mercy to you and your compatriots, provided you and they will submit to the King's justice once we return to England."

Thomas had expected a grateful acceptance, even after all the apathy the man had displayed so far. He was shocked when Briggs hawked up a mouthful of spittle, revoltingly loud, and let it fly onto the bloodstained deck by Wickerham's boot. "There for yer King's justice," he snarled. There were flecks of his own saliva caught in his beard, making him look rabid.

Harris' arm came up, twisting the sword to point directly at Briggs' chest. He almost certainly would have run the man through there and then, all sense driven out of his head by fury, but Wickerham stayed his hand. "Steady, Fred," he murmured, with remarkable stillness in the face of his own, more general anger.

"But sir— "

"Enough, Lieutenant." Wickerham drew himself up, and Thomas felt a rush of pride fill his own chest. Not for the first time he felt the thrill of the honour it was to be serving this man, this hero of the navy, who had more honour and chivalry in his right hand than any pirate could ever have dreamed of. He made a fine picture, despite — or perhaps by virtue of — his general disorder. It was a rare occasion to see him so much as rumpled, even after months at sea. Even today he had somehow managed to put on his coat, though most of the men having been roused from their beds in the dead of night had thrown on only shirt, breeches and boots without stopping to put on so much as stockings. But with his coat shorn in two, blood down his shirt and the gash over his eye, there was a wild nobility to him now that a royal portrait artist could only hope to capture. Thomas fixed the sight in his mind. If he remembered it well enough, perhaps he could sketch it, and try his hand at fixing it in oils once they were back on land. Wickerham wouldn't thank him for it, but perhaps no one else needed to see it. He had a dozen such paintings at home, completed during his brief stays on land, for his own eyes only in times of wistfulness.

Wickerham waved both of his Lieutenants towards the rail. They hurried to keep up with him, with Harris still holding Briggs at sword point. Gower had directed the survivors of the pirates' raid into two lines facing the quarterdeck. They did not stand to attention. Some of them were almost doubled over, clutching at seeping wounds, others still being supported to stand. It might be a long time until they were seen to, Thomas thought, and chided himself for his pity. He knew there was nothing to be sorry for. He was sure that if the pirates had succeeded in their senseless scheme, the entire crew of the *Courage* would have been slaughtered and tossed like rubbish into the sea without even a word said over their corpses. Or perhaps taken as slaves, a fate Thomas could only imagine to be considerably worse than an honourable death in battle.

"What was your ship's name?" Wickerham demanded of Briggs.

The man sneered as though prepared to spit again, but the point of Harris' blades between his ribs clearly made him think better of it for the moment. "*Queen o'Heaven*," he snarled.

"Blasphemy," Harris muttered. Wickerham's look silenced him.

The admiral turned to the assembled men. "Crew of the *Queen of Heaven*," he announced. His voice carried clear and easily on the breeze. "Since your appointed leader has refused to speak for you, I make this offer. Since you are not navy of an enemy nation, I cannot grant you parole. However, if you agree to stand surety for each other, I shall make the conditions of your captivity as comfortable as possible. We will care for your wounds and make sure you are decently fed." He leaned forward, his hands resting on the rail on either side of his body. "Not all men would make you this offer. It is not given lightly. Should any man of you disobey the orders of my crew, or make any attempt to escape, I shall have that man executed and any who aided him, and rescind all the privileges I had theretofore bestowed upon the rest. Should you behave well and honourably, I shall speak favourably to the magistrate on our return. I hope I make myself clear."

Thomas shivered. Wickerham did not need Harris' temper to be intimidating, but it didn't frighten him. Quite the opposite. It thrilled him.

*

Lieutenant Thomas, who had been christened Charles but rarely used the name, was still a young officer. He had only just made Lieutenant, having come up as a midshipman under Wickerham's service. He had shown himself during that time to be a decent sailor and a good swordsman, but what distinguished him most of all was his popularity among the men. Though he was younger than most of the ordinary sailors, he was well-liked among them and they never baulked at taking his orders. Raised a gentleman, as were all officers, his manners were always perfect, and he could count on one hand the number of times he had used anything other than respectable language. This might have been in direct contrast to the coarse nature of some of the sailors; still, he had an easy, sociable manner and sense of humour that endeared him to all in spite of it. The other officers appreciated the ease with which he could settle a debate; his mother had always said he could charm birds out of the skies. He had a mop of reddish-gold Irish hair, from his mother, and his father had gifted him a long, straight nose and hazel-brown eyes. His skin was fair and sadly freckled, though he took care to avoid direct sun as much as possible, having no desire to take on the red-faced appearance so common among seamen. He kept his clothes as clean and pressed as they were new. Such fastidiousness was not unusual on the *Courage*, where the majority of the officers took after their captain's example, but it was also a point of personal pride, especially now he was fourth — no, third now — in command. He wanted badly for Wickerham to not just approve of him, but to respect him as well. Unlike Harris, who privately spoke of one day commanding a ship of his own, Thomas had no great ambitions of being made post — a captain himself — at least not just yet. In moments like this, he thought he could happily have remained under Wickerham's command for the rest of his life.

*

None of the pirates made any noise, not even to acknowledge the admiral's offer of mercy. Thomas found himself getting angry, as well, an emotion he was usually not quick to feel — these men should be begging at Wickerham's feet for forgiveness, not standing there like so many sullen lumps. Before he could do or say anything, however, Harris had stepped forward. "If you accept the terms, let us hear you say 'aye'," he ordered, glaring at them with glinting eyes.

There was a low rumbling of 'ayes' from the pirates, but at the same moment — too late — Thomas realised that in stepping forward, Lieutenant Harris had let his sword point drop.

Briggs moved like a snake. He pulled a dull knife from somewhere within his oversized coat, and stabbed Harris in the side of the neck. Blood spurted everywhere. It flew into Thomas' eyes, so that, blinded, he could only fumble in midair as he tried to seize the pirate's arm. He heard a cry from Wickerham as chaos erupted once again all around them. Thomas found himself grappling with Briggs; still half-blind he somehow managed to get both hands around the man's wrist and slam it down onto the rail, again and again until the pirate howled and the knife went clattering away across the deck. The sailors reached them just as Briggs landed a sharp punch just under Thomas' ribs; they grabbed him by the arms and dragged him back while Thomas fell to one knee, winded, rubbing his eyes clear.

Harris lay spreadeagled on the deck, his eyes glassy and unseeing, blood saturating the left side of his coat from the deep neck wound. Thomas swallowed and looked away, still trying to catch his breath.

"Call Mr Smythe!" someone shouted. Thomas straightened on still-shaky legs and opened his mouth to tell them there was no need, Harris had gone. But then he saw the cluster of men gathered around another collapsed form on the other side of the quarterdeck.

Admiral Wickerham was holding a hand tightly to a wound in his side. Despite his best efforts it continued to gush blood from between his fingers. As Thomas staggered over to him, the colour was already draining from the admiral's face. Fear started building in the pit of Thomas' stomach. He hadn't been afraid throughout the battle, even when he had been disarmed near the end and had used both his pistols. Dying to protect the *Courage* and her men was an honourable prospect, and it did not frighten him. But seeing unbreakable, immortal Wickerham in such a position was enough to send a rush of horror through him.

"Where is that surgeon?" he demanded, turning on his heel with every intention of routing the poor man out himself, but Smythe was already tearing towards them with both arms bloody to the elbow. Thomas stood aside to let him pass, and watched anxiously as Smythe went to work, replacing Wickerham's shaking hands with his own.

"Harris," the admiral gasped, looking up at the sky as though he couldn't find a face to focus on among the men that surrounded him.

Thomas swallowed. "He's dead, sir," he managed, swallowing bile.

"Murder, by God," moaned Wickerham. His breathing sounded rough and uneven.

"Sir?" Thomas moved one of the sailors aside so he could kneel by the admiral's side. Wickerham's eyes darted about until they settled on Thomas' face. He lifted a trembling hand and Thomas took it, his heart in his throat. "You'll be all right, sir," Thomas said firmly, forcing himself to believe it. "This isn't what gets you."

"This scratch?" the admiral wheezed. "I should hope not."

"The scoundrel must have punctured a lung," Smythe muttered. "The captain cannot breathe properly. We must get him below decks immediately if I have any hope of repairing the damage."

Thomas waited for a moment until he realised that Smythe was waiting for orders, and he was the only man left who could give them. "Yes," he said quickly, looking around at everyone who was standing anxiously by. "Rogers, Bowery, fetch a stretcher. Hurry — your captain's life may depend on it."

"Thomas."

Thomas looked down once again into Wickerham's ruddy, bloodstained face. "Captain?"

"Are you hurt?"

Thomas looked down at himself. He was covered in blood, but it wasn't his. Most of it had belonged to poor Harris. He could feel it drying already on his face, crusting in the soft hairs on his chin. He must look monstrous. "No sir," he said, miserably. "I'm sorry, sir."

"Blast it," Wickerham coughed, his fingers tightening for a moment on Thomas' hand. "What on earth for, boy?"

Thomas knew he had to be honest, though he did wish they were not surrounded by nearly all the other officers. Gower and a few others were still guarding the pirates, who had been forced to lie on their stomachs with their arms stretched over their heads. Thomas could just see them laid out on the deck from where he knelt. "Sir, I wasn't quick enough," he admonished himself, feeling wretched. "I ought to have warned Harris, or I should have leapt on Briggs before he could attack you... I should have seen that he had a knife hidden..."

"The prisoners were Harris' charge," the admiral managed through harsh breaths. "It was his duty to search for weapons, not yours. Charles — "

"Enough," Smythe chided them both. "You must stop speaking now, Captain."

The two sailors returned with the stretcher and Wickerham was transferred, painstakingly slowly, onto it. Two more men then helped to carry him below. Thomas caught Smythe by the arm as he was about to follow. "Will he live?" he demanded, in an undertone.

Smythe's face was unreadable. "I shall do everything I can, but the wound is grave," he said, speaking so that no one else nearby could hear. "Let me do my work, and I suggest you occupy yourself with setting all this to rights."

As Smythe hurried away, Thomas looked back over the mayhem that had erupted at Briggs' attack. Poor Harris still lay with his arms and legs splayed wide to either side, dead eyes gazing up at the sky. Feeling sick, Thomas waved over a couple of sailors. Like all the men, they were fellows he had once been on friendly terms with, until his promotion had made carousing and gambling below decks inappropriate. Now they looked at him with unease. "Have Lieutenant Harris laid out with Lieutenant Masterman," he instructed them, a slight tremor coming into his voice. Without a word, they saluted gravely and went to it, lifting Harris as respectfully as they could under the arms and knees.

"Mr Gower," Thomas called out, his throat dry.

"Sir!" Gower saluted from where he stood over the prostrate pirates. "Shall I have them taken down to the brig, sir?"

"We 'ave wounded," one of the pirates spoke, a large black man with a thick neck scar, his accented voice muffled from where he lay face-down on the bloody deck.

"We have one surgeon," Thomas replied, his anger at the attack on the admiral making his voice cold and unfeeling, very unlike his usual friendly tone. "And wounded of our own. Since your man saw fit to reject our offer, your surety is revoked. You are lucky I *don't* have you all thrown to the sharks." He took a breath. Some of the men around them had paused in their work to stare at him. He cleared his throat and looked away. "Carry on, Gower," he said.

Looking over the starboard rail as the pirates were forced to stand and march single-file down to the lower decks, he could see that his threat had not been entirely idle; dark fins were circling around the *Courage*, no doubt drawn by the blood blown into the sea, or perhaps not all the pirates had made it off their ship before it went down. Having had a taste of human flesh they were now hungry for more.

Having made his own orders, Gower came over to stand by Thomas' side. "What about Briggs, sir?" he asked, cautiously.

Thomas considered. All his instincts said that Briggs deserved death. Having murdered a British officer and gravely wounded one of its admirals, there was no chance whatsoever of him being spared by a magistrate, and frankly he doubted whether any of the others would also survive their own judgement. What was the point in shipping them all to England? He couldn't help feeling that poor Harris had been right after all; the pirates would only eat their supply and use too much of Smythe's valuable time and resources, being nursed back to full health only to be shot like the criminals they were.

The law, that was the point. He doubted any man on earth would fault them for executing Briggs there and then, but it was still dishonourable to kill an unarmed man, except by the law.

He had been thinking too long. He cleared his throat again. "The admiral must decide," he said. "When he is well." He refused not to think about what would happen if Wickerham did not recover. "Put Briggs in the brig for now — separate from the others, if you can. And then..." he looked around again at the deck of the *Courage*, her boards gleaming red under the glow of the sun. "Put every man we can spare to swabbing this damn deck."

"Yes sir," Gower said, with some relief. He was a seaman of thirty or more years, no doubt as perturbed as Thomas was by the sudden change of command. His new acting captain was nineteen years old. Things might have been different if they had been sailing with the rest of the fleet, where there were officers to spare, but circumstances and delays in repairs had seen them set off from Cape Town alone.

"I'm going to need your help here, Joe," Thomas added, keeping his voice low. "No one could have anticipated this. I don't know what to..."

"The admiral trusts you, Thomas," Gower said quietly, slipping perhaps unconsciously into a more informal mode. For a moment they were two midshipmen again, content to stand in each other's company with no boundary of nice manners between them. Thomas would have liked to have remained friends with the man, despite the seperation demanded by the difference in rank, and especially now. He was going to need more than a few friends if he had any hope of commanding the *Courage* for so much as a few days. But it made a strange situation, to be giving orders to a man so much older, who had once been his senior officer and then his equal; in such situations it was only a strict adherence to the chain of command that kept men from falling into resentment. Perhaps a true friendship was now impossible.

"Very well," he said finally, putting back his shoulders. "Let us put on full sail, and get as far away from this godforsaken patch of ocean as we can. And send someone to find my sword."

$$-\ 2\ -$$

There was simply no way to preserve so many bodies as needed to be put to rest, so the funerals had to be hastened. They stopped just after midday to relieve themselves of the burden of over thirty dead pirates, weighed down but without so much as a scrap of sailcloth to preserve their corpses. As it was they had to be careful with rationing the weights; there was only so much heavy metal scrap to be spared, and no one could have foreseen so many losses that they would need barrowfuls of stones. No one suggested wasting cannonballs on the pirates; these were reserved for the sixteen navy men who had died; Masterman, Harris, two midshipmen, the ropemaker, five of the gunners who had been on watch, and four sailors. And finally, Tom Ridley, the smallest bundle, a boy of only thirteen who had set sail with them eighteen months ago on his first voyage. A shocking toll, especially considering the total four officers. The bodies made a sad line on the lower deck, laid out in yellowing linen.

By evening they had sailed into calmer ocean where they could weigh anchor, and, after washing themselves of the blood, shaving their faces and putting on clean bandages, those who could still stand gathered on deck. One by one the carefully-wrapped bodies were lowered slowly and respectfully into the sea. Father Murray, the ship's chaplain, had spoken himself hoarse by the time it was over. The sun was setting, the red glow making the ship look bloody once more, though half the crew had spent most of the day scrubbing the boards clean.

"A terrible thing," Murray sighed when Thomas went over to thank him. "But what can we expect when men turn their face away from Christ? To live in sin is to live in infamy. Not all men who turn to a life of crime out of desperation are evil in their heart, but to live a sinful life is to become sinful."

Thomas nodded uncomfortably. His mother had been a devout woman, but he always found himself rather uneasy around the clergy, particularly when they began on the topic of sin. It made him think back to being whipped as a boy by the priests who had taught him religion and history. He had always been more interested in art and mathematics, which those men never seemed to find appropriate for a young boy of good standing and modest heritage. "Do you think any of them can be saved, Father?" he asked, reminding himself that he could not be whipped anymore for asking such questions.

"In this life, I very much doubt it," Murray sighed again. "It remains to be seen whether the gates of heaven will be open to any of them."

Thomas walked below decks with Murray. "Can there be any hope of that at all?" he wondered aloud.

"The Lord's house and its laws are not subject to our understanding," Murray said. "Farbeit from me to presume His mind. Perhaps I can bring some of them to Christ before we land in England. We still have time to save their immortal souls."

"But not Briggs?" Thomas suggested.

"No," Murray said, darkly. Like surely nearly every man aboard, the chaplain loved and respected Admiral Wickerham. Below the vibrations of grief that carried over the ship, there was an ever-present murmuring of fury, no actual words spoken, but still audible in the very air as men worked silently, stung by the insult to their ship, their captain and their service. Thomas realised that he would have to put extra measures in place, if Briggs was to survive the rest of the voyage. Not that he would be at all grieved for the pirate's sake, but it would be a great shame to have to punish any of his own crew for taking the task upon themselves.

"I must go and see to the wounded," Thomas said, as they reached the turn of the stair.

"Of course." Murray nodded politely. "I will go to pray for the admiral, and for all of us."

"Thank you," Thomas said. He wasn't sure how much good prayer would do, but by this point he was willing to accept any help he could get.

Having taken his leave of the chaplain, he made his way down to the sickbay. He found it almost full, with several men badly injured in the morning's action. Thomas knew Wickerham would certainly have visited them all, had he the chance, and now he must do it in the admiral's stead, but it felt very disconcerting to be the one going from bed to bed and wishing them well. He had been in here himself after a battle, and remembered the way Wickerham made it possible to laugh away a sword cut or a broken bone. He was sure that, while the gesture was appreciated, his own words of encouragement could not have quite the same effect.

"Are you the captain now, sir?" asked little Pasco. The third son of a Spanish officer now serving in the British army, he was the youngest aboard, being only twelve, and young Ridley had been his constant companion. Under the bandage wrapped about his head, the boy's face was blotchy with tears, though to his credit he did not cry in front of his superior officer.

"Not at all," Thomas assured him, blanching inwardly at the very idea. "I will only mind the ship until Captain Wickerham does well again. You must not trouble yourself over it."

"Oh, I wasn't," murmured Pasco, embarrassed by his naive outburst.

"Never mind," Thomas said, low. He put a hand on the boy's shoulder. "Try not to be too grieved. You were a credit to the service today."

"Not really," Pasco sighed shakily. "I only helped hand the powder down to the guns. Ridley was helping them load." His voice shook. "He only went on deck to take a message. One of them shot him as he was coming up the stairs."

"Pirates," one of the other wounded men muttered. "Murderous savages. Slayin' a mere boy before he could even draw sword."

A murmur of agreement went around the room.

"Lieutenant?" Mr Smythe had appeared at the door to his cabin.

Thomas patted Pasco on the shoulder, nodded around to the men, and went over to the surgeon, who held the door open for him. This room was where Smythe kept his tonics, tools and books, and also where he slept. He had had Wickerham laid in his own bed, the cot looking rather small against the admiral's broad, tall frame. "How does he do?" Thomas asked, anxiously noting the pale colour of Wickerham's cheek where it had so recently been red with colour. The wound on his head had been washed and dressed, the other was hidden under a thick blanket that rose and fell ever so slightly with each shallow intake of breath.

"He lives," Smythe replied, shortly. "Other than that I am afraid I cannot say. It might be several days before we know for sure. But I am hopeful."

"Thank God." Thomas sighed and took a half a step forward. "He looks so very still."

"I have given him laudanum," Smythe explained. "He will sleep for some hours yet. Come tomorrow morning, and you may speak to him then before I give him another dose."

*

Thomas went to his cabin. He was keenly aware that both the great cabin and those reserved for the first and second lieutenant would be unslept in that night. Sea chests left open, letters left unfinished. It was a devastating state of affairs. He took off his coat, wincing as his whole body protested the day's treatment, bruises throbbing, and wondered whether he ought to draft the captain's letters to Masterman and Harris' families, or if that was presumptuous. Surely he ought to wait to do such things until they knew for sure whether Wickerham would recover.

He sighed, sitting on the edge of his bunk in half-open shirt and breeches. He had put on clean ones for the funeral — the others were ruined and would no doubt have to be burned — but he still felt as though there were blood all over his skin, drying, making it painfully taut and itchy. He almost dreaded the thought of getting into his bunk and spreading that feeling to the sheets. He felt bone-tired, but at the same time he knew it would be quite impossible to sleep. His mind was too busy. His chest ached where Briggs had hit him.

Before he could gather himself enough to finish undressing, there was a knock on the cabin door. Thomas felt the hair on the back of his neck prickle. He knew who was there before he even stood to open it.

"Hello Bill."

Bill Blake was an able seaman with over ten years on Thomas. He had been on Thomas' first ship, the *Queen Charlotte*, and it was not by coincidence that their paths had converged. Blake had been a mentor of sorts to the promising young gentleman he had been, and when Thomas had been made midshipman on the *Courage* at sixteen, he had recommended Blake for a more prestigious posting among her crew. It was a friendship that he cherished, in a strange way, but they were hardly equals anymore, and he had a growing sense of discomfort in the pit of his stomach as he looked up at the man's hard face.

Blake came in and shut the door behind him, without waiting to be given permission to enter, or even so much as a bow or a salute to his lieutenant. In private, there had never been any adherence between them to the manners required by rank, but it was still a shock to the system to have the huge man grip him by the arms and hold him there without so much as a moment's hesitation. "Charlie… are you all right?" he asked, practically glaring. With difficulty, Thomas squirmed his way out of the big man's grip. Blake had huge, thick arms that could barely be contained by his shirt, and he was so tall that his head grazed the roof of the cabin which, while not luxurious when compared to the great cabin, was notably larger than those shared by the junior officers and certainly more spacious than the sleeping quarters for the seamen. Bill's jaw was dark with two days' growth; many of the men had not had time that day for so much as a shave.

"Quite well, thank you," said Thomas, trying to straighten his shirt while half the buttons were still undone. "Not even a scratch; just a bruise to the ribs."

"You know that isn't what I meant," Blake said, gazing at him hotly. "I saw what happened, with Harris. You could have been killed."

"Bill, you shouldn't be here," Thomas blurted out, losing in a moment any sense of his own station.

"Oh?" Bill's lips twitched into a wry smile. "Now you have command of the entire ship, you mean?"

"No!" Thomas stared at him. "No, that's not… surely someone would have seen you come up here…"

"No one has before," Bill pointed out. "And if they have, they haven't said anything. You know how it works aboard ship."

Thomas knew very well how it was, but it did little to curb his anxiety. Indiscretions, particularly ones which would be unseemly in the extreme to mention, were often ignored at sea where they would most certainly not have been otherwise. It was the unspoken knowledge of all seamen that some men, deprived of female company for so many long months, might turn to their shipmates for some physical means of relief. Even some high-ranking officers carried a secret which was not quite so secret as they might have liked, given the general lack of privacy and discretion available in the confined space of a ship's quarters. But that didn't mean it was good for a man's reputation, and while it was all very well for a captain who had already reached the peak of his career to become a little careless, a young officer who wished to be looked on favourably by the admiralty board might not.

Blake took a step towards Thomas and folded his arms around him. Thomas sighed, and let him. He was so tired. And it was nice to be held, as though he deserved at least some comfort for having been suddenly thrust into deep water, his head barely staying above the surface. Just for a moment to be allowed to be the boy Charlie, instead of Leiutenant Charles Thomas, commander by circumstance.

"You were covered in blood," Bill murmured into his ear. "Thought I might have lost you."

"I was not even hurt," Thomas said, but his voice shook.

Bill lowered his head and kissed his neck, firmly, possessively. His beard scratched against Thomas' jaw.

"Bill…" Thomas tried, daring to breathe.

Blake shushed him, one big hand holding tight to the back of his head, keeping him still with fingers tangled into Thomas' touseled gold hair. "Let me take care of you," he said, practically growling.

Thomas swallowed. It would be so easy, to pretend nothing had happened, to pretend everything had not changed. He pushed half-heartedly at Bill's broad shoulder. "I can't..."

"Let me." Bill's other hand moved to shift Thomas' breeches, the fastenings coming apart easily between his fingers. Thomas felt his body stir of its own volition, his groin straining towards Bill's hand. *No.*

He forced himself to stumble back, ducking out of Blake's grip... "Bill," he hissed. "This — we cannot do this. Not now. Everyone will be watching me, all the officers, Father Murray." He drew himself up, heart thumping in his chest. "If... if you are my friend, you will leave now and not re-enter this room without my permission until I say otherwise."

Bill straightened up, his expression changing rapidly to one Thomas did not like. He had seen it before, but that didn't make it any easier to face now, not when it looked down on him from such a threatening height. "Your permission?" Blake repeated Thomas' words with a low growl of incredulity.

"Yes," Thomas said, firmly. Out of Blake's embrace, chill bumps rose all down his arms. His heart was pounding, but not as much as it might have if he had had this conversation yesterday. It was impossible to tell if it was the exhaustion that made him suddenly brave, or the authority of his borrowed rank, or the very real danger of any of the men coming to look for him and finding them together. "My permission, *Mister* Blake."

"I see." Bill's glare darkened. "*Lieutenant.* When you were a junior officer it was all right, but now you're too good for me, is that so?"

Thomas felt another lukewarm flash of anger. He was too tired to be more polite, and Bill was not a man who took rejection well.

He should have known this would happen. He should never have opened the door. "I was fourteen when this started," he hissed in an undertone, "hardly older than little Ridley. If I heard of anyone approaching *him* in such a way —"

"Poor boy probably died a virgin," Blake grunted.

Thomas went breathless with shock. There was a long moment of tense silence until he gasped out: "*Bill*. How can you?"

Blake, at least, had the decency to look a little ashamed. "I only meant — "

"We lost *sixteen men* today — "

"Which is all the more reason not to waste any more time," Blake insisted, taking a step forward and reaching for his arm. Thomas twisted away again, his cheeks flushing hotly.

"Bill, I said no. I am not a boy anymore, whom you can manipulate for your own ends; I am your commanding officer. If I am going to bring this ship safe to harbour, I need you to respect that position. If I have to ask you one more time..." he trailed away, set momentarily adrift.

"Well?" Bill raised an eyebrow.

Thomas glared at him. The man knew perfectly well that he couldn't be punished in any official way, not while Thomas was as complicit in the crime as he was, himself. "Get out," he demanded, keeping his voice low.

Bill's expression darkened still further. Thomas waited, doing his best to look as though he expected his command to be obeyed. He imagined what would happen if it was not. If he called out, someone would come running. Blake would be arrested. Blake would tell anyone who would listen that Thomas had accepted his advances up to now. Wickerham would hear of it, and every man aboard. Even if no one believed him, he would be heard. Word would spread. He could ruin Thomas' chances of ever making post-rank, even if there were no charges laid on either side, which was unlikely if they were caught in the act. No. Blake had him in his pocket, and he knew it. If Thomas only could reverse time, if he could tell his younger self, naive and inexperienced in the ways of the world, what he was getting into, perhaps he would not be in this position now. Powerless.

"Very well," Blake said at last, very reluctantly. He bowed, and backed away, and Thomas was finally able to catch his breath. "I won't force myself on you. I'm not that kind of man."

Thomas said nothing.

"But you know where to find me, should you change your mind," the man added. He hesitated a moment, as though he would have liked to say something else, and then he left, closing the door softly behind him.

Thomas fell back on the bed, shaking. *Well Charlie, now you have your own ship*, he thought. His inner voice sound remarkably like his father's, or as well as he could remember it, and slightly mocking. *Isn't that just what you wanted?*

His sketchbook was lying neatly on the small writing desk beside his bunk. He opened it to the last page. Only the day before he had been bringing to life his memory of the three deck hands hauling an enormous grouper on deck; the successful fishing expedition that had resulted in Admiral Wickerham calling for extra rations. The feast had sent them all late to their beds, so that no one but Masterman and the five gunners on watch had been awake when the pirates made their advance.

He closed the book. He might never finish that drawing now. Wearily he stripped off the rest of his clothes and, without caring to put on so much as a nightshirt, crawled between the sheets to dream fitfully of Harris' blood in his eyes, and the *Queen of Heaven* slipping mercifully under the waves to be claimed by the bottomless sea.

— 3 —

He woke to someone knocking on the door. It was past daybreak, he realised; he must have slept through the first bell. As he sat up, the events of the previous day came pouring back into his head like a flood. It felt as though he hadn't really slept at all, only closed his eyes for a moment. His heart pounding with the suddenness of his waking, he threw the sheets aside and scrambled to dress. "Who is it?" he called through the door.

A moment's hesitation, then: "It's Gower, sir."

Haphazardly he pulled on the stockings and breeches he had had on the previous night. He had laid them carefully over a chair, but they were still hopelessly rumpled. It would have to do. He could not be seen to have been sleeping the day away. Blearily he wondered how he had ever thought he could do this. A nineteen-year-old officer, who had only been made third lieutenant out of necessity in the first instance thanks to a bad bout of pneumonia that had forced them to leave several good officers on shore before they had even set sail out of Portsmouth.

This voyage is cursed, he thought, before quickly shaking off that ridiculous notion. He hoped nothing of the sort occurred to any of the hands, who happened to be the most suspicious members of the crew. He had no desire to have to battle demons and ghosts as well as everything else. However was he to manage it? "What is it, Joe?" he called through the door, straightening his coat by what he could see of his reflection in the port window.

"It's the prisoners, sir," was the reply, and Thomas felt his blood run cold. He ran to the door and yanked it open.

"What now?" he demanded.

"I'm not sure, but there's something going on down there," Gower said, somewhat breathlessly. "Cole here says there's a fight broken out."

Thomas noticed the boy standing behind Gower's shoulder, a fifteen-year-old midshipman with freckles even thicker than Thomas, and too-long hair bleached blond by the sun. "You saw this?" Thomas asked.

"Yessir." The boy nodded frantically. "We were taking down food and water, but then they started shouting and brawling… I thought I ought to fetch another officer. I left Rogers to watch…"

"They're fighting among themselves?" Thomas wondered aloud as they made their way with haste down to the lower decks. "Not trying to escape?"

"I don't think comradeship is prized very highly among them, sir," Gower said, with a trace of humour in it that Thomas recognised, though he wasn't sure whether or not he should find it amusing. It was becoming increasingly clear that the damn pirates were a lot more trouble than they were worth.

The ship's gaol in the lower deck was not built to contain thirty men, and it was very tight quarters. The ragged men, crowded together with barely enough room to all sit at once, let alone to lie down — quite impossible — had already made a stink of the place with their filth. Thomas swallowed and tried to breath through his mouth, though it made little difference. The only one with any relief was Briggs, chained instead to a thick iron ring on the opposite bulkhead, separate from the rest. There was a large purple bruise covering most of his face, and he hardly stirred, apparently knocked senseless.

There was indeed a fight, though by the time Thomas, Gower and Cole came down the ladder, it had downgraded from a brawl to two men making wild, clumsy swings at each other while the rest tried in vain to stay out of the way. Seaman Rogers, standing guard near the door, was helpless; he could do nothing through the grating without injuring one of the other men or, more likely, getting hurt himself. Thomas knew he could not let any more of his men be injured for the sake of these prisoners. He did not think that even Wickerham would blame him for taking matters into his own hands, if it came to that.

"What is the meaning of this?" he shouted, trying to put the strength of a bellows into his boyish voice.

"I'm sorry sir," Rogers said helplessly. He was older than Thomas only by a few years, an excellent shot with any type of gun made, but a little slow of thought. "One of them came and tried to tell me something, and t'other one leaped on him, like." Behind the grated bars, the two men continued to grapple at each other. One was the big, dark-skinned man who had tried to speak to Thomas on deck. He had jet black tattoos winding about his bare shoulders; he wore no shirt, or perhaps it had been torn off during the skirmish. The other was a squat, muscled seaman, buck-toothed and one-eyed, an evil-looking specimen. There was blood pouring from his nose, staining the rags he wore. Neither man was able to inflict any really dramatic damage on each other in such close proximity, but it was only a matter of time before one of them bore the other down to the ground to be trampled.

Thomas found he had reached his limit. Drawing his sword he rammed the hilt up against the grate, startling the pirates into attention. Distracted by the noise, the two fighters were at last able to be pulled apart by their fellows. "That is *enough*," Thomas despaired. "Have some damn sense, before you all crush each other to death. What on earth is behind this?"

"Sir —" the big man made an attempt to speak, but the one-eyed creature spat and lunged forward.

"Shut yer mouth, Aggie, fucking traitor cunt!" Spittle flew from the corners of his mouth.

Thomas grimaced and turned his head away, out of range of any stray saliva. He recalled some of the stories he had loved as a child; Blackbeard, Calico Jack, Don Benito. Pirates with manners, pirates with honour, brigands who despite their blatant criminality at least *behaved* like gentlemen. Perhaps such men were tales only, or they were simply all gone now, leaving behind only the very dregs of their abysmal society. Certainly no such men were to be found amongst this unhappy band. "Mr Gower," he called over his shoulder. "Bring one of the gun crews down here. We will have some order."

"Yes, sir," Gower said in solemn approval, and got back on the ladder.

"You," Thomas snapped, pointing at the man One-Eye had called Aggie. "Tell me."

"Sir, one o' our boys is hurt bad," Aggie said, making no attempt to strain against his crewmates hold on him, while One-Eye continued to rage and spit insults. Aggie had a thick Jamaican accent, so that Thomas had some trouble understanding him. "I was goin' te ask yer man to ask yer mercy, sir, just for 'im, you unnerstand, he bein' on'y a lad. But Babber dere want to keep him down 'ere. Won't leddim go, sir. Sir, he gone to die down 'ere."

"We're all gonna die down here, ye fucking yella-livered mongrel," sneered One-Eye. "Might as well 'ave some fun widdim in the time we got left —"

"Better yella-livered dan black-'earted, Babber!" Aggie growled, his large muscles bulging under the restraining hands of his fellows. "You let de boy alone!"

"Daw, Babbs's right!" someone else shouted, a murmur of agreement rumbled around the group, as though they had all forgotten that Thomas and Cole were standing there. "He's gonna die anyway, it's a waste!" Some of them sniggered nastily.

Thomas did not know what was going on, but he didn't like the sound of it whatsoever. Footsteps started pounding towards them on the deck above, and within moments one of the gun crews was descending the ladder, armed with fully-loaded pistols. "Where is this boy?" Thomas demanded of Aggie, and the few men holding him who appeared to be on his side.

"He back dere, sir," Aggie jerked his head towards the back of the cell. "Please sir, dey'll crush 'im 'fore too long."

One of the men made a grab for Gower from behind the bars with a filthy black-nailed hand, and laughed when the midshipman took a hurried step out of his reach. "Wot a big brave navy man," he jeered. He had overlarge ears sticking out from the sides of his bald, tattooed head. Gower glared back at him, pistol raised. "Give us a kiss, navy man."

"Get back," Gower warned, to more jeers.

"Stand away, all of you," Thomas ordered, waving his own men forward. "Gentlemen, separate the prisoners until we can retrieve the injured man. Bring him out here."

Faced with the pistols, the pirates were forced to stand aside, some of them being hauled out of the cell to make room, the others pressing back against the grate, sneering as the sailors shoved their way through them. Eventually they made their way back, two of them half dragging, half-carrying a thin, ragged figure. Once the men were out, the remaining pirates were pushed back into the brig, being struck around the head and shoulders with pistol butts if they so much as strayed off course. Three of the men slammed the iron door shut and rammed the bolts into place.

The injured man was still conscious, panting hard with the effort of trying to hide his pain. The crew laid him down on the opposite side to Briggs, allowing Thomas to get a real look at him. He was indeed quite young, perhaps Thomas' own age or only a little younger. Barefoot and filthy, like all the others, he had black hair grown long to his shoulders, tangled and matted, crusted grey in places with white salt where seawater had dried. His snub nose and pouting lips were indeed boyish, more suited to the face of a society gentleman than a ravaging corsair. The ragged sleeveless shirt he wore was a dark colour that might once have been a rich purple or navy blue, but was now almost black, which perhaps explained why his injury had gone up to now unnoticed. He was holding one trembling hand to a long, deep gash that ran from shoulder to hip, poorly dressed with more of the same filthy fabric, apparently the sleeves which had been torn off for that very purpose. Blood covered the whole affair, fresh and dried, and the stench was extraordinary. Thomas was about to turn his face away for what little relief that might give him, when the boy looked up, staring at him. Their eyes met, and for the briefest of moments Thomas found himself transfixed. The eyes were blue and bright as sapphires, and they struck him temporarily dumb with their piercing intensity.

"Pretty isn'e?" Babber sneered from inside the cell. Gower slammed the butt of his pistol against the grate, rattling it loudly, as though he were trying to quiet a cage of rowdy dogs.

Thomas could not look away from the boy. Babbers' jibe had made it all too clear why the pirates had been fighting over him, and the insinuation was one that at once didn't bear thinking about, and yet made it impossible to think about anything else. They stared at each other, the boy's face full of pain, and something else… fear, perhaps, but it was impossible to tell. And then the pirate's eyes finally rolled back in his head, and he fell limply back to the floor.

"Sir?" Cole prompted, anxiously.

Thomas shook himself, dragging himself back to the task at hand. "The wound is deep — it will need to be cleaned properly, and stitched. Take him to Mr Smythe — take Rogers with you and guard him closely. Tie him down, if you have to."

Cole saluted, and he and Rogers together started to carry the unresisting boy up the ladder.

Still trying to rid himself of the indescribable feeling brought on by those penetrating eyes, Thomas turned back to the rest of the pirates. They stood sullen and muttering, nursing their new bruises.

Aggie limped forward, putting four fingers of one large hand through the grate. The smallest finger was missing entirely. The whites of his eyes, though yellowed and bloodshot, shone very bright in the relative darkness of the lower deck, and there was no mistaking the fear in his face. "Thank ye, sir," he said, with genuine gratitude. From behind him, Babber and several of the other bloodthirsty-looking band glared, furious at being robbed of their prize. It was strange to see such a big fearsome-looking man afraid, Thomas thought. Still, it was the first act of kindness he had seen from any of the pirates, if kindness it could be called, and he had no desire to see the man beaten to death for it.

"Mr Gower."

"Yes, sir." The older midshipman stood to attention at his side.

"Have at least two men on guard down here at all times, with pistols." The look on Gower's face gave him only a moment's pause. "Any more of this behaviour, and the offenders are to be shot." He turned his gaze back on the men in the brig. "I hope I make myself understood." There was only a low muttering from the cell, no acknowledgement, but he had not really expected any. "And have Mr Smythe look at Briggs, when he has a moment," he added, reluctantly, looking at the slumped form against the other bulkhead. "He ought to be conscious by now. No — never mind. I am bound there this morning in any case; I will tell him myself."

— 4 —

Mr Smythe was still thoroughly occupied when Thomas eventually made his way to the ship's hospital after a hurried breakfast, a shave, and reports on the ship's progress overnight by the sailing master. Men nodded respectfully to him as he passed, and he nodded back, though he couldn't help but wonder if there wasn't a little irony in their show of deference. That the situation was unforeseen and necessary did not seem to matter; no one was sanguine at the thought of such a green officer commanding a second rate, and, he was forced to admit, a ship which had had an unusual and harrowing string of bad luck recently. He couldn't blame them for thinking that his sudden battlefield elevation was just another event in that downward spiral; certainly he thought he himself might have thought the same, had he been in their position. It felt painfully isolating.

A few men had been released from the sickbay, their minor wounds having been pronounced non-debilitating. More had been confined to their own quarters for the time being. Others, the even more badly hurt, still lay on the cots where Mr Smythe and his harried assistants moved among them, checking each man for signs of improvement or deterioration. Young Pasco had been allowed to rise from his bed only to be pressed into service by the surgeon, carrying trays and instruments to and fro, undeterred by the fresh bandage around his head. Thomas smiled to see him; better kept busy here than left to brood over Ridley's death. He was sure Smythe had appointed him for that reason, and not just because he was badly in need of more assistance.

"Should you require any more help, please see fit to apply to me," Thomas told the surgeon as Smythe led him through the rows of wounded men. "I shall give you as many hands as you need."

"We do better now that some of the lucky ones have retired to their own beds," Smythe said, waving a hand. "With less to care for we should have time enough for all the other wounded. Though I heard that you would like me to examine the captain's would-be murderer," he added, with no hint of irony or even distaste in his voice.

"As far as I am concerned there is no urgency," Thomas said, darkly. "Let us make sure to care for our own men, first."

"And the boy you sent up with two guards?" Smythe reminded him from under a raised eyebrow. "Had you forgotten?"

Thomas sighed. He had not forgotten. "I would rather not have to dispose of any more corpses, if it can be avoided," he said, flatly.

"He will live, I expect." Smythe said, unflustered. "A long cut, but only skin-deep. Provided no infection is allowed to fester, you shan't need to send him over the side for the time being."

"Very good," Thomas nodded. He felt more relieved than he had expected at the news. "I will have a look at him when we are done here."

Smythe frowned a moment, but then said, "Very well. Let us go and see the admiral — he has been asking for you." He reached the door to his cabin-cum-study, and opened it enough to allow Thomas inside.

Wickerham was lying on raised pillows, quite pale and still but otherwise looking awake and alert. Thomas' felt his heart lift immeasurably at the sight. "Captain!" he exclaimed, saluting.

"Ah, Thomas." Wickerham's voice was thin and wheezy, perhaps the result of the lung injury Smythe had mentioned. Thomas could clean and dress a wound, but that was about as far as his medical knowledge would stretch; he wasn't sure he could even reliably remember where the lungs were in relation to the other organs. "I've been waiting for you."

"Yes sir," Thomas replied, unable to hide his beaming. "I am overjoyed to see you looking so well."

Wickerham waved a hand dismissively. "Well, indeed. I feel weak as a newborn puppy." He coughed. "Sit down, boy."

Thomas pulled up the nearest chair, still elated despite the admiral's protestations. Smythe had been so reluctant to assure him of the prognosis that he had been dreading the sight of his captain on the brink of death. Perhaps, he thought hopefully, he would not have to master the ship all the way back to England, at all.

"How does the *Courage*?" Wickerham asked once Thomas was seated, fixing him with his gaze.

"Very well, sir," Thomas assured him, sitting up straight. "We have her set on a north-westerly course, and Mr Days has her well in hand. The men are making repairs to the upper deck where the first cannon hit." He paused, sobering a little at the memory of that terrible roar; that no man alive had seen but all had heard, the noise followed by the screams of the men on watch who had narrowly survived with shards of glass and scrap metal dug into their flesh by the blast. The force of it had torn to shreds part of the larboard rail, the heavier pieces embedding themselves in the boards themselves, making an entire ten-foot square area dangerous to walk on even in boots.

"Mr Smythe has given me the report on the casualties," Wickerham said soberly, perhaps sensing the shift in Thomas' mood. "You laid the dead men to rest?"

"Last night, Captain," Thomas said, suddenly uncertain. "Should I have waited for you, sir?"

The admiral hesitated a moment, frowning deeply, then shook his head. "No, there would have been little sense in having them wait so much as overnight, even if I could have been on deck this morning. Well done, Lieutenant."

Thomas nodded acknowledgement, feeling his throat stiffen a little at the unnecessary praise. "I'm very sorry about Mr Harris, sir," he said. "And Mr Masterman, of course. It is a remarkable stroke of bad luck."

Wickerham scoffed. "It is no such thing," he said. "Not when it is brought on by thieves and murderers. I hope the survivors are kept secure?"

"Yes sir," Thomas replied, then, battling with his impulse to honesty he added: "There was some trouble this morning, but I have put an extra guard below and I hope there will not be more."

"I see." Wickerham sighed. "Will you close the door?"

Anxiously, Thomas stood up and closed the cabin door which

Smythe had left ajar as he returned to his other patients. He could not recall ever having been alone with Wickerham before, not even to receive admonishment. His heart pounded.

"I hope," Wickerham said as Thomas sat down again. "That you will not think I regret my having promoted you when I did, for I certainly felt — and still feel — that you possess all the skills and experience required of a senior officer, despite what some might call a tender age…" Thomas swallowed, trying not to show his very real concern on his face, for that was certainly a fear he had been nursing beneath all the other, more urgent concerns. "But," Wickerham went on. "I admit some remorse only in the sense that you are so very young to have this responsibility thrown on you in this fashion. I hope you will tell me if you do not feel yourself up to the task, and I shall make arrangements, with absolutely no recrimination or dishonour on your part."

"Sir?" Thomas said, dismayed. He found himself running through everything he had done over the last day, all the orders he had given, every decision he had made, looking for the fatal mistake that might have prompted this suggestion.

"Don't look so doleful, lad," Wickerham sighed, a smile pricking at the corners of his mouth. "I am not punishing you. You have earned the right to the command. I only wish to give you the option. If you feel it is too much, there are a number of older, more experienced men on board to whom I could divide some of the responsibility."

Thomas, feeling not particularly encouraged by this explanation, forced himself to consider it. It was true that he suddenly had a great deal to manage, and being suddenly the most senior officer on board able to fulfil the duty was discomforting, to say the least. But he could only imagine the humiliation implicit in accepting an inferior post, to be given as good as a demotion. On the other hand, surely he had to think about what was best not for himself, but for the ship and its crew. That concern, he realised, was from whence Wickerham's concern came, not out of any personal feeling. That realisation however, did little to make him feel better or more confident in his own competence. "But surely you will be on your feet soon, sir?" he asked, to cover his own distress, as much as that was possible.

"Your optimism is warming to an old man's heart," Wickerham rasped. "I can hardly breathe, I'm afraid. Mr Smythe is preparing to nurse me all the way back to England."

Thomas sat back. The prospect of commanding the ship for the next few months was daunting in the extreme, but he had somehow already resigned himself to it, in the back of his mind. He had also, in the far far recesses, begun to imagine how his success would be received by the admiralty. With Wickerham's recommendation he might be made a captain, surely one of the youngest men ever to do so, perhaps given command of a small frigate or a sloop-of-war. And if not anything quite so dramatic, he could at least expect a promotion to second or even first lieutenant on his next voyage. He had even dreamed in some wistful way of being asked by Wickerham to stay on as his next in command. A better compliment he couldn't hope to receive. An offer that surely would not be made, if he decided now that he could not do the task. "Sir, I would never do anything to put the *Courage* at any risk," he said, finally, with a heavy heart. "If you think it best…"

Wickerham held up a hand, silencing him. "No, no, I see it will not do," he said dismissively. "Carry on, Lieutenant. Only do not be afraid to look for advice where it is needed; no one will think any the worse of you, you know. I do not plan on dying in the immediate future; I expect daily reports."

Thomas swallowed. "I… yes sir," he managed finally.

"The ship is yours, Commander. Treat her well."

"I won't let you down, sir," Thomas said, breathless with emotion. He stood up and saluted. "We will bring her safe to port."

"It will be a long time before you'll have to think about landing at all," Wickerham pointed out, laying back on his pillows. "Only keep her steady, and all will be well."

Smythe had appeared like a phantom behind Thomas' shoulder with a small cup in one hand. "Time for you to rest, Captain," he said, with all the authority of an experienced naval surgeon. He held the cup to Wickerham's mouth, and the admiral held it with a shaking hand, drinking until it was empty, and closed his eyes.

"He will sleep now for a while," Smythe told Thomas, ushering him out of the cabin. "It is best that the wound stay as undisturbed as possible while it heals on the inside."

Thomas still felt as though all his emotions were caught in his throat; it was all he could do to clear it and say, "Very good."

"Your next patient is over there," Smythe indicated with one hand to the far corner where Cole and Rogers stood a nervous watch. "You must excuse me while I see to mine." He was gone before Thomas could even thank him.

He made his way over, stopping occasionally along the way to return greetings from the other wounded. Many of them he knew well, and a few he had even lost money to in card games before his promotion. Others he knew only a little, or just by name, but he tried not to stay too long with any one man, giving them all equal favour.

Rogers and Cole saluted him as he approached. On the bed between them the young pirate lay with eyes closed. Having been stripped of shirt and breeches, he lay with the sheet drawn up as far as his waist, a white bandage wrapped tightly about his chest; the area having been thoroughly cleaned was several degrees lighter than the rest of his skin. His arms were tied down to the bed rails on each side, thin ropes snaking about his wrists and knotted expertly. "Trouble?" Thomas asked, looking at his men.

"Aye sir," Seaman Rogers began, while Cole said, "No sir."

Eyebrows raised, Thomas looked between them. "Well, which is it?"

Cole reddened; he was an officer and outranked Rogers despite his tender years, and it was not unusual even for more inferior men to speak for Rogers, who sometimes took more time than was necessary to form a sentence in his mind before he spoke it out loud. Still, Cole clearly felt as though he had been caught out, somehow. Rogers was frowning, puzzled by the contradiction.

Thomas looked the boy in the eye. "Cole, you tell me," he said.

"He was cooperating sir, let us undress him and everything," Cole babbled. "Never even said a word. Only he started screaming when Mr Smythe tried to clean the wound, fighting him off.

We had to hold him down. Then you should've heard the noise he made when he got sewed up." He winced at the memory. "I was glad it were him and not me, that's for sure."

"Did no one think to give him laudanum?" Thomas asked, mildly appalled. "Or brandy, at least?"

Both men stared back at him, equally shocked but apparently for opposite reasons. "To a pirate, sir?" Cole said eventually, frowning.

Thomas stared back at them, letting his disgust at that comment show on his face. "If you fail to understand me, I suggest you ask the same question of Father Murray," he said, "and he shall remind you of our Christian duty." He understood the sentiment, he did, particularly when stores were low and so many other men were in need, but there was also a nasty bit of greed in it. Cole at least had the sense to look abashed; Rogers, he thought, would need a few more minutes to catch up. "Away with both of you," Thomas sighed eventually. He didn't have the heart to punish them for their feelings, and he didn't like to think what the reaction of the rest of the men would be if he did. "He can hardly go anywhere tied to the bed."

They obeyed, albeit with a little hunching of shoulders and indiscrete muttering. He was sure he heard Rogers asking Cole to explain what had been said.

He looked down at the pale, bare figure. Without the filthy clothes and in such a peaceful repose he might have been one of the *Courage*'s own crew, if one ignored the tangled, overgrown state of his hair. Thomas reminded himself that it was foolish to judge on appearance alone, and that this boy along with all the rest of them had surely been fighting to kill, the previous morning. He might well have been responsible for the deaths of any of the sixteen men they had put to rest. But he did look so very young and harmless in sleep, despite the slight crease that furrowed his brow, brought on perhaps by some dark dream.

Or was it? Thomas frowned also, realising as he looked closer that the boy's chest was very still under the bandages; too still. He had seen enough people sleeping, in close quarters as a boy in his first few years aboard ship, to know that people breathed slowly but deeply when they slept. The pirate boy was either dead, or playing dead.

Amused despite himself, Thomas leaned over and blew in the boy's ear, one short blast of air. The blue eyes flew open and the boy flinched away, straining against his bonds. He was able to lift himself up slightly on his elbows, but that was all the movement the ropes allowed him.

"Enough, you aren't hurt," Thomas chided him. "Not more than you were, anyway." He positioned himself carefully so that his body blocked the boy from view by the rest of the patients. He noted with approval that Smythe put him in the bed farthest from the door, an attempt to shield both parties from any misconduct on either side. Though being tied down, the boy could do very little even to defend himself. "I am Lieutenant Thomas," he said, making himself look straight into those enticing, accusatory eyes. "I am in command of the ship. What is your name?"

The boy stared back blankly, saying nothing.

"Are you mute?" Thomas asked. Several of the most outlandish stories he had heard about pirates mentioned their penchant for cutting out men's tongues. On the other hand, he thought Mr Smythe would have mentioned the discovery of any such deformity.

Still the boy remained silent and sullen. His face, Thomas observed, was perfectly symmetrical, heart-shaped, being broad at the eyes and narrow at the chin, a pretty softness to his lips despite his half-starved, wasted appearance. Here in the sickbay, where there was a lot more light than the cell down below, the eyes were not quite so startling — but still unusually bright for a grown man. Scarcely any hair grew anywhere except for his head, so that a number of scar marks stood out visibly against the skin on his arms and torso, some which might have been from blades, and others that looked like puckered burn marks. Such anomalies were not unusual for anyone who lived a harsh life at sea — Bill Blake, for example, was covered in them — but it *was* strange to see so many on someone so young.

"Very well," Thomas said, when it was clear he was not going to get any reaction to his questions, let alone answers. "I cannot spare more men to guard you. I expect exemplary behaviour from you, or I shall have you returned to the brig. Is that understood?"

For a long moment, he thought the boy would only continue to glare, out of either stubbornness or incomprehension. But then, slowly, he nodded, a lock of matted black hair falling into his face.

"Good." Thomas nodded in return. Perhaps the boy was only feeble-minded, he thought. It was possible that he had never developed speech. Thomas had come across a few such men over his naval career, men who had chosen a life in the lowest ranks of the navy over vagrancy or an unhappy servitude on land. They tended to be targets for mistreatment, being unable to defend themselves, and too often were taken advantage of in many ways. He could only imagine, if such things took place in the navy, what someone in the same position might be exposed to aboard a pirate ship. The vile comments made by the boy's own crew left Thomas in no doubt as to some of the abuses he had already suffered. He felt a pang of sympathy, however misplaced it might have been. "You should be safe here," he said, his tone a little softer than before. "If you have any trouble, only shout and Mr Smythe will be here in a moment."

The boy looked over to where the surgeon was speaking to a patient with a splinted arm, and then back to Thomas, frowning.

"Yes," Thomas said firmly, and then, a little slower to make sure he was understood, "Mr Smythe will be treating your wound. You must not resist him while he does his work, for you will only make it hurt all the more. And don't do that," he added, when the boy tried once again to strain against the ropes, twisting his wrists in what must have been a painful contortion. "We will not have time to nurse you when you have injured yourself further. Only stay still and do not make a nuisance of yourself."

The boy took a breath and let out through his nose, like a blowing horse, and fell back limply onto the pillow.

"Good show." Thomas waited just one more moment, to see if there would be any more effrontery, but the boy only turned his head and stared blankly towards the bulkhead. Deciding that was as good as he was going to get, Thomas sought out Smythe to let him know he was leaving, and made his way back up on deck to seek out Master Days. He passed Bill Blake on the way, heading down towards the first gun deck. The man looked as though he would have stopped, to speak — but Thomas pretended not to see him.

— 5 —

The sailing master was one of the oldest men aboard, a highly experienced officer who had sailed with Wickerham for many years. He knew exactly how far to turn a ship to get the best possible wind in her sails, and his navigational skills were legendary. He wore a thick black beard, unusual for an officer, and it had been streaked with grey for some time. When Thomas found him, he was standing with one hand on the ship's wheel, gazing out over the ocean with a frown creasing his bushy brows. Thomas had once served directly under Days, as midshipman, and even as third lieutenant the man had still been his superior. Now their roles were awkwardly reversed. He did his best to shake off this discomfort yet again; if Wickerham was indeed going to be bedridden for some time, he was going to have to get used to it. He and Days had conversed briefly the previous day on the ship's course, and the niceties had already been observed, so there was no need to stand on formality. "Something wrong, Days?" he asked, coming up beside the old sailor.

Days looked around. "I'm not sure, Thomas," he said, in his usual gruff manner. "I have a feeling there's a storm coming on, only take a look at the sky. Clear as you like."

Thomas looked out over the ship's bow. It was indeed a very

clear day, the sun shining brightly above them as the *Courage* rolled easily over the calm ocean waves. "It wouldn't be the first storm to come on without introduction," he said lightly. "We would be fools not to trust your instinct. Should we make ready?"

"Ordinarily I'd say no," Days still looked uncomfortable; perhaps he simply wasn't used to being so uncertain. "But we're coming up on Cape Verde. There are a number of rocky islands up there. I should hate to get caught trying to navigate them in the midst of a gale. It might be better to be safe than sorry, if you catch my meaning."

"I do." Thomas nodded. "Whatever you think best. Would there be anywhere to put in for supplies, do you think?"

Days grimaced. "Only if you like to eat birds and lizards," he said, with a distinct lack of enthusiasm. "I suggest we hold out until Madeira."

Thomas knew the comment was not a reproach, and that Days and Wickerham often spoke together in such a way, in private, but he couldn't help feeling that the laugh he heard from somewhere behind them was directed at him. He supposed it had been a foolish suggestion. "Very good," he said, trying to shake off the feeling that perhaps he ought to have taken Wickerham up on his offer. After all, that was what the sailing master was for, to steer the ship and give advice to captains who had never had much of a head for mathematics, or preferred to spend their time planning attacks on enemy ships without giving much thought to how they could be managed. "Please do whatever you think is best."

After that, his day became filled with one problem to be solved after another. For one thing, Wickerham had always delegated much of the ship's major responsibilities between his three lieu-tenants. Now that Thomas was commanding the ship, there were three vacant positions, meaning that every little concern seemed to come directly to him. He could not promote anyone, as acting captain, certainly not without Wickerham's approval, and Smythe would not let him see the admiral until the next day, so he was forced to divide the tasks piecemeal among the midshipmen and the petty officers and try to deal with whatever else came up on his own. He made sure to consult with the quartermaster and the ship's cook to ensure that they had enough to feed the crew and the prisoners, at least until they reached port at Madeira. Since they had lost sixteen men of their own, the numbers were not a great deal increased even if they were to feed the pirates on full rations, which no one had any intention of doing. With some fishing, he was told, they would indeed manage. That was a relief. He stopped only long enough to remind them that the young pirate in the sickbay was to be fed according to Mr Smythe's orders, not their own feelings, before moving on to the next thing presented.

After the remaining officers had sat down to dinner, their con-versations darkly dominated by the likely fate of all the unhappy men in the cell below, they dispersed, some to their beds, some to their duty, others to take some air on deck. Thomas joined this latter group, taking a moment of rare quiet to lean over the rail, letting the sea breeze soothe his anxious mind. He thought about Masterman and Harris, lost now in the ocean far behind them. He had never been close to either of the men, both having been his superiors for all the time he had known them, but he missed them now. Harris had had a quick temper, but there was no one on board better at military strategy, and he had been an expert marksman. Masterman had risen up in the ranks from master gunner, and while somewhat cold and taciturn, he had always had meticulous control over the day-to-day running of the ship. As third lieutenant, Thomas had been little more than their go-between, learning as much from them and Wickerham as he could about the intricacies of command. He supposed there was something to be said for learning under fire, as he was now, but it was not at all to be recommended in his view.

His thoughts drifted, unbidden, to the blue-eyed pirate. He was still unsure whether he had done the right thing, and while none of his fellow officers had upbraided him for it, which they could scarcely do, they had not commended him for it, either. But if he had left the boy below, at the mercy of his fellows, he had no doubt what would have happened. Aggie was a big man, but he could not be any truly adequate protection. He shuddered as he imagined it. What kind of people had so little feeling that they would abuse their companions, let alone in front of all the others? It was enough to make his blood run cold, and it had the unfortunate effect of making him feel sorry for a pirate, which was a position he did not like. He made a solemn promise to himself, as he stared up at the moon hanging in the night sky above. He would keep the boy safe until they got to port. If he was in command, he was going to do what he thought was right, and let the others mutter amongst themselves as they liked.

The breeze picked up for a moment, sending a waft of salt air past his face, and he looked up. There was no way to see the clouds in the night sky, but there was a scent on the breeze that took him back to the conversation he had had with Days. It was the smell of rain coming over the horizon.

*

By the following morning the sky was dark with clouds, and the crew was busy battening down the hatches and putting out most of the shipboard lanterns, in case one of them should break and start a fire. Thomas went to Wickerham, whose cheeks were still uncharacteristically pale, and received his permission to make Gower his acting first lieutenant. Wickerham also suggested two other men to act as seconds and to ensure the storm preparations ran smoothly.

On the way out of the sickbay he looked in on the blue-eyed pirate, who was once again making a pretence of sleep, and Thomas was too busy with the running of the ship to spend time trying to engage him; he had to smother his curiosity. Smythe confirmed that the pirate had kept his silence throughout the re-dressing of his wound, but had not tried to fight the surgeon this time, which seemed a good sign. He was also apparently eating ravenously all that he was given. "You would think he had never seen food before," Smythe commented. "But it can only do him good, skin and bones as he is. Still, it seems a shame to fatten him up when it's so likely to be a waste."

Thomas could not agree, although he saw the logic and reason behind the sentiment. "No one has bothered him?" he asked, absent-mindedly.

"No, this crew would no more fight in my sickbay than in a church," Smythe said coolly. "But I cannot account for his safety once he is well enough to leave. I expect you don't plan on having him returned to the brig, but he can hardly bunk in with the men."

Thomas sighed inwardly. "I'll cross that bridge when we get to it, if it's all right with you sir," he said, allowing himself the slightest trace of irony.

Smythe took it well, at least. He smiled and waved Thomas away, indicating that he had more important things to do than to entertain him all morning.

Days was confident of their crossing through the islands of Cape Verde, provided there was no sudden change in the weather. He planned to get through the most dangerous stretch before the worst of the storm hit. Thomas listened carefully to the explanation, making sure he understood every aspect of the sailing master's plan, before telling him to carry on. The wind picked up over midday, and by early evening it was all a man could do to stand upright on the deck, with the sails full to bursting and the ship skimming along over the water as fast as an arrow in flight. Some of the younger boys, giddy with adolescent glee, went up to stand over the bowsprit to feel the spray in their faces and revel in the delight of such magnificent speed. Thomas couldn't help sharing in their enthusiasm; there was nothing like feeling one was master of the elements, taming them to one's own ends. Still, the last thing he needed was to have one of them swept overboard, so he quite spoiled their fun by ordering them all below. It was not long after that that Days ordered most of the sails furled and secured; it was too dangerous to continue with full sail on their current course.

They did not hold a dinner for the officers that night, the men instead choosing to have their meals in their rooms. Thomas did not stop so much as to eat from a plate; he sent for some biscuit and ate it hunched under a tarpaulin as he watched Days personally manoeuvre them around the rocky, volcanic shapes in the distance, almost invisible against the roiling black sky. The giant, black rocks stuck straight up out of the sea, some of them broken off to sharp points like spearheads. What could be seen of them all looked far apart from their position aboard ship, but he could understand Days' former reluctance; it wouldn't take much more than a strong gust of wind on the wrong side of the sail to send them careening towards one of those rocky points. The islands looked further away still, and Days steered well clear of them, ignoring the howl of the gale and the pounding rain that was now coming down so hard that it bid fair to drown any man who stood on the wrong side of the tarpaulin. The deckhands scurried around on deck, miserable, checking the ropes and checking them again.

Looking out over the starboard rail, Thomas was starting to think they might be out of the thicket of rocky obstacles. Just as he was about to congratulate Days on a job well done, there was the sound of commotion from down below. Thomas grit his teeth; he hoped fervently that none of the boards had sprung a leak under the relentless pounding.

"Bowery," he called to the boy who was standing idle, gazing out over the waves. "Go and see what they are about, down there."

The boy saluted and vanished.

"Steady she goes!" carried the voice of one of the seamen from the stern.

"Furl all sail!" Days announced, waving his men into position.

"This storm isn't going to give us more time!"

There was a shout from across the deck — one of the men had lost his grip on one of the thick hawser ropes, slippery with the deluge of rain. The rope's end flailed about wildly in the wind, threatening to do serious harm to anyone who got in its way, as the dismayed man ducked about trying to get it back under control. Thomas hesitated a moment only before going to help, finding himself drenched in moments as soon as he left the protection of the tarpaulin. It took three of them to leap on the rope before it could be secured, and they all came away with painful burns on their palms. When it was done, Thomas hurried back to the wheel, realising as he went that the noise from below, while muffled under the deafening deluge, had become louder. Where on earth was Bowery with the report? He would have to go down there himself, once he had made certain things were secure on deck.

"Is all well, Mr Days?" he asked, as soon as he could reliably be heard under the din.

Days, one hand still on the wheel, turned to look at him and opened his mouth. His expression twisted for a moment into one of horror, just at the moment a crack of thunder rang out — and then he was clutching at his throat, gasping. At the same time, Thomas put a hand up instinctively to his ear — it stung terribly all of a sudden. *Hail?* he wondered, stupidly.

Mr Days fell back, eyes still open wide in that awful expression, as though he had seen a demon rising from the depths of hell. Some black substance like tar was pouring from between his fingers, and as his hands dropped limply and he collapsed onto the wheel, Thomas saw clearly that there was a gaping hole in his throat beneath the bushy beard, and the blackness was blood, leached of its colour by the near-pitch darkness. Realising far too late that the sound he had heard had not been thunder at all, Thomas whirled around and saw a dark figure hurtling across the deck towards him, inches away. He threw himself to one side, drawing his sword as he scrambled upright and turned to face his attacker. The man threw the spent pistol aside and in one quick movement pulled Days' gun from his belt. Thomas sprang forward — the man raised his new weapon and fired. Thomas ducked — but the pistol failed, dampened by the downpour. As the man tried fruitlessly once more to get wet powder to light, Thomas whipped his sword around, spearing the attacker through the ribs. Lightning ripped across the sky in that moment and, up close, he saw the man's face clearly for the first time. He was undoubtedly a pirate, his eyes set so deeply in his gaunt face that the white-blue light of the storm made him appear like a skeleton given life. He smiled, revealing a mouth full of rotten or missing teeth, and coughed blood onto Thomas' face. Appalled, Thomas drew back, using his boot to slide his attacker off his blade and letting him fall onto the deck beside Days with a sound that could barely be heard over the din.

When he looked around, there were similar struggles taking place on the deck as other pirates tried to get to the wheel. Fortunately Days had already tied the spokes in place, and the *Courage* remained on her course. The attack had happened so quickly that Thomas hadn't had time to comprehend what it meant; now his heart was in his throat.

He vaulted over the rail onto the quarterdeck, heading for the stairs. His own men were holding their own against the pirates; he saw one go down as he went past, flailing wildly with a stolen sword. "Guard the wheel!" he called over to the two men who had dispatched him. There was no time to stop and help them.

The lower decks were chaos. The crew of the *Courage* had the numbers, but having started below decks and worked their way up, the pirates were using the tight corners and bottlenecks at the stairs and ladders to their advantage. They had clearly gotten their hands on plenty of weapons, and the navy men who had not yet taken to their beds were taken by surprise yet again, attacked from behind or shot before they could draw swords, their crumpled bodies creating obstacles for their fellows.

Thomas himself nearly tripped over someone slumped over on the stairs to the gun deck. It was Cole, swaying limply as he poured blood from a wound in his thigh. "They killed Rogers, sir," he gasped when Thomas dropped his sword and went to one knee beside him, trying to assess the damage. "It was Briggs, sir, he must've slipped the chain somehow, and he killed Rogers and let loose the others…"

Thomas held his hand against the wound, trying to staunch the heavy bleeding, but the stair under them was already black with blood, and as he scrambled for something to use as a makeshift bandage, the boy went limp in his arms. "Cole?" he tried, shaking him. Nothing. Cole's face was pale.

He stood up and staggered back, trying to think through a fog of panic. This was no navy battle, where boarding was rare and hand-to-hand combat was hardly needed. It was like fighting inside a multi-layered maze, with all his men spread out over the ship and no way to unite them, or even to give them orders.

Then there was an almighty noise, ten times louder than a cannon and more ferocious than a thunderclap, and Thomas was thrown off his feet, slamming up against the bulkhead. His skull thudded painfully against the heavy oak boards, and for a moment he saw nothing but stars as he tried to struggle to his feet. He need not have bothered. Seconds later the same awful, crashing sound echoed around his ears. This time he managed to hold onto the stair rail, gritting his teeth so hard he thought he felt his jaw crack. The ship pitched and groaned ominously, and the distant sounds of panicked shouting could be heard. Cole's body had been tossed to the foot of the stairs where it lay like a discarded rag doll.

Somehow Thomas managed to drag himself upright, holding onto the beams for balance, and stumbled down the corridor towards the lower decks, picking up his sword as he went. He had to step over two more dead men wearing blue coats whose guns and swords had been ripped from their belts; he forced himself onwards without daring to look at their faces.

The lower gun deck was already flooding. Some men who had managed to make their way out in time were grappling with two pirates at the stair. Howling in the very depths of his mind, Thomas tightened his grip on his sword and slashed the throat of one of them; the man screamed and went down. The other snarled and turned on him, but Gower, fighting at the head of the gun crew coming up from below, managed to slice open the man's belly before he could advance. There was a foul stench as the pirate's guts spilled out onto the boards and he keeled over. Between them Gower and Thomas cleared both men away so that the crew could get up the stairs. "How bad is it?" Thomas panted, and saw the answer in Gower's face before he spoke.

"Bad." His face was white. "Whatever we hit took out the bow cabins, and we're taking on water fast. I don't know if we can save her. What does Days —"

"Days is dead," Thomas said.

Gower swallowed hard, eyes wide, then nodded. "Your orders?"

Thomas knew that there was nothing he could do. There was no telling how many men they had already lost in the impact. There would be no patching up that much damage out of dry-dock, even if they weren't in the midst of a gale and under attack by marauding pirates. "We shall have to try and make it to the boats," he said finally. "As many men as you can."

"What about you, sir?"

Thomas spoke before he had time to even realise his own thoughts — "I must go to the sickbay. We must save the admiral if there is any chance."

Gower nodded. "The pirates will probably be heading for the boats, too, sir," he pointed out.

"Then," Thomas said, including all of the men around them in his fiery look. "We shall have to get to them first."

The men, as one, drew their swords, determined despite their fear. "The King," Thomas said, as he shook Gower's hand.

"For the King!" they chorused.

Thomas stood aside to let them pass, and they charged forward. He stopped only long enough to look over the stair rail. The water was already lapping the third and fourth step, rising with every second that passed. There was no more time to waste.

As he reached the infirmary, following a different path to the one Gower's men had taken, he saw the injured already being supported out of the door. Relief flooded Thomas as he saw Wickerham, dressed only in loose trousers and shirt and held up on either side by Mr Smythe and Dolson, one of the hands. It was Smythe who was bellowing orders to the men, and they obeyed by instinct the voice of authority, staying in single or double file to one side of the corridor so that they did not cause a crush in their haste to escape.

"To the boats!" Thomas called to the men. "Head for the boats!"

"Abandon ship?" Wickerham gasped. Thomas felt physical pain in his chest at the look on his captain's face, but there was no time to dwell on it.

"Yes sir," he said, looking around to meet Smythe's eyes. The look in the surgeon's expression was just as easy to read. Thomas knew better than to tell him his work. They both knew the likelihood that Wickerham would survive the night on a roiling sea in the pouring rain in a cramped, uncovered lifeboat was miniscule at best, and that was assuming they all made it that far. "Are they all out?" Thomas asked instead.

"All but one," Smythe jerked his head back towards the door. "I'm sorry, but I could not risk it."

Thomas realised immediately what he was talking about. If the blue-eyed pirate were released, with no one to keep him in check, surely he would turn on the injured men, or Smythe, before rejoining his own crew to wreak more havoc. To put the boy's life over those of Thomas' own men would be foolhardy and even illegal — the admiralty board would certainly see it that way. On the other hand, Thomas thought with a kind of wild dread, the chances of any of them having to face the admiralty were becoming slimmer by the minute. Tied to the bed, the boy would drown, and those damn blue eyes would haunt Thomas for whatever time he had left on earth. "Go," he told Smythe, indicating the corridor to the stairs that led to the upper decks. "Find Mr Gower, he will see you safely aboard."

Smythe looked as though he might have liked to argue, ignoring any technical obligation he had to obey, but Wickerham's groan made him think better of it. "Try not to get yourself killed, boy," the surgeon muttered instead. He and Dolson lurched forward, planting every step with consideration to avoid being tossed aside by the ship's heaving, unnatural movement. Time was of the essence, but if they fell, they might not be able to get Wickerham up again.

Thomas hurried inside. The cots here were thankfully nailed down, so he could grab onto their posts with both hands to keep his balance, moving crab-like from one to the other for the greatest speed. On the far bed, the blue-eyed boy was tugging frantically at the ropes that bound his wrists to the bed, bracing his feet against the mattress and trying to gain leverage enough to force his hands through. It was having very little effect; poor Rogers may have been a slow-thinker, but he had made excellent knots. As Thomas staggered forward the boy looked up at him, his expression even more fearful at the sight of him holding his sword aloft.

"Hold it tight!" Thomas ordered, with no time for explanations. The boy's eyes widened in surprise, but he did as he was told, pulling one of the ropes as taut as it would stretch. One swing from Thomas' sword cut it through. He was about to go around to sever the other, but to his surprise the boy reached over and undid the complex knot one-handed with incredible speed. Thomas kept his sword levelled, warily, as the young man untangled himself from the ropes and scrambled off the bed, hindered only by the bandage across his chest. The wound clearly pained him; his face twisted into a grimace as he stood. Smythe had found him a clean pair of breeches somewhere, but that was all he wore, and it would have to do. "The ship is sinking!" Thomas had to shout to be heard over the noise. "You must follow me if you wish to live, and if you try to stab me in the back I shall make certain you get left behind. Is that under— "

Before he could finish, the boy ran past him. Cursing, Thomas followed. To his surprise the boy paused in the doorway to wait for him; apparently he had not been trying to escape, only unwilling to stand and wait for Thomas to finish his speech. Standing, Thomas realised in the midst of his growing panic that they were almost exactly the same height. "Stay behind me," Thomas chided him, wondering why on earth he expected a pirate to obey. Or a better question, why was he doing this in the first place? He could argue to those who would chide him that it was profoundly unchristian to leave any man to face certain death, no matter his provenance. But they would surely tell him, perhaps rightly so, that the risks outweighed even a heavenly reward. But it was done now, and short of killing the boy himself there was nothing he could do to change that.

He felt uneasy with the pirate bringing up his rear, but he could hardly do otherwise; the boy was unarmed and there was no question of forcing him to go ahead. He made his way cautiously along the passageway, his boots splashing and sliding with every step in seawater that was now rising around their ankles. The pirate seemed to be having an easier time of it without boots, but Thomas was not about to go similarly barefoot and risk a worse injury than a few bruises. They seemed to be the last to evacuate the middle deck; on the upper gun deck he could hear men shouting and the occasional sound of pistols. As they came out of the water and up the stair, running footsteps pounded over their heads — impossible to tell whether friend or foe. Thomas put up a hand, signaling to wait, until he judged the sound to have moved far enough away, then he charged up the stairs.

He knew every inch of this ship. He had sailed on her now for three years. He had climbed these stairs a thousand times, and yet it had never seemed so far from one deck to another as it did now. Ahead in the near-darkness he could see men grappling, stumbling as the ship veered wildly about, some unable to keep their feet, others flailing with weapons to either side, cutting down anyone in their path; it was too dark and too chaotic to even recognise his own men.

He drew his sword and hurried forward, catching the first man by the ragged collar of his shirt and drawing him back, knocking him aside with a blow to the side of his head as he tried to wriggle free. The sailor he had been beating upon scrambled back and away, running.

A strangled cry from behind him made Thomas look around. A dark shape had come up out of the chaos and had the pirate boy from behind, armed with a large, heavy-handled knife which must have been filched from the galley. The boy's eyes were wide — but not frightened, Thomas thought in the split-second of time he had to take it all in, only furious — struggling as well as he could with the wide blade at his throat. Thomas didn't stop to think; he brought his sword up, nicking the man's arm, and as the attacker howled and momentarily loosened his grip, the boy shot back a hard elbow and ducked away. The pirate snarled and reached for him — Thomas flicked his sword again — once — and there was a gasp; blood began to pour sluggishly from a thin but deep throat cut. The man scrabbled at his neck, trying to staunch the flow, but it was already pouring out his life. His legs staggered and failed under him; he went down.

Thomas felt sick. As the light died in the man's single eye, he recognised him at last — it was Babber, the man who had fought with Aggie to keep the boy in the brig. The young pirate stared down at the body, wide-eyed, rubbing at his own neck as though in sympathy, though Thomas could not imagine why he would have any.

"Come," Thomas said, hoarsely. He sheathed his sword and turned to go — the water was already starting to slosh around their feet, chasing them, gradually becoming a river of blood. To his horror, however, the boy had knelt beside Babber and began rifling through his clothes, looting the body. "Stop that!" Thomas cried, so shocked by this barbarous behaviour that his exclamation came out sounding more like the constant admonitions of his old governess than a military officer.

The boy ignored him, tugging at the one-eyed man's tattered shirt until the seam around the neck tore, revealing a tobacco-stained upper torso covered in patches of dark hair and blood. The boy's fingers searched around the man's ruined throat; there appeared to be something hanging there on a cord. "Enough," Thomas said, managing to put some authority into his voice this time, and reached for his arm to drag him away. The boy ducked nimbly away from his grip, despite the pain his injury must surely be giving him, and stepped away, having successfully lifted the trinket over Babbers' lolling head, bringing it away whole. His fingers were stained with the man's blood. He glared at Thomas as though daring him to try and take his prize.

Swallowing his disgust, Thomas turned and hurried back to the stairs that led to the quarterdeck, following the sound of the rain hammering on the boards. By now he found he didn't much care whether the boy followed him or not; he wished only to get to the ship's boats before they launched without him.

Then, just as he reached the final step, the gates of hell finally opened all the way. Something hit the starboard side of the *Courage* with such force that she was almost instantaneously split in two. The deck smashed apart under Thomas' feet; in the same moment he felt something hit him hard from behind, and he had the briefest sensation of flying away, up into the emerging darkness.

$$— 6 —$$

Thomas' lungs were burning. He choked, and the next thing he knew his stomach was emptying what seemed an obscene amount of water and muck onto the soft, shifting surface under him. *Sand,* he realised blearily as he tried to make his body follow his commands. His limbs felt as though they were weighted down with lead, and there was a terrible stabbing pain right at the base of his skull. He had been lying face down on the sand, and it had found its way into his eyes, nose and mouth. He spat, drily, and shook his head, ridding himself of the worst, and tried to make his knees bend under him. After a minute or two he was able to lift himself onto his hands and knees, but his coat was so stiff with salt and sand that he could hardly move his arms. He coughed again, vomiting another mouthful of seawater, and tried to look around. His vision was blurred, but he could tell that it was daylight; the storm was over, and he was on land.

How on earth had he not drowned?

"Hello?" he tried to call out, but his voice emerged only as a strangled husk. His body swayed.

Fighting the urge to simply lay down and fall once again into blissful unconsciousness, he leaned back onto his heels and tried to struggle out of his coat. This was difficult to do at the best of times, and was now almost impossible. A dress coat certainly *would* have been impossible, and he praised small mercies that he had only been wearing his navy uniform, which had not been starched since they had put out to sea. Gradually, painstakingly, he eased out one arm, bending it painfully backwards as far as it would go, and then the other, letting the ruined garment fall unceremoniously onto the damp sand. His fingers almost numb, he managed to tear off his neckcloth also. Exhausted by this simple task, he fell forward onto his forearms and rolled over, landing on his back. The sun was very bright overhead and it pained his eyes; groaning, he covered them with the back of one sand-caked arm. He licked his parched lips and turned his head to either side, trying to make out anything that might give him some idea of where he was. It was all a blur of dirty yellow and green.

The sun beat down on him with a heat that grew gradually more unbearable, until he knew he had to move or be cooked slowly. Grunting with every movement as he forced life back into his muscles, he rolled back onto his hands and managed a slow crawl, painful but steady. Eventually the damp sand under his hands gave way to dry, rocky stuff that then became dirt and roots under his searching fingers. When he felt the blazing heat shift off the back of his neck, it was far enough. Groping, he found the trunk of the tree he had crawled under, and set his back against it. He brushed his shaking hands against his breeches, ridding them of the worst of the sand, and carefully — very carefully — did his best to wipe his face. The movement stung the sensitive skin under his nose and around his eyes, but when he was done he could see a little better. He had crawled into what appeared to be a shaded copse on the edge of the shoreline, the earth covered with large, boat-like green leaves that seemed to be the offshoots of some kind of vine. The tree he had found was a short, stumpy palm, a thick cluster of yellowish coconuts hanging from the base of its wide, green fronds. A couple of riper ones had fallen onto the ground within his reach, but when he picked them up they fell apart in his hands, rotten.

A movement caught the corner of his eye and he looked up. He could see no signs of life anywhere. Perhaps a bird or some native creature had simply stirred in the underbrush. He lay back, pretending he had not noticed, and paid close attention to his peripheral vision — there, again, he saw a flicker, not of any plant or small creature, but something big enough to be human, moving between the trees.

"Hello?" he called out again, hoarsely. "Is someone — " He stopped, cursing himself for a fool as he realised his mistake too late; if the figure who approached was one of the pirates, he would be dead before he could move. Clumsily he fumbled for his sword, but it was gone, both blade and sheath missing.

Helpless, he watched as a figure emerged from the trees. At least it did not come all in a rush, which was only mild relief, and then, as it grew closer, he recognised it. "*You*," he croaked, a peculiar shiver going down his spine.

The blue-eyed pirate stopped, looking down at him. He was holding something that glinted in the dappled sunlight. Thomas squinted at it. "Is that my sword?" he asked. His voice was unimproved by the untold hours he had spent baking in the sun; there was no moisture in his mouth at all.

The boy was holding the blade by the hilt in one hand, the scabbard in the other. He held it low, but not in the manner of one who knew how to use it; had he been upright and at full strength, Thomas might have knocked it out of his hands in a moment. Like Thomas he was covered in sand, most of it having sloughed off his bare arms, but it had stuck in patches to the bandages wrapped around his chest. These were now coming apart, as apparently even Smythe's expert work was unable to stand up to the rigours of being thrown overboard in the midst of a hurricane. His hair was in a worse state than ever, hanging over his shoulders in four matted grey clumps. Thomas could not see clearly enough to gage his expression, but he did not need to; his danger was already clear enough. "Are you well?" he asked, hoping to keep the boy off his guard by distracting him with questions. "Have you seen any other survivors?" As he spoke, the wave of grief he had been avoiding threatened to rise in his throat. Days. Cole. Rogers. All dead, and he had no doubt that many of his crewmen, perhaps most of them, were gone as well. He wondered if Gower had managed to load any of the boats. Perhaps it would not have made any difference.

The pirate did not answer, only frowned and took another cautious step forward. Thomas managed to keep his eyes fixed on the boy's face, not daring to focus on the sword's point unless the next thing he saw was it plunging into his own chest. "How is your wound?" he asked. The boy looked down at his mess of bandages and then back up again, quickly, as though suspecting he had been tricked. Still, he did not move to attack. Thomas suspected that if he was going to make a move, he would have done so already. He could only hope.

"I won't hurt you," Thomas promised, trying to make his ruined voice sound gentle. He decided not to add that he was too weak to be any danger, in any case. "Have you been far?" he asked instead. "Could you find any fresh water?"

The thin brow over those blue eyes furrowed thoughtfully, and their gaze flickered upwards. After a moment's consideration, the boy stuck the sword blade-first into the sand beneath the living bed of leaves, and picked his way over to Thomas' tree, not looking at him but focused on the canopy above. Thomas watched as, with a look of determination, the young man took a hold of the tree with both hands and began to shimmy up it like a monkey. Thomas had seen native men do this in the Portuguese colony in Brazil, and if he had been awed by it then, he was even more so now. The pirate made good use of his bare feet, clinging to the irregular surface of the tree's bark as he hopped feet first, his arms following a second later. Fortunately it was not a very tall tree, and he reached the top before he could lose momentum and go sliding back. Thomas squinted and turned his head away as the brightness from between the palm fronds pained his eyes; he could hear heavy rustling from overhead, and in a moment there was a *thunk* as a large yellow fruit landed on the ground beside him, bouncing off into the undergrowth. Before he could try to go after it there was another, and another. They all fell a little outward from the tree, as though the boy were deliberately swinging them away, making sure they did not drop directly onto Thomas' head.

Presently the boy came scrambling back down the trunk, his

descent rather clumsier than his climb. He landed awkwardly on his rump, letting out a short, pained exclamation. "Are you all right?" Thomas asked him, without wondering at his own concern. "That was an incredible climb. Where did you learn it?"

He didn't know why he asked the question, as he had no expectation of being answered, but then to his surprise he heard a voice say: "Tortuga." The voice was quiet but no less masculine for it; it had a softness rather than a hoarseness.

"So you do speak," Thomas said, surprised. *Perhaps he only knows a few words*, he thought. "What's your name?" he tried.

A moment of hesitation, then the answer came, simply: "Jim."

"Jim," Thomas repeated. "Why did you not speak before?"

Ignoring him, Jim cast about on the ground for one of the coconuts. He reached over suddenly and Thomas flinched, half expecting to have his head bashed in with the thing, but the boy only rapped the coconut against the tree trunk, knocking as though checking for something. Then he picked up the sword again and began making expert hacking cuts near the hilt. It made Thomas wince a little, for the condition of the blade as well as for the lack of care the young pirate had for his own fingers, which were less than inches away from being sliced off. Having chopped his way into the interior, the boy seemed to hesitate a moment, regarding his handiwork. Then he offered it forward, waiting for Thomas to take it in his stiff, unyielding hands before snatching his own back, as though he were feeding a lion in a cage.

"Thank you," Thomas said, stunned, but Jim was already picking up another, tapping it expertly against the trunk in the same way, and starting on the work. Eagerly Thomas lifted the fruit to his lips, tipping his head back and letting the sweet, refreshing liquid fall onto his tongue. He took first a carefully-measured mouthful, which he swilled around his cheeks to wash away the sand, and spat it out before drinking the rest. At the moment, it was more delicious than any fine wine he had ever tasted.

Jim finished his own coconut and reached for another. "Perhaps we ought to save them?" Thomas suggested, with some reluctance. His voice came out a little clearer.

Jim stared at him, his blue eyes narrowed with what seemed more like condescension than confusion, and motioned with his free hand to the trees surrounding them in three directions, as if to say there was clearly no shortage.

Thomas understood, and he could hardly argue. When Jim, a little more cautiously this time as though he were afraid of being refused, offered him another coconut, he took it and drank his fill. "Thank you," he said again, already feeling stronger. Jim once again did not answer; he was focused on digging out the meat of his coconut with his sticky fingers, caring little or nothing for the grains of sand that transferred onto the white flesh as he spooned it into his mouth. Occasionally he reached up to scratch under his shoulder-length mop of matted hair.

Probably has lice, Thomas thought with private revulsion. He suddenly remembered the body of the pirate he had killed back on the *Courage*, and the blue-eyed boy's fingers digging under the shirt of the corpse, coming away bloody. The blood had since been washed away, but the memory was not at all comforting.

His desperate thirst now sated, he took a moment to consider the situation. He was alone on what he had to assume was a deserted island in the middle of the ocean — at least, alone in the sense of having none of his own crew beside him. His unlikely companion was a pirate. He had been one of the crew whose ultimate escape and attempts to take over the *Courage* had certainly resulted in her being smashed to pieces on the rocks, the deaths of perhaps all her crew but himself… but Jim had not been a part of that escape. Neither had he done anything, thus far, to make Thomas fear him, other than the theft of his sword which might understandably be considered a precautionary act of self-defence. On the contrary, his actions had only served to contribute to his survival. His only motivation might be a simple-mindedness that made it impossible for him to discern between friend or foe, but that was no reason to treat him as anything other than an ally in such a desperate situation. He may very well try to loot Thomas' body in the event of his death, but there was nothing left to find in any case.

"Jim," Thomas prompted, leaning forward to gain the boy's attention. "Tell me, did you walk far? Do you have any idea what kind of place this is?"

Jim looked up once more, one cheek pulsating slightly as he chewed — thankfully with his mouth closed. He shrugged, non-committally. Thomas grit his teeth in frustration. Looking up, he tried to gauge the position of the sun overhead. How long since they had been thrown from the deck of the *Courage*? Eight hours? Perhaps more? The dark realities of the previous night — the storm, the shipwreck, the massive loss of life — started filling his chest with emotion; he shoved it back, forcing himself to focus on survival. He had loved Crusoe as a boy, though he sometimes had skipped what he felt were the least interesting parts in favour of those chapters with the most action. Whether he had actually learned something from Defoe would remain to be seen, he thought wearily. "We must search for more survivors," he decided aloud. "And a source of fresh water… and a way to signal, in case the boats are nearby." This, he had to admit, was scraping the heights of optimism. Even if anyone had managed to launch the lifeboats, and he did not think there had been enough time, they would hardly be sailing around in circles looking for him. The boats had charts and compasses stored aboard them, wrapped in oilcloth and stowed away in case of emergency. Gower surely would head for the nearest land if he had the chance. But while he was an experienced navy man, even if Smythe was not, there were too many obstacles in the way of his finding safety on land; the ferocity of the storm, the lack of men to row, sailing blind in the dark… "perhaps we should light a fire," he thought, and didn't realise he had said it aloud until Jim frowned and shook his head vigorously.

Thomas stared at him. "What? Why?"

Jim looked at him as though this ought to have been perfectly obvious. "Will… be seen," he said, after a moment. The words did not sound stilted, or slow, only soft. Cautious.

"Of course someone will see," Thomas exclaimed. "I mean to signal anyone who can help us, unless you should like to be stuck here forever. Wherever *here* is," he added. "Although perhaps on second thought it would be wiser to take a turn about the place; try to get some idea of our direction. If you would just — "

Jim's eyes went very wide, all of a sudden, and he reached

over, clapping his hand over Thomas' mouth. Thomas couldn't stop a startled exclamation; it came out muffled. Jim ignored him, looking around wildly in all directions; then he tugged on Thomas' shirt with his free hand, almost dragging him behind the tree on the inland side. Trapped between Jim and the tree, Thomas could see or do nothing, only sit there listening, trying to hear whatever had startled his companion. For a long moment he heard nothing. He breathed through his nose, the sound too-loud in his over-sensitive ears. Jim was crouching over him on one knee, his bare foot on the other side of Thomas' waist, very close, and he was perfectly still. His hand smelled strongly of fresh coconut, and Thomas did his best to focus on that and not the sour stench of the poultice emanating from the bandages which had not all been washed away.

After a moment of nothing other than his own heartbeat, he heard the distant sound of voices, harsh and guttural. Then he felt more than heard the footsteps through the earth under him. He tried to turn his head, to see, but Jim held him fast, shaking his head quickly.

"T'aint much more t'an a Godf'rsaken spit o' land," someone was cursing as the voices came close enough to comprehend what was being said. "How we gonna get out o' this?"

"Shut yer face," growled another. Thomas thought he recognised that voice as the one who had jeered at Gower from the cell, the one with the large ears. "Better stuck on some rock than in that fucking ship, or in some hole in a British gaol."

"How?" demanded the first. "We gon' die either way."

"Druther die wit' sun on me face," said a third, calmer voice.

Thomas saw Jim's head twitch around. It sounded like Aggie, the big black man who had insisted on having Jim's wound treated. "Wuddn't be so bad to be buried out 'ere, near de sea." The voices now were close enough that surely Jim, peering around the edge of the tree, could see the men walking along the line of trees.

"Oh aye, an' who'll bury you?" demanded Big Ears. "Like as not your bones'll be left out to dry in t'sun."

"Still better'n bein' hanged."

"What's that?" the first pirate said, with an air of discovery. Thomas' heart leapt, but the man didn't sound excited or angry, only curious.

"Ooh." Big Ears laughed wickedly. "Wot a nice coat. Try 'er on, Gappy." Thomas, remembering the stained and shrunken article he had left abandoned on the beach, swallowed hard and closed his eyes in a silent prayer. Jim's hand came slowly and carefully away from his mouth, but he did not dare move.

"'Ow do I look?" the first pirate asked, after a moment's shuffling about — Thomas was surprised anyone could have put the ruined coat on, after the effort it had taken him to take it off.

"Be careful, someone could mistake ye for a navy man!"

"Mebbe he who dropped him still 'round 'ere," Aggie rumbled.

"Ye ever see a navy man take off 'is coat?" Big Ears laughed again. "E'd be so pale unnerneath you'd see 'im a mile off."

The first pirate snorted. "Let's 'ave a look 'round then."

Thomas opened his eyes in panic. Jim looked back at him; their eyes met. Thomas knew what Jim was going to do seconds before it happened — he reached for the boy, trying to grab him by the loose waist of his breeches, but Jim slipped out of his grip easily, standing up with a grunt and stepping back. He grabbed the hilt of Thomas' sword where it stuck out of the earth. For a moment Thomas was sure he was done for, his mind full of a vividly gory vision of being slaughtered with his own blade, but Jim only gave him one final look, twisted the hilt in his hand so that the blade pointed toward the ground, and broke away.

Thomas waited, heart in his throat. He could not run. He had no real confidence even in his ability to stand. He heard Jim hurrying through the undergrowth, it seemed to him deliberately careless, when he had been so nimble and stealthy before. "Wassat?" one of the pirates exclaimed, followed by a chorus of laughter from the others.

"Aw, s'only Jim," rumbled the first voice.

"'E's alive!" Aggie exclaimed joyfully. "Where you been, Jim?"

"Oooh, lookit 'is fancy blade," sneered Big Ears. "Where'd ye get that beauty, maggot?"

"Gah, stop asskin 'im questions," sighed the first pirate. "Ye know 'e won't answer ye."

"Show us the blade, maggot," Big Ears coaxed. "Go on, let's see it."

"Let 'im alone," Aggie protested. "Lookit 'im all swabbl'd up… is 't bad, Jim? I t'ought you were gone for sure."

"It's *swaddled*, ye halfbrained idiot," sighed the other. At least, Thomas thought, there seemed to only be three of them. He wasn't surprised that Aggie had made it out — it would take a lot to kill a man that size, he thought — and perhaps they had taken one of the boats to save themselves from the wreck. "C'mon, I've seen enough o' this pile o' sand," the pirate continued. "Let's go inland, see if we can find anythin' worth livin' on."

The footsteps started to move towards Thomas. He bit his lip and locked his jaw; his teeth were chattering despite the heat. "Oi!" the first pirate yelled. "Watch what ye're doin' wi' that sword, boy, afore I show ye where to put it!"

"Aw, Gappy, 'e on'y tryin'a tell ya somet'ing," Aggie protested. "Mebbe he see'd a lion."

He isn't speaking to them, Thomas realised, even through the haze of fear. *They don't even expect him to speak. But he spoke to me.*

"It's an island, mudbrain," 'Gappy' snarled. "Ain't no lions on a liddle island like this'n."

"'Ow'd you know?" Big Ears put in, sounding nervous. "No one could'a seen where we were goin', in that storm. We could of washed up all the way to Africa."

"Gah, that's 'undreds of miles away," Gappy scoffed. "I'm tellin' ya, it's only birds an' insects an' maybe a nice fat seal if ye're lucky. I'm goin' in."

There was a rustling sound, too close, much too close. Thomas braced himself; he would have to try to run, no matter how futile. Then he heard a startled exclamation. Unable to help himself, he turned his head just far enough that he could peer out to the edge of the treeline. Jim was standing in the way of a tall, skinny man in a knee-length, bloodstained article which, with no belt to cinch it about his waist, gave him the appearance of wearing a nightshirt, with Thomas' salt-stained blue coat slung haphazardly over it. He was thin enough that the stiffness in the fabric appeared to give him no trouble. Jim had Thomas' sword in his hand and was, while not pointing it directly at the man, waving it around in a dangerous fashion, gesturing as though he were holding a cane and not a razor-sharp weapon. Just visible behind the man, who had to be Gappy by process of elimination, Big Ears and Aggie stood a cautious distance away. "Put that bloody thing down, ye mad little shit!" Gappy yelled, stumbling back. "Someone take it from 'im."

Aggie laughed, a bassy, rich laugh. "You can try it! Lose all yer fingers!"

Big Ears beckoned to Jim. "Coom on then, maggot. You show us. See if ye can find us somethin' te eat, eh? Make yerself useful."

Jim lowered the sword and stepped towards his comrades.

Thomas hadn't realised he had been leaning out of his hiding place to listen. When his head swam suddenly, he put his hand down, out of instinct, catching himself before he could fall. It was a tiny noise, but enough to make Gappy flinch and jump back a half a step. "What's that now?" He rounded on Jim. "You see anythin' out there?"

Thomas jerked back behind the tree and braced again, feeling as though he were already so tense that his spine might snap. He started to wish they would just find him, and get it over with. Except pirates wouldn't just kill him, he reminded himself. Pirates were notorious for their desire to inflict pain and suffering on all they encountered; and so far he'd seen very little to convince him otherwise. *But Jim helped me*, he thought. *He didn't have to*. But at that point, Thomas might have been Jim's only chance at survival. Now he was back with his friends — if they could be so called — surely no such consideration would occur to him? Or was he giving the boy the credit of more intelligence than he was due?

"It's just a bird," Big Ears said finally. "You're the one who said there ain't nothin' else out here."

Gappy hesitated, it seemed, but finally Thomas heard him spit on the sand and turn, his footsteps and those of the others beginning to move away.

Thomas let out a long, painful breath. It had hurt his weakened lungs to hold it in, and his chest burned as he gasped, sucking in much-needed air. He was alive, through some miracle. Then again, he thought as he looked with some despair around at his surroundings — green, but desolate — probably not for very long. He was stranded alone — now truly alone — on an island with a gang of pirates, his own crew all dead or gone, and with only an empty scabbard to defend himself. What was he going to do now?

— 7 —

It did not take Thomas too long to come around from his despair. After all, he reasoned, if some pirates had survived, perhaps there was more chance that some of the *Courage*'s crew also lived. It was certainly too much to hope for that they had all landed near each other, but he remembered quite clearly being thrown from the ship like a bullet from a gun — it made sense that he could have travelled quite far. He had not yet seen any sign of the *Courage* at all — not even a stick of wood or scrap of sail — it followed that wherever the ship or her lifeboats were, there would be the best place to start searching.

It was a little longer before he could gather strength enough to get to his feet. It was difficult, and his head ached horribly, but his legs seemed to be able to hold his weight once he had got them planted. He used the sturdy palm tree as a support as he dragged himself upright, finally steadying himself with both hands while his head cleared of its vague disorientation. He felt oddly as though the storm had sent him all the way through the earth, and that everything was suddenly upside down. But at least his mouth was no longer bone dry.

His boots squelched uncomfortably. Despite the heat surrounding him they were still damp at the soles. Removing them was out of the question, however, so Thomas would have to bear it. He looked around at the harvest of fresh coconuts; he doubted he could stumble across a similarly fresh crop elsewhere, and he did not like his chances of finding his way back to the spot every time he needed to eat. His eyes fell on the wide leaves of the creeping plant. Gingerly, wary in case the dizziness came on again, he tugged one of them free. It was as long as his arm span and almost as wide when flat, but it curled up on either side, looking rather like a canoe. Into it he fit four coconuts and turned up the corners. It packaged well enough, once he took a strip of vine and bound it together. More vine, wound carefully around the bundle and secured with ship's knots, made it possible for him to sling it over his shoulder. Then he picked up the last coconut he had drunk from, and pinched at the flesh with his fingers, the way Jim had. He was surprised at how easily it came apart. When he put it in his mouth and chewed, it was plain-tasting, but pleasantly so. He was hardly in any condition to stomach any rich food, although, he thought wistfully, a glass of wine might not have gone amiss.

Ridding himself of thoughts of food and wine both, he set his jaw and set off into the trees. He dared not follow the waterline for fear of coming across Jim and the pirates. He decided to head west instead, in the opposite direction from the beach, in the hope of making his way eventually to the other side of the island.

Once he started walking, the pain in his head lessened somewhat, making it easier to focus on his task. He only ate a few bites of the coconut, saving the rest. He was not really hungry, but he knew it would not be long before he was.

The trees were not thick, but other plants were grown in large patches around and between them. Though he tried to follow the sun, there was no path, and he was forced to turn and change his course frequently. It forced him into an abysmally slow pace, to the point where he was beginning to regret not risking the pirates after all. He walked for a few hours, doing his best to ignore the strain in legs used only to short distances aboard ship, and the blisters forming on his toes. His shirt had dried in the heat, but when the sun reached its peak, it started sticking to his skin once again with sweat. He stopped and took shelter under another tree, taking advantage of its shade to finish the meat from his coconut. He found dew collected in the curve of another large leaf and tasted it, drinking just enough to wet his lips and hoping it would not make him ill. His face burned uncomfortably with sun exposure.

He lay back against the soft covering of leaves. Desperate as his situation might be, he couldn't help noticing how peaceful it was. All he could hear was the breeze rustling through the palm tree fronds, and the distant sound of seabirds. Not a human noise to be heard, no bells ringing, no sails flapping, no men calling to each other amidships, no sound of guns. It ought to make him feel isolated and lonely; instead it was almost a welcome relief. The last few days had been so full of noise. He had thought he would never get the stench of blood and gunpowder out of his nose — now, the air was clean and fresh. He closed his eyes.

When he woke, the sun had set. He sat up quickly, imagining he heard the ship's bells tolling an alarm. How long had he slept, out here in the open at the mercy of anyone who could stumble across him? Furious with himself, he got to his feet and lifted his bundle of coconuts. His stomach rumbled uncomfortably, but he ignored it. He had wasted too much time to stop and eat.

Walking was actually easier in the cool of the night, but it was also less peaceful. Nocturnal creatures, unseen in the darkness, made otherworldly noises that caused him to stop every few minutes, frozen, expecting someone or something to come rushing at him out of the trees. At some point he realised that the ground had stopped sloping steadily upwards and had evened out. He decided he must have reached the high point of the island, but it was too dark to see anything on either side.

It took him some time to work out how to cut into a coconut with a sharp rock, and he made rather a botched job of it, but he managed to save most of the juice inside. Resting against a tree, he considered as he sipped carefully, savouring each refreshing mouthful as long as he could before letting it go down to soothe his dry throat. If he were to wait until morning, he might have a better view, perhaps get some idea of where he was going. But then he would be wasting several hours that he could have spent searching for survivors. What would Admiral Wickerham do? he wondered.

In the end, selfishly, it was his aching, blistering feet that decided him. He took the time to make a shelter by folding some large leaves over two low plants, enough to disguise him should anyone glance casually at the area. Then he took off his boots and lay down, hoping that he didn't miss the sunrise and sleep all through the day.

Unlike before, when exhaustion had dragged him in near-unconsciousness, his sleep was troubled. His dreams were full of his ghostly crewmates, reprimanding him for his failure. He should have got them safely through the storm, he should not have let the pirates escape. The *Courage* was destroyed again and again in front of his eyes, and he woke several times with the horrible jolting sensation that his body was flying through the air. When he opened his eyes and the sky was orange-grey with the early light of dawn, he sat up.

His boots had finally dried overnight, and he put them on, wincing, realising as he did so that he must look a horrific sight. His stockings were bloody and torn, his breeches not any less so, and his shirt had come loose, flapping in the wind. He made to tuck it in again and changed his mind; there was no one about to see, and the breeze was pleasant against his sweat-soaked skin. It was still much cooler than the dry heat of the day, but the muggy oppressiveness that covered everything now was not a great improvement.

Finally he stood and looked around. There was indeed a better view from here, though the angle was not good enough for him to see much more than the expanse of sky above and the distant spread of darkness that was the sea in the poor light. Frowning, he looked about for something to climb, and saw a small rock formation not far away that might be enough to allow him to see over the trees. Resolutely, he set out for it, putting all his remaining determination into getting there.

It was a difficult climb. He left his coconut bundle at the base of the rocks, and took it one hand and one foot at a time, freezing with a jolt to his stomach every time he almost slipped. He was used to heights, and they did not bother him, but this was something other than climbing a rope ladder to the tops aboard ship. Here there were no convenient handholds, only jutting rocky ledges that he reached for, trying to spread his weight evenly. Finally, panting, he rolled onto a pitted ledge.

He stood up shakily, looking outward. The sun was now rising in the east, and the island was bathed in an orange glow, the view hindered only by birds wheeling overhead. When he looked towards the sun, the way he had come, he saw greenery covering the land until it sloped down to meet the sea. The other side was similar, if dotted more frequently with rocky outcroppings like the one he had climbed. The waves on the western side lapped not against a sandy beach, but a sheer cliff. He watched shadows move over the land, glad that he had not tried to walk all the way there overnight. He would have trapped himself there, unable to go further without wings.

He looked south then, and something caught his eye immediately. There was a dark smudge on the shore, something large that did not look like it came from nature. It was too evenly shaped to be a rock, he thought. It was possible that it was a beached whale, but it seemed unlikely. Far too small to be the *Courage*, but perhaps some poor part of her had washed ashore.

Suddenly feeling much more alive than he had on waking, he scrambled back down the face of the rock, trying to contain his excitement long enough to keep from foolishly stumbling and falling to his death. It was good after all that he had saved his strength, as he would have to move fast to reach the site before night fell again.

Buoyed by the sudden sense of purpose, he trotted down the

hill as far as he could before the vegetation once again became too thick for him to charge through it. He returned to painstakingly picking his way through, cursing the necessity that forced him to slow down as he navigated his way around the cliffs to where he could descend more easily. The blisters on his feet burst and bled, but he did not stop to tend them or even to eat, only cracked open another coconut and munched on it as he walked, finding a sharp stone he could use to get all of the flesh away from the husk. The only time he allowed himself to stop was to make sure he was on the right course, each time that he found a tree at an angle that he could climb a little way. He even forced himself to go on through the heat of the afternoon, pressing on grimly as sweat soaked his entire body, the sun stung his face, and the pain in his weary feet began to extend up to his knees, making each step an even deeper stab of discomfort. All this however was almost nothing compared to the insects that buzzed around his head, seeking any opportunity to land on his neck, face or hands. At first he slapped them away, flinching at every sting, but eventually it became impossible. He grit his teeth and resigned himself to being bitten alive.

By the time he reached the rocky shoreline, blissfully free of any trees or plants to get in his way, the sun had lost its relentless heat, although the air was still just as thick and torpid. The dark shape in the distance became clearer as he drew closer, and his heart leapt as he realised what it was: one of the ship's boats. It was lying haphazardly on its side with the keel pointing inward, towards the cliff. It was surrounded by a number of other dark shapes.

It was not a survivor's camp.

Thomas' pace slowed as he recognised the still forms of human bodies, some of them still in their blue coats, lying in twisted positions on the rocky sand. Before long he could smell the acrid, coppery stench of blood. His throat felt tight, choked with grief and horror as he forced himself to continue to put one boot in front of the other, his footsteps crunching over the dry sand the only sound other than the waves crashing, and the wheeling birds above.

There were perhaps twenty men lying in bloody heaps on the ground. Their fatal wounds were not from the wreckage; they had been stabbed, in chest or belly, some had had arms or legs severed away, and most had had their throats slit. Around each figure the sand was stained black-red with blood. Thomas knelt hesitantly beside the first body, lying face down. There was a large stain on the back of his coat where he had been run through. Grimly, steeling himself, he put a hand on the man's shoulder and heaved him onto his back. It was Joe Gower. Insects had already begun to eat their way into his eye sockets.

Thomas' stomach heaved. He twisted to one side, vomiting chunks of half-digested coconut onto the sand. Blearily, as he looked up, he could make out other faces, faces he knew, faces of men he had once counted among his closest friends and comrades in arms. Some were wearing only their smallclothes or even nightshirts, having been dragged from their hospital beds into the boat in the hope of safety. His crew, who had been under his command. And they had been slaughtered like animals.

He didn't know how long he knelt there on hands and knees,

stricken with grief. It was long enough that the sun had set over the western side of the island by the time he pulled himself out of his sorrow long enough to think rationally. He was alone. He would have to fend for himself. Shakily he got to his feet and staggered over to the upturned boat, picking his way carefully between the bodies, avoiding looking at any more faces. Boxes and bags wrapped in oilcloth to keep them dry had been strewn over the sand, knocked loose perhaps by the rough landing. He stopped at the nearest box and went to open it; only then did he see that the protective covering had been sliced open, and the lid removed, its contents vanished. With growing desperation he checked the next package, and the next. The supplies were gone, with not so much as a blanket left behind. Whoever had slaughtered the crewmen in the boat had also looted it, and effectively.

Pirates, he thought, his heart hardening to stone as he remembered Jim robbing Babber, and the way the one called Gappy had claimed Thomas' own coat for himself. Of course they would have taken the opportunity for anything they could steal. Once again he looked around at the bodies, this time with a closer eye, as much as it pained him. He could not see a single weapon, no swords or pistols. Perhaps some of those without coats had had those stolen too; it was hard to tell. Fury filled him like a raging bonfire; he threw his head back to the sky and yelled an oath.

There was a noise from behind him, a kind of low keening. Startled, he whirled around, but nothing had approached him unseen. The sound came again, and with a gasp he realised it had come from further along the beach, a spot that had been hidden from view until now by the boat. He ran towards the sound, calling out. There was another body here, and it was stirring slightly. "Charlie?" it muttered as he came near, looking up at him through glazed eyes. "Is it you?"

Tears streaming down his face, Thomas fell once again to his knees. The man was almost completely covered in sand, further obscuring him from view and making him almost unrecognisable, but he would have known the voice anywhere. It was Bill Blake.

"It's me," he said, forcing out the words through a throat that was still painfully tight. Bill was pale under the coating of sand, and his eyes were strangely unfocused. "Where are you hurt? Let me help — "

Bill closed his eyes, his breathing coming in very shallow, and slowly shook his head. "Never mind," he said, low. "These last hours I had thought I would never see another living soul. And here you are. That's enough."

"No," Thomas said shakily, brushing the sand away in his attempts to find the injuries. He had survived this long. Surely something could be done. "Bill, you must tell me what to —"

"Stop," Bill hissed, and Thomas flinched back, instinctively. The man's lips were a dark red in his ash-white face, and his big, sturdy arms were lying limply to either side, as though he could not so much as move them. "Enough, boy. There's nothing you can do." His next breath was raspy.

"No," Thomas said again, trying and failing to stop the tears. He was a grown man, an officer. Had he not already lost hundreds of men, his entire crew? Why now could he not be stalwart in the face of death?

He was my friend, he thought, in the voice of a child. *And I loved him. Or I thought I did.*

"There has to be something," he said, in little more than a whisper. His breath caught in his throat as he saw that in the moonlight, Bill's eyes were misty and grey. "Do... do you see me?"

Bill sighed. "No," he murmured. Thomas watched, horrified, as the unseeing eyes flickered from side to side. "Charlie... listen. They did not kill us all. They..." he coughed, wetly, and closed his eyes again.

"Bill?" Thomas gasped, confused. "What do you mean? Did someone escape? Where are they?"

"Listen," Bill managed. Thomas found himself putting his hand under Bill's, holding it palm-to-palm with the thumbs curled around each other. "They took some of the boys... I heard them. And the... "

"The pirates?" Thomas felt a terrible twisting pain in the pit of his stomach, as though someone were wrapping their hand around his guts. "Where? Bill, where did they go?"

Bill grimaced. "East," he said, his voice barely audible. His hand tightened in Thomas grip; or perhaps Thomas only imagined it did. "They took them east, when the sun was rising..."

Thomas felt fresh tears begin to run down his face. Bill, his friend, his only lover, was dying, and the last thing he had said to him was to push him away. "I'm sorry," he said, holding back sobs. "Bill, I'm sorry. For what I said. I was wrong."

Bill blinked, and he stared up in the direction of Thomas' voice. "No," he said finally. "You were only a boy. You were right. I... took advantage." He heaved again, a rough, ugly-sounding breath. "Promise me you won't be like me," he said then, the faintest hint of a smile at the corner of his mouth. "I used your innocence. Forced you… into a life like mine…"

"No," Thomas said quickly, shaking his head so roughly that his hair fell forward into his eyes. His breath caught in his throat. "No, I didn't mean… that's not… Bill…"

Bill's head lolled to one side, and he was still. "Bill?" Thomas whispered. "Bill?"

He was gone.

Thomas pulled the big man's head into his lap and wept. He felt all at once the insufficiency of his nineteen years, only a boy himself, and Wickerham should never have given him the command. He was utterly, agonisingly alone, and the sun shining down on the bloody sand was a mockery, as though the Lord on High were glaring down on him, saying:

Look what you have done.

$$— 8 —$$

They took some of the boys, Bill had said. For what purpose, Thomas could only guess, and guessing was scarcely encouraging. His heart railed against leaving the bodies of his men to rot in the sun, but he had no time now to dig twenty graves.

He wondered as he set off again back in an easterly direction, trusting to the darkness to keep him covered as he trudged along the rocky shoreline, whether what he was doing was quite mad. After all, he had spent all of the last two days doing everything in his power to avoid the pirates, and now here he was trying to find them, reversing his course entirely. But, as he reminded himself furiously as he walked, he had no choice at all. The wreck of the *Courage* was his responsibility, and so were the lives of every man aboard her. He had been in command. Even if it meant his own death, and he was almost certain that it would, he had to try and rescue however many of his men could be found. Besides, what were his other options? He could hardly hide away on the island forever, awaiting an unlikely rescue. Neither could he escape on his own. With a few more men, perhaps, they could man the lifeboat for long enough to find an inhabited port, somewhere from whence they could get word to the navy of the disaster.

The futility of this thought was not lost on him, but any hope of escape was ultimately a secondary goal. He had to save his men. With this firmly in mind, he pressed on, but eventually he felt his eyelids begin to close of their own accord, and suddenly he found himself sprawling on the ground, spitting sand. He glared back at the obnoxious tree root he had tripped over. Begrudgingly he decided he would have to rest. He had reached a point where the vegetation had once more begun to creep down to the shore, and he began digging his way back through it, far enough that he could no longer see the sea. Judging this to be a safe enough distance, he made a similar shelter to the one he had made the night before, and finally let himself collapse into it.

*

The sound the Courage *made as it was torn apart was the sound of demons screaming. As his body was thrown from the ship, faces of the dead appeared to him — Bill Blake, Gower, Days, Smythe, Rogers, Cole, Wickerham, and Father Murray. Their expressions were full of fury. We trusted you, they said as he tried to get away, but his limbs were frozen. You have killed us.*

*

This time he woke in daylight to the distant sound of voices. He kept himself still, not daring to make any sudden move that might announce his presence.

"If that fella thinks I'm portagin' that boat all the way back this way, 'e's got another thing commin," someone was moaning. "Why'd 'e think we left it in the first place?"

"Yew could of filled it up again and rowed it back, halfwit," muttered a second man. "There were enough o' you."

"Naw, half the oars were missin'," shot back the first man. "Won't go far wiv on'y half the oars. Not agin' the current. Halfwit yerself."

"Stop yer whinin', both o' yer," a third pirate broke in. "Better jus' do what the Cap'n says."

"Cap'n?" someone exclaimed, with a tone of incredulity. "What Cap'n? 'E can't be Cap'n now just cos he told everyone 'e was."

"Well, someone 'as to be. We can't jus' be wanderin' about wiv no Cap'n."

"Briggs?" another voice put in. "He's the maddest of all of us, and that's saying somethin'. He ain't anythin' like ol' Cap'n Draffus."

"That oaf weren't no real Cap'n," muttered one. "Just some merchant who fancied 'imself King o' the Ocean. *Queen o'Heaven*, pah." The man spat. "Anyway he's dead now, inne? I'm with Briggsy. He might be a mad ol' cutthroat, but who among us ain't? He's the one who got us off that stink'ole of a ship. I didn't see *you* doin' the rest o' us any favours."

"Yah well, I was stuck in there wiv you, wasn' I?"

Thomas let out the breath he had been holding as the men moved out of earshot. So, they were going to collect the boat — or not, depending on what was decided among the obviously disorganised band. Now he was glad he hadn't stopped to put his men to rest; that would only have alerted the pirates to the fact that someone else was alive on the island. He could only hope that his footprints had been brushed away by the wind, or erased by the tide.

Wearily he sat back to wait for their return, looking around him for anything he might be able to make into a weapon. The time for sparing lives out of mercy was long over. There were not any large sticks, or anything heavy enough to do any real damage, the trees being mainly trunks and fronds, and the plants being mostly vines and leaves. He set his jaw. Following the pirates back to their camp was the obvious plan — it was far preferable to wandering around aimlessly only to stumble blindly upon them, if he was lucky — but how exactly was he going to rescue his men, when the enemy was armed with stolen weapons and he had nothing but an empty scabbard?

There was no time to come up with an alternative plan, however. All he could do was wait.

It was mid-day by the time the pirates came trudging back along the beach, carrying the boat on their shoulders, six to a side. Thomas had found a hiding place where he could watch; he was surprised to see so many men, though he realised there must have been more than the four survivors he had already seen, enough to massacre the *Courage*'s crew with no casualties on their side. Still, even with twelve men they moved slowly, as the lifeboat was a heavy load even without its stores. It wasn't difficult to keep them in eyesight once they had moved far enough ahead that Thomas could follow them without being heard as he moved through the trees.

Fortunately the camp, such as it was, was not too far away from the place he had stopped to rest. It was only an hour's walk or so before he heard more voices. He was not surprised at all to note that it sounded like yet another argument — he almost pitied the pirates for the lack of discipline that seemed to lead to such an indulgence of discord. The camp had been set up among the trees near the shoreline, and as the pirates portaging the boat turned towards it, Thomas was forced to find another place to hide. Fortunately the grunting and stomping of those men muffled any sounds he might have made as he hurried to crouch on his heels behind a low bush, peering as cautiously as he could through at the camp. There were perhaps twenty pirates all told, including the twelve who were returning with the lifeboat. It was shocking to see so many, perhaps two thirds of those who had escaped the brig. Drawn up to the edge of the camp was another of the lifeboats; they must have all commandeered it before the men of the *Courage* could reach it. Anger filled Thomas' chest once more like a pot over a spitting fire, threatening to boil over; he forced it down. As the portagers heaved the boat off of their shoulders and into the sand beside the other, Thomas looked around anxiously for his own men. His heart sank as he realised there was no sign of them; the only men he recognised were Aggie, his big dark shape very recognisable where he sat making vine ropes with surprisingly nimble fingers, and the one he had internally dubbed Big Ears. He couldn't see the man who was wearing his coat. Neither could he see Jim.

"Well, there 'tis," announced one of the portagers. It sounded like the one who had been complaining earlier about Briggs' leadership. Reminded, Thomas searched for Briggs among the crowd. He did not have to look far. A makeshift fire pit had been dug in the centre of the camp; it showed signs of having been lit at least once, but for now in the heat of the day there were only the remains of smouldering embers. They had found some logs from somewhere, perhaps the leavings of palm trees blown down by the gale, and placed them around as seats, where several men were huddled in low conversation. From one of the logs stood Briggs, his black eyes glinting so that even Thomas could see. He was still wearing his large brown coat, and he made no effort to hide the sword he held deftly in his right hand. It was no pirate's cutlass; Thomas could see even from his hiding place that it was good steel, and well cared for. He wondered bitterly which of his slain crewmates it had belonged to.

"There, that weren't so hard now, was it?" Briggs called back, a sickly sweet mocking tone in his voice. The coat looked bulky; Thomas realised that Briggs' left arm was not in its sleeve but bound up against the chest, perhaps to protect an injury.

"Gaw, go boil yer 'ead, Briggs," snapped the complainer. "Next time ye can be yer own fetch'n'carry boy, an'all."

An uneasy silence settled over the camp. Thomas heard someone nearby mutter a hushed curse. Briggs took a step in the man's direction, smiling nastily. "Oh aye. Hard work, were it? Our *deepest* apologies," he added, in a mocking imitation of a gentleman's voice, as though he were play-acting a magistrate. "Ye have a problem wiv carryin' out me orders?"

The man spat grossly again, dangerously close to the tip of Briggs' boot. "Aye. Mebbe I do. You ain't really our Cap'n, you can't just go orderin' us around."

"Oh?" Briggs looked around at the other men. "Anyone else

feel like Podunk 'ere? Anyone else want te *register a complaint*?" His head whipped around, his oversized coat flapping about his shoulders. No one else volunteered an opinion. Briggs spat. "Aye, just as I thought. Cowards, all o' ye. Podunk, you wanted to be Cap'n, did ye? Maybe ye should 'ave been the one to give yer name to those navy bastards. Ye could've. Any of ye could've. But no, I was the only one of ye man enough, an' I didn't see any of *ye* puttin' a sword through their Cap'n's guts neither."

Uneasy looks went around the camp. Apparently no one dared dispute this.

"Aye, ye did that," one of the others piped up, nodding enthusiastically. "An' ye killed that other'n and let us out o' that gaol. So I'm 'appy to call ye Cap'n, an' I'll fight any man who don't."

A chorus of 'ayes' followed this, which left Podunk the only one still looking uncomfortable. Briggs sneered as he sauntered over to him, turning his sword expertly around in his good hand. "You got anythin' else you want te say?" Briggs demanded.

Podunk let his defiant gaze drift away. "No, Cap'n," he said, sullenly.

"Good." In the next second, Briggs' hand had whipped up, his sword slicing audibly through the air. Podunk screamed and fell back, clutching at his face, blood streaming from between his fingers. Briggs' next blow took him through the throat, and he gurgled wetly in a heap on the sand. Watching with his heart in his stomach, Thomas forced back a mouthful of bile.

"Right." Briggs lowered the bloody sword and sat down once again. "Now, if any of ye want t'ever get off this island, ye'll set yerselves to makin' oars for those boats. An' as for Froggie and

Bob," he added, his face darkening, "Anyone sees 'em, make 'em show you te the prize and then shoot 'em in the arse. Mutinous fuckers. Aggie! Where's yer boy?"

The big man looked up from where he was sorting through a pile of pilfered supplies. "Jim come and go," he said, warily, shrugging. "Ain't seen 'im since las' morn'.'"

Briggs leered. "Shame. The little maggot might be the last thing on this island worth fucking. Tell him I wanna see 'im when he shows his face."

Behind the trees, Thomas put a shaking hand over his own mouth, swallowing an angry exclamation and forcing himself to calm. He wanted to put paid to the whole damn lot of them, but he knew he'd be dead before he moved three paces into the clearing. He had to find his men.

Briggs went back to his companions, and the crowd that had gathered when there was a chance of a fight began to dissipate. Thomas spotted a flash of blue, and looked quickly — but it was only Gappy, carrying a bag that was no doubt filled with the supplies looted from the lifeboat. The stolen coat was still stained badly, but it was dry, and no longer a heavy, cumbersome burden to whoever tried to wear it.

Where *were* the prisoners? Thomas' heart sank as he wondered suddenly whether Bill might have been imagining things, confused by the pain brought on by his injuries. Perhaps he had only thought he saw boys being captured.

There was a sound behind him, almost imperceptible, but his senses were on such high alert that it was enough to make him jerk his head around. There didn't seem to be anything there, but he wasn't about to take the risk. He had already stayed in the camp too long.

He crawled a short way, staying hidden behind the jungle of low bushes and other vegetation. When he judged that he would be invisible from the camp, he stood and stepped hurriedly behind the nearest tree, whereupon he found himself staring down the length of a blade.

Not just any blade. It was his own sword, the one his parents had gifted him when he had made midshipman, the year they had died. It was a good make, perfect for a boy just coming into his manhood; efficient but not elaborate.

He looked up from the razor-sharp edge pointing directly at his heart, and saw a pair of hauntingly familiar blue eyes, glaring at him.

He did not give Jim time to think. The boy was clearly an inexperienced swordsman, and Thomas had a few dozen pounds over him. Quickly he feinted to one side, then, when the sword followed him, darted back and under, catching Jim's arm at the wrist and forcing the blade aside. It was the work of a moment to have Jim's back pulled flush against his chest, and to have his hand take control of the sword, bringing it up against Jim's throat. He put his other hand up to cover the boy's mouth. "That was foolish," he hissed. "You shouldn't attack with a weapon you don't know how to use."

The boy made no sound, only panted uncomfortably into Thomas' hand, trying not to move for fear of nicking his own throat on the blade. Thomas suddenly wondered what on earth he was going to do now. "Walk forward," he said finally, settling for getting as far away from the pirate camp as he possibly could. "Make a sound and you'll never make another. Understood?" He drew the blade away just a fraction. Jim nodded, slowly. "Good," Thomas muttered, and took his hand away. "Move."

Jim moved slowly, but Thomas did not try to rush him. Slow and quiet was favourable to fast and loud. He also needed to focus much of his concentration on where he put his feet — he could not afford to trip and fall — so it was all he could do to keep his sword up. He didn't want to take any chances by stopping too early; he kept them both moving until they had gone at least half a mile, and it was impossible for anyone in the pirate camp to hear them even if they shouted. "Enough," he ordered Jim when he was satisfied. They had walked into a small area that was at least partially clear of trees, with enough space to sit down. He took a small step back, lowering his aching arm so that the sword was pointing at the back of Jim's neck. "Get on your knees and give me your hands."

Jim hesitated, but after a moment he obeyed. He was still dressed only in borrowed sailor's breeches, so perhaps he hadn't been able to find a coat to fit him out of all the spoils. The bandages had come off, leaving unbound and unprotected the wound which could now be seen clearly, a thick black line of stitches from the right shoulder to the left hip. Thomas went carefully to one knee in the dirt, hastily unravelling his leaf bundle. There was one coconut left in it; he had quite forgotten to try and eat for hours now. He put the coconut to one side and took the vine rope he had made, winding it tightly around Jim's wrists. He was quite satisfied with the result. "Sit," he commanded. Jim looked around, glaring at him, but Thomas raised his sword, pointedly, and the boy shifted awkwardly onto his backside with his legs out in front of him. Keeping one eye on him, just in case, Thomas hacked away another long section of vine and began weaving it into another rope. "What were you doing lurking outside the camp?" he asked as he worked, sitting on a nearby mound, his sword stuck into the sand within easy reach. Jim only glared at him. "I know you can talk," Thomas reminded him, flatly. He no longer had any sympathy for his prisoner, not after seeing the massacre on the beach. "I'm sure you know more than the five words I've heard you say so far."

Jim's nose twitched and he looked away. Thomas tied off the end of the rope and set about binding the boy's ankles together. "Very well," he said, picking up his sword and sitting down again. "I have one more question for you, and if you don't answer me it'll be the last one you'll ever hear, understand?" Then, when Jim looked doubtful, he added, "don't think I'll spare you now just because I did before. I saw what you and your crew did to my men on the southern shore."

Jim's blue eyes went suddenly wide, and the uncertain look went away just as quickly. He looked down at his knees. "I... understand," he said, finally. There was something odd about his voice, something other than the strange softness with which he spoke, but Thomas couldn't quite put his finger on it.

"Here it is," he said, leaning forward. "I was told your men took prisoners from the lifeboat. They weren't at the camp. *Where are they?*"

Jim blinked. He did not look surprised, only hesitant. Thomas stood up angrily. "I know you know," he said, all sense of decorum lost in the midst of his grief and fury. He pointed his sword directly between the boy's eyes. "Where are they?"

Jim shrank away from the sword, his matted hunks of black hair falling over his face. The blade near the hilt was quite dull from cutting into coconuts, but the tip was still mortally sharp. "Yes… I know…" he said, in little more than a whisper, and then again, "I know…"

"*Where?*" Thomas demanded again. In his desperation he took a half a step forward — the blade caught on the boy's cheek and left a shallow red line in its wake. Jim hissed in pain and pulled his head back.

"Not far," he muttered. "I can find them. I can take you."

Faintly horrified at what he had done, Thomas tried to keep his face unreadable. He had not really wanted to harm the boy unless he had to, but he could hardly apologise for it now. "Good," he said, sticking the sword once again into the ground. It was disrespectful to a blade which had served him well, but he wanted it close to hand. "You will lead me. Any attempt to escape or to alert your crew…"

Jim nodded quickly, a trickle of blood making its way down his cheek to his chin. "I understand," he said again, that same soft, hesitant inflection.

Thomas stared back at him. He would never have thought of taking a pirate prisoner in return, if the event had not stumbled upon him in such a way, but perhaps he should have. He did not trust Jim not to run away, not after the last time, but he also had difficulty imagining the boy attacking him. He had after all been at the advantage twice before, with the sword in his hand, and Thomas was still alive and relatively unharmed.

"One more question," he said, sitting back on the knoll and adopting a less threatening posture. "Why did you not hand me over to your crew, two days ago? You could very well have pointed them to where I was."

Jim looked away again, some of his teeth visible where he bit the corner of his bottom lip. "Blood for blood," he said, looking down at the mess covering his chest, and spat on the sand. "Life for life."

Thomas grimaced at this obviously barbaric notion, but it did serve as some explanation for the bizarre behaviour. It was just the sort of thing pirates would consider righteous; a simple exchange of services rendered was as far as honour would go. Well, then. "I saved your life at least twice, if I recall," he said, watching Jim's face. "Does that not mean I am still owed one in kind?" He raised an eyebrow as the boy slowly shook his head. "Oh? Why not?"

Jim hesitated. Thomas considered him. He doubted that the boy did not know what to say, he only would not — but Thomas could guess. He had already considered that it was very strange that he should have woken, undrowned and unhurt, in the middle of an empty stretch of beach — and Jim had after all had time to take his sword.

"Did you pull me out the of the water?" he asked, low, eyes narrowing.

Jim shifted uncomfortably and tugged, perhaps without conscious thought, at the vine ropes around his wrists. He did not meet Thomas' eyes.

Thomas waited only until he thought he had caught his breath. His heart, which had been pounding out of his chest since he had crept into the pirate camp, was finally starting to slow. He had a goal and a means to attain it; he would save whoever was left and get the hell off this godforsaken island. Somehow. "Very well," he said, leaning across to untie the ankle rope before he curled it over his shoulder. "Show me the way."

Even with his wrists tied in front of him, Jim moved through the jungle-like terrain as easily as if he had been born there, as though he had been raised by whatever small creatures could survive on such a small rock in the middle of the ocean. These could not be many. Clearly the plant life was flourishing, and they saw some birds and insects as they picked their way through the thick vegetation, but Days had been right when he said there would be no larger game. Thomas felt the eerie sense of being one of the first human beings on an uninhabited shore, a place perhaps where God had never intended man to go. But the blue-eyed pirate padded almost silently through it all, unconcerned by sharp rocks or the uneven surface under his bare feet. He either moved so instinctively that he could avoid harm, or the soles of his feet were calloused and hard enough that he might as well have been wearing boots. The wound across his chest seemed to bother him only when it came to climbing over a more significant obstacle. One of these was a large tree which had fallen across their path. It was stuck between two large hillocks; the boy seemed to consider going around the thing before sighing and hauling himself up and over, his bound hands pressed together on the trunk as he performed an impressive vaulting manoeuvre, landing with a grunt and a grimace.

"Are you well?" Thomas asked, scrambling over with much less grace. Jim was bent over double with pain, breathing heavily, but he shook his head and moved away when Thomas offered a hand to help straighten him. "You must be careful not to pull the stitches," Thomas told him, following on behind when he started walking again with determination. "If the wound opens you are sure to get an infection."

Jim only shrugged and kept on, without even looking back.

"Suit yourself," Thomas muttered, swatting away an irritating insect that flew into his face. He might as well have been talking to himself, but it made him feel a little better. "I'm sure I don't know why I should care. If you get sick there will be no one to nurse you back to health. I certainly won't."

As they walked, getting deeper and deeper into the under-growth, he started to wonder if he had been more foolish than he realised. He had long since lost track of their direction, the tree cover so thick that it was hard even to see the position of the sun — though that was a welcome relief from the direct heat on his face and shoulders. Jim seemed confident in finding his way, but for all Thomas knew he could simply be leading him as far away from the camp as possible, perhaps then to find a way to escape, leaving Thomas utterly lost with little hope of finding his way back.

After another hour of what increasingly seemed like aimless wandering, he reached out and grabbed Jim by the arm. The boy flinched and pulled away, the scratch across his cheek very red as he turned. Thomas ended up holding him by the wrist as Jim tried to stand at arm's length, glaring, inhibited by the vine ropes. "Where are we going?" Thomas hissed. "Do you even know where we are?"

Jim glowered and tried to tug his hands away, jerking his head in the direction they had been heading. There seemed to be no landmarks by which he could have been navigating, and Thomas' heart started to pound again. Why would the pirates have taken their prisoners all this way? Had they even had time to learn the island, while Thomas had been trying to get from one side to the other? He started to think he had made a real blunder. What had he done? He rounded on Jim. "If you've been leading me down a false trail..." he growled, his hand tightening on his sword hilt.

"Hey Froggie." A voice from somewhere out of the forest ahead. "You 'ear somt'ing?"

Thomas froze; Jim's head whipped round. There was the sound of someone moving through the trees towards them. "Oh aye," another voice, mocking. "Go on in 'dere, Bob, see if'n ye ever find yer way back agin!"

Jim tugged forcefully at Thomas' grip, shocking him into movement. He allowed himself to be dragged deeper into the undergrowth, doing his best to follow the boy's near-silent footsteps, but kept a tight grip on him. He wasn't going to let him slip away again.

There was a clumsy crashing, as though someone were swiping furiously at the undergrowth with a blade. "Somewhere through 'ere," the first man grumbled, his voice nearer than before.

Jim stopped behind a thick tree trunk and raised his bound

hands to put a finger to his lips. Still holding him by the wrist, Thomas was pulled close. The trunk was between them both and the sound of the onslaught — they might not be seen unless someone looked closely.

"See anythin?" came the call from afar.

"Too many damn bushes…" came the muttered reply.

They were standing chest-to-chest, so that Thomas could feel the ridges of the wound's stitches against his own skin, could feel the ends of the matted, lice-ridden hair tickling his neck. When he looked down, Jim closed his eyes. Thomas stared at him, despite himself, despite the danger approaching still closer and closer every second. The boy didn't seem at all afraid. Perhaps he knew that even if they were found, he would be safe. The pirate would simply kill Thomas and release him. But then why wasn't he calling out for help? Why hide at all?

When Jim opened his eyes again, Thomas found himself staring into them. There was something so strange about them, and about this semi-mute young man who acted simple but did not *seem* simple. Thomas had experience with simple men, who found work on ships or in shipyards; none of them had eyes that burned, that looked right through you the way these did. For a moment Jim stared back at him, silent, somehow daring, and then his gaze flickered downwards. Thomas frowned, but Jim was lowering his hands, reaching for Thomas' belt. Thomas let out a sharp, shocked breath — and then he realised the boy was going for his sword, not trying to grab at it but tapping it pointedly, raising his eyebrows. The crashing was almost upon them.

Thomas let go of Jim's wrist and stood back. When the pirate came past, Thomas' sword came up between his ribs before he could so much as cry out. The body slid off the blade even as the man let out his last shuddering gasp, his own sword falling uselessly from his fingers into the dirt, his heart pierced through.

Thomas' stomach rolled. It had been so easy. The pirate was rake thin and must have been wounded earlier; there was a black bruise swelling around his eye and red blood crusted under his nose, as if he had been punched, but the eyes were already dead and staring. Swallowing a sudden tightness in his throat, Thomas looked up at Jim. The boy only stood there, still flush against the tree, and blinked back at him, apparently undisturbed by the sudden and violent death of his crewmate.

"You're helping me," Thomas breathed, still holding the bloodied blade in one shaking hand. "Why?"

Jim hopped off the mound of tree roots and stepped over the dead pirate's arm without looking down. Silently he held out his bound hands, a question in his eyes. Thomas looked down at them, and then back up into that unnerving gaze. He remembered suddenly the man back on the *Courage* that had tried to stop them — Babber. The way Jim had robbed the body, coldly, without hesitation. "No," he said flatly. Jim only sighed and shrugged, which made Thomas abruptly and irrationally angry. "Why won't you just —" he started, too loud, and suddenly Jim's hands were over his mouth, one on top of the other.

"Froggie," he whispered.

"What?" Thomas tried to say, his voice muffled behind Jim's fingers.

"Bob?" the first voice called out, distantly. "You got lost?

Tol' ya not t'go in dere!"

Thomas swallowed. Jim let go his mouth and stood back.

"Right," Thomas muttered. "Is that where my men are?"

Jim nodded once.

"How many?"

A hesitation. "Two of yours… I think," Jim said, his eyes flickering away at last, then he added: "I… didn't see them. I was hiding."

"But you knew where they were?" Thomas asked, quickly. He wasn't sure why, but he felt the urge to keep the boy talking now he had started. He remembered the names Froggie and Bob, the ones Briggs had sentenced to death as mutineers.

Jim's mouth twitched, he was looking out through the trees in the direction of the voice. "No… just heard them talking. Briggs and the others."

"About these men taking the boys?"

Jim nodded.

"Then how did you find them?"

"Followed the trail."

Thomas blinked. He had not seen anything resembling any kind of trail as they staggered through miles of thick jungle forest. But he was a seaman, not a hunter, and Jim *had* got them here. "Why did they leave the camp?" Thomas muttered, not really expecting an answer. Surely it made more sense for the pirates to stay together, particularly when the shore-side camp had all the supply they had stolen from the lifeboats. "Why take the boys?"

Jim shrugged again. "Wouldn't share them," he said.

Thomas gasped, and instinctively went to slap the pirate

across the face. He just managed to stop his hand an inch away from Jim's cheek, panting with the effort of restraint. The boy stared back at him, but did not move, or try to get away. There was a long silence while Thomas tried to get his sudden, uncontainable fury under control. He remembered what Briggs had said about Jim, and found he couldn't quite look the boy in the eyes.

"Very well," he said at last. "Only one man. We will approach from the rear. I will overpower this… Froggie." His lips twisted in disgust. "You will stay back until I have secured the camp. Understood?"

A flicker of expression passed across Jim's face; a frown perhaps, of distaste or of disappointment. He looked as though he would have liked to argue, but he indicated with a short, spasming nod of his head that he understood. Thomas picked up the dead man's blade and secured it in his scabbard, keeping his own sword ready in his hand.

They made their way quietly back the way they had come, trying to find the easiest path to where the voices had first come. Now that Thomas knew what to look for, the fresh path the dead pirate had taken was made obvious by traces of footprints in the soft earth, and plants leaking green sap where they had been haphazardly chopped aside. Eventually Jim stopped and pointed ahead to where the trees began to thin, a shaft of daylight coming through a wider gap.

Thomas took a step forward, but Jim reached out and caught him by the sleeve of his shirt. When Thomas turned to look, the boy actually opened his mouth to speak, perhaps the first time he had done so without prompting or threats, but it could not have been more unwelcome in that moment. Thomas put up a sharp hand to stop him, and repeated the gesture, motioning for him to stay where he was. He would have liked to do something to make his prisoner more secure, but he couldn't risk the noise or the time it would take. He could only hope the wrist bindings were enough deterrent from any mischief the pirate might like to get up to.

Stepping as softly as he could over the crunch of vines and fallen palm leaves, he made his way to the gap between the trees. Beyond it was a small clearing. A makeshift shelter had been set up to one side, a simple scrap of canvas draped to form a crude tent.

On opposite sides of a single tree near the far side of the clearing, two small figures were sitting limply, tied and gagged. Squinting, Thomas recognised young Pasco, his Spaniard's complexion easy to make out against his grubby shirt. He at least was stirring a little — the other captive, partially hidden by the tree they were tied to, seemed to be unconscious; long fair hair stained red-brown with blood.

The remaining guard was standing looking out at the trees, no doubt wondering where his companion had got to. He called out "Bob?" just as Thomas burst upon him.

A long knife flashed in the man's hand as he whipped around, catching Thomas on the forearm. Thomas fumbled and stepped back, catching the next blow just above the hilt of his sword. The man had an unexpected strength for his weight, and the blow jarred Thomas' arm — there was blood coming from somewhere, but for the moment he felt no pain, only a rush of adrenaline as out of the corner of his eye he saw Pasco strain against the ropes, eyes terror-wide and staring right at him. He grunted and tried to shove his attacker back, but he succeeded only in extricating his sword, ducking the next swing that came dangerously close to his head. Then it was frantic, too-close clumsy fencing as he tried to gain enough distance to be able to use his blade at all effectively, and the pirate kept lunging at him, stabbing at his chest, his arms, his eyes. He managed to manoeuvre himself around, hoping to trap the man between himself and the forest, but he couldn't batter the man back in such close quarters.

The pirate's eyes were wild, animal-like. He was fighting for his life with a blade that was too short and too awkward; his own blood stained his fingers in places where he had already nicked himself. But he was faster and stronger than Thomas, and Thomas hadn't been prepared for this ferocious onslaught. For a moment he felt a thrill of terror such as he hadn't felt since his first battle, a realisation — *this is how I'm going to die.*

He was too focused on the knife to notice movement from the trees to his left, until Pasco managed a muffled warning shout. Thomas risked a sideways glance — it was Jim, stepping quite calmly into the clearing. The other pirate had turned to look as well, and his distraction was the only moment of advantage that Thomas needed. He knocked the knife aside with a sweep of his sword, slicing through the man's ragged shirt and deep into the flesh in a line under his belly. For a moment the pirate staggered on his feet, gasping and putting both hands to his stomach to try and slow the flow of blood and organs that were starting to spill from the incision. Then he fell to his knees, and, groaning, keeled over onto his side on the ground, gasping out his life as the blood soaked into the earth under him.

Thomas stood, panting, his hands shaking, and turned his face away. He felt as though he was being choked, it was so hard to get enough air, as though in the moment of accepting his own death his body had forgotten how to live. When he finally turned away from the body, Jim was just standing there, looking at him. "I thought I told you to stay out of sight," Thomas said, roughly.

Jim shrugged and motioned to Pasco and the other prisoner. Remembering his mission, Thomas hurried over to them. Pasco was staring at Jim as Thomas pulled down his gag and began trying to undo the knots that bound him to the tree. They were hard, tight knots, and they did not give. "What's *he* doing here?" the boy asked. There were teartracks just visible on his cheeks through the dirt, but Thomas pretended not to see. "Is he your prisoner, sir?"

"Yes," Thomas said simply, going around to look at the other of his men who had been taken. He winced; whoever it was had been beaten around the face so severely that it was quite difficult even to identify him. "Who is it?" he asked, breathlessly.

"It's Peter Cole, sir," Pasco said, straining his head around and seeing the stunned look on Thomas' face. Thomas remembered holding Cole as the life went out of him, back on the ship… or had he only dreamed it? "I think he's alive — he was moaning, earlier… but he's hurt badly. He… they were… they tried to…" He turned his face away, blinking furiously. "He hit that other one and they beat him blue," he managed, hoarsely.

"We must get both of you away from here at once," Thomas muttered almost to himself as he found Cole's thin wrist and felt for a pulse. Fifteen years old, he thought. Cole was fifteen, and an officer, and look what they had done to him. His stomach twisted with anger. At least little Pasco seemed to be mostly unharmed — there was a red gash across his forehead just above his right eye, but it was a few days old and healing well. Cole was alive, but barely — as Thomas pushed his bloodied hair out of his face he stirred a little.

"C-could you get out us out of these ropes, sir?" Pasco asked, prompting.

Thomas went back to considering the bindings. "The knots are tight," he muttered. "I suppose I shall have to cut them… it's a shame we can't make use of the rope." That rope was no doubt pilfered from the wreck of the *Courage*. It would have to do in shorter lengths, he supposed. He stood up, thinking he would use Froggie's knife for the purpose.

"I can do them," Jim said, surprising both Thomas and Pasco both.

"I thought he couldn't talk!" Pasco exclaimed, glaring up suspiciously at the skinny pirate with the long red wound slashed across his bare chest.

"It appears he is only stubborn," said Thomas, eyeing Jim with suspicions of his own. "The ropes are quite swollen," he said, meeting Jim's eyes. "I doubt they will ever come apart."

"I can do them," Jim repeated, with a hint of impatience. He held out his bound hands expectantly.

Thomas narrowed his eyes, but so long as there was no risk to the boys, he might as well let the pirate try, though he knew he ought to be whipping him for disobeying his orders. "I should have bound your legs," he muttered as he undid his vine rope easily, keeping one hand on the hilt of his sword.

"You would be dead," Jim said flatly, going to one knee beside the tree trunk. Pasco flinched away from him, but the boy did not appear to notice, running his nimble fingers over the ropes. "Froggie is — was — one of the best fighters in the crew. I did try to tell you."

Struck dumb by the boy's cheek, not to mention the most words he had ever strung together in a sentence, Thomas could only stand and watch as Jim picked at the knots. It did not appear at first that he was having a great deal of luck with them either, but he only cocked his head a little and turned to Pasco. "Push back into the tree," he told the boy, who glowered at him. "Make it slack."

Pasco looked instinctively up at Thomas; it made his heart sink a little to see the boy's complete and utter trust. He nodded a short agreement and Pasco grunted as he dug his heels into the earth, pressing his body tight to the trunk of the tree.

"There." Jim tugged at something in the tangle of ropes, and they went suddenly loose. Thomas hurried around to steady poor Cole, who sagged to one side, and Pasco started struggling again in an almost panicked attempt to free himself. "Stop that," Jim told him.

"You don't tell me what to do, pirate," Pasco spat, boyishly defiant.

"Be still, Diego," Thomas said absentmindedly. He was trying to get the half-conscious Cole to sit for himself, and Pasco's wriggling was setting the midshipman's head lolling grossly from side to side. "Try not to jostle him."

"Oh." Chided, Pasco settled back enough for Jim to unwind the section of rope. There were two more knots, but these offered very little resistance under the pirate's skilled fingers. Pasco scrambled up as soon as he was free enough and jumped away from the tangle left behind. "Will he be all right, sir?" he asked, keeping one wary eye on Jim as he calmly wound up the rope.

Thomas wasn't sure how to answer. Cole's eyes were slightly unfocused, but they were open. "All right, lad?" he asked, trying to keep his real concern out of his voice. "Peter? Do you hear me?"

Cole let out a low groan. His jaw was swollen out of shape, blood dried on his lips and crusted around his eyes. There was a deep cut on his brow where the skin had split, only a few freckles just visible on his cheeks. He was wearing only shirt and breeches hanging open, now stained brown all over, and all his things were torn in multiple places. "Peter, it's Lieutenant Thomas," Pasco said, coming around to put a hand on Cole's shoulder. "He's come for us."

Cole reached up; his hands groped their way blindly up Thomas' arms and found his shoulders, holding onto them for dear life. He opened his mouth to speak, but all that emerged was a low rasping sound. "We must have water," Thomas said, looking around the clearing without much hope. Jim was still standing there, holding the looped rope over his arm. Kneeling on the ground as he was, Thomas knew instantly that if he chose, the boy could make off easily into the forest with no expectation of being pursued. He could have done so already; he had had every opportunity. Neither he nor Pasco could leave Cole, now, and it might be some time before the midshipman was ready to be moved. Still, the young pirate only stood there, watching at a safe distance. Their eyes met. "Will you — ?" Thomas began, not sure how he was going to phrase such a request under the circumstances, but Jim only nodded and moved away and out of the clearing, carrying the rope over his shoulder.

"Sir —" Pasco protested, but Thomas shook his head. It was done now, and if the boy never came back he could call himself a fool, but they would scarcely be worse off than they were already.

"Those pirates who were holding you, did they have any supplies?" he asked instead, trying to lift Cole into a more comfortable position. Now that he was calmer, the wound on his arm stung painfully. He ignored it as best he could. "Food? Weapons?"

"I — " Pasco began, stammering nervously. "I — yes sir, I think so. But there were two of them — "

"The other is dead," Thomas assured him. "I already have his sword. See what you can find. Anything would be better than what we have."

"Sir," Pasco tried again, his lips trembling. "Sir, the rest of the crew on the lifeboats — Mr Gower —"

"I know," Thomas said, feeling a chill go down his spine once again at the memory of the south shore. "I saw them."

"Oh, sir —" Pasco bit his lip, fighting back tears.

"Enough." Thomas wished he could stand, his legs were already burning from the painful crouching position, but he could hardly force poor Cole to let go of him. "Be thankful that the three of us yet live; and by god if we should get the opportunity we shall make sure their lives are paid for in blood." It was a heartier speech than he felt he had the right to give, but he said what he thought would have given him courage, at Pasco's age. He was, Thomas reminded himself, only twelve, and the last six months had been his first at sea. What a miserably short end to a naval career, and what a waste, if they were never to make it off this island.

Pasco straightened his boyish shoulders and sniffed, and then went to rifle through the pirates' paltry pile of plundered supplies. Thomas concentrated on keeping Cole upright, listening with one ear to the distant sound of soft thudding. He wasn't surprised when Jim returned carrying an armful of coconuts, but Pasco jumped almost out of his skin and had to try to pretend he hadn't been afraid. Jim ignored him. He dropped his coconuts into a pile and looked around a moment before going around to the dead pirate and prying the knife out of his bloody grip.

"Sir — " Pasco said nervously.

"Never mind," Thomas said. He didn't know how he was suddenly so sure of their safety, but he felt no fear. He only murmured what he hoped were encouraging words into Cole's ear while Jim cut open one of the coconuts, before taking it from the pirate's offered hand and holding it up to the boy's lips, letting the liquid trickle little by little into his open mouth. Out of the corner of his eye he was aware of Jim opening another, and handing it to Pasco, whose thirst must have superseded his fear and suspicion; Thomas heard him slurping loudly.

It took a bit of coaxing, but eventually Thomas managed to get Cole to hold the second coconut himself, in both hands. Jim disappeared again, and came back with the first coconut shell filled with brackish water. "Don't drink it," the boy ordered directly, as he knelt down and poured the water carefully over Cole's bloodied face. Pasco offered a scrap torn from his own shirt, and Thomas used it to wipe the crusted blood out of Cole's eyes. When they opened, they were bloodshot, but focused.

"Can you stand?" Thomas asked him, and Cole grimaced, but nodded. Thomas called Pasco over, and together they managed to lift him to his feet. He had to put most of his weight on one leg.

"I don't think he can go far," said Pasco.

"Nevertheless, we must get as far away from here as we can," Thomas said solemnly. "I imagine it won't be too long before the other pirates come looking for their fellows."

He looked at Jim, feeling uncertainty in his conscience. Jim had done him and the boys a great service, and for whatever reason was not immediately making his escape. Not for lack of opportunity. Thomas thought it would be wrong to take him again as prisoner, now, even were he not too burdened with Cole to physically overpower Jim before he could get away. But neither could he simply leave him behind to rejoin the pirates, perhaps to carry tales of the three of them back to Briggs. He liked to think that he would not, considering the abuse which Briggs had quite openly wished to do upon him, but word might still get out — and besides, he was not quite ready to trust Jim so far, not when he had already been wrong so many times, not when the ultimate consequences of his decisions had led to the wreck of his ship, the death of so many of his men...

No time to think of that now. No time for agonising.

"Will you come with us?" he asked Jim.

Jim looked surprised to be asked. He hesitated, his body tensed, and for a moment Thomas thought he really would take his leave, this time. Then he nodded, the same movement, so small and quick it was barely more than a blink. If Thomas had not been watching him so intently he might have missed it. He nodded back in grateful acknowledgement.

"Where do we go, sir?" little Pasco asked, looking up at him with unwavering trust.

They needed somewhere to hide, Thomas thought. Somewhere not too far away that was out of sight, where Cole could rest until he was ready to travel. Somewhere he would have time to think clearly enough to come up with some kind of plan of escape. Failing that, though, *away* would have to be his first consideration. The opposite direction to the main pirate's camp, as soon as possible. He had gotten quite turned around, but he knew they had been travelling roughly North-West; perhaps the best thing was simply to continue in that direction until they found a suitable shelter — if one was to be found. Of that, however, they were not at all guaranteed.

"We head for the northern shore," he said at last, hoping he sounded more confident than he felt in the moment. "We shall go as far as we can before night falls again, and rest under cover of darkness." He looked around, but no one offered any objections. Even Jim only looked back him with a blank expression, as though he had no opinion on the matter. Thomas set his jaw, shifted his arm under Cole's shoulder until he had good leverage, and together they set off into the forest.

— 10 —

It was painfully slow progress. Pasco and Thomas did their best to help keep poor Cole on his feet, but the boy would drift occasionally out of consciousness, losing his footing, and it was all they could do together to hold him up. It was uncomfortably uneven, with Thomas being half Pasco's height again, and they were forced to walk lopsided with Thomas' neck stretched painfully to his left while Pasco had to walk in some places on his toes. Cole had no shoes and the rough terrain bit terribly into his feet whenever he did manage to hold his own weight. Thomas would have given him his boots, but Cole, in a brief moment of lucidity, admonished him. "We won't get nowhere far if you can't walk either sir," he said, hoarse and breathless. "I will do, only I don't know I will get much further before I fall asleep again."

"Courage, Peter," Thomas said to him, doing his best to imitate the tone of voice he had heard Wickerham use so often when speaking to injured or dying men. "Night is not far away, now."

In fact, it seemed impossible that the day should have gone on so long. It seemed a lifetime ago that he had woken alone by the rocky outcrop on the peak of the island. Since Bill Blake had died in his arms. Since taking a pirate prisoner.

Said prisoner was now moving ahead of them, not out of calling distance, but he could after all move much faster without a man to carry, and he was making himself useful by moving aside any logs or other fallen debris to make their way easier, without leaving any permanent marks that might have left a trail. At first this seemed incidental to Thomas, until Jim deliberately stopped to hold aside a large leafy bush, rather than simply stamping it down. He knew what he was doing, and he did it well. No words were exchanged; none were needed, and once they were past the difficult stretches he would move on ahead again, looking for the next obstacle, his head twitching around at each woodland noise. At one point he stopped dead in the middle of the path, his hand going to the knife which he had secured at his waist with one of the shorter lengths of the rope, the rest having looped over his bare shoulders. Thomas stopped still in response, watching, heart pounding, until the tension visibly left the boy's thin frame and he straightened up again. "What was it?" Thomas asked him quietly as they caught up to him.

"A bird," Jim said simply. "I thought I could catch it. It would make good eating. But it flew away." Then he continued on northward into the forest on almost silent feet, leaving them behind again.

Pasco scoffed as the trio made their unsteady way after him. "Catch a bird, hah," he muttered. "You can't catch a bird with a knife, not 'less it's hurt already or it can't fly. I don't care how good he is at finding coconuts."

Thomas wondered at it as well, but it was a sobering reminder of their sad lack of supply. Though they had Bob's sword,

Froggie's knife and the short coil of rope, Pasco had found nothing edible among the pirates' belongings. Thomas had eaten only coconut meat the last two days, and the boys had not had even so much. Pasco was putting a brave face on it, but both he and Cole would have to eat soon — something more substantial than the local trees could provide.

"He is very resourceful, that's for certain," he said after a moment, realising that he had left an uncomfortable silence, and Pasco had also gone quiet; perhaps imagining by his officer's lack of response that he had overstepped his bounds. It had not been so long ago that the two of them had been separated by only one rank, less meaningful than the social chasm between ship's boy and acting captain, and Thomas had slipped out of habit into a less formal mode. He shook his head, trying to rid it of the strange heaviness he suddenly felt.

"Can we trust him, sir?" the boy asked after another minute.

"We have very little choice," Thomas pointed out, wincing as they squeezed through a narrow gap between two large boulders. "He has been of material help so far, but I find him quite… unpredictable."

"But he's a pirate," Pasco protested. "Why would he help us?"

As to that, Thomas had no real answers, and this was not really the time for such a conversation, in any case. "Let us make sure to watch our feet and save our breath," he said instead, and then, not wanting the boy to think he was being chastened, added, "you are doing very well."

Pasco bit his lip, and straightened his back as best he could under Cole's arm.

Night fell, and the going got even harder. It was impossible to see where they were landing their feet, and they had to feel their way inch by inch, judging their direction by instinct and the brief glimpses of stars they could see occasionally through the canopy. Pasco was breathing heavily and raggedly, and stumbled badly more than once, risking further injury. Thomas would have liked to ask Jim to take a turn on Cole's other side, but he could tell from the way Cole shrank away every time Jim approached that it would not do. Besides Jim seemed to have little difficulty in finding his way, as though he had owl's eyes capable of seeing in the dark. They now truly needed his guidance, as obstacles were visible only as outlines against the moonlight through the thick forest. There came a point where Thomas thought they could not possibly go any further; he kept finding himself half-asleep on his feet, and he could only imagine how either of the boys were still managing to put one foot in front of the other. They had not found any shelter, and Thomas was just thinking despairingly that he must call a halt anyway and let the boys sleep where they fell, regardless of the danger, when Jim came loping back to them between the trees, his soft footfalls the only real warning they had of his approach.

"I can hear water," was all he said.

Thomas blinked, feeling slow and stupid with fatigue. The island was not so large that the constant rushing of the ocean was inaudible even this far into the interior; he had long since ceased to notice it. "What do you mean?" he asked finally. "A waterfall?"

"No, like a river," said Jim, his voice low. "Up ahead. Stay here and I will find it."

"But —" Thomas began, but the boy was already gone, slipping silently into the thickest part of the forest where they could never have made a usable path. Surely there could be no rivers, he thought, dizzily. Not on this scrap of rock. He felt a rush of annoyance; what time might be lost on such a fool's errand?

Still, there was no sense in going ahead to where Jim might not be able to find them again, so he and Pasco let Cole down on a soft piece of ground, and he ordered Pasco to rest also. "I hope he has not gone far," he muttered aloud to himself as he stood looking out uselessly into the blackness. He could barely see his own hand in front of his face. "Damn him. If he gets himself lost we shall all be in even worse straits than we were already."

"He seems to know what he's about," Pasco yawned shakily, forgetting his manners once again in the face of sheer exhaustion, slumping against a tree with his legs outstretched. "Even if he isn't very good at waiting for orders. But maybe pirates aren't, as a whole. I've never met one before."

"Neither have I," Thomas admitted. "There are scarcely any pirates anymore, you know, not like there used to be. Those that are left are poor bands of bandits living off the scraps of the sea, like this lot."

"In the stories they always have chests of gold, and treasure maps and so on," Pasco murmured. "But I suppose those are only stories. I always liked them, before now. But the ones who attacked us are all evil."

"Yes," Thomas said, low, thinking of the southern shore.

"Except for Jim, I suppose," the boy continued sleepily, his eyes already closing. "He doesn't seem evil. And he did help save us from those other ones. Don't worry, sir... I'm sure he'll come back."

Thomas smiled wryly to himself at the optimism of the young. "Better get some sleep," he said, but Pasco had not waited to be given permission. Cole was very still also, his chest rising and falling slowly, either asleep or still half-conscious.

There was no good place to sit, as an attack could conceivably come from any side, but Thomas reminded himself that any pirates who might like to attack them would be just as blind as they were themselves, and resigned himself. He sat against the tree beside the sleeping boys, with his own sword bare across his knees, the other still sheathed ill-fitting by his side, and tried to keep himself awake by reciting shanty songs in his head. It seemed to have the opposite effect, however, and more than once he jerked himself suddenly awake after drifting too far, his heart pounding. He was so tired. The wound on his arm ached, but he had nothing to clean or dress it with, so he ignored it.

After perhaps half an hour, though it was impossible to tell for certain, Thomas jerked himself out of yet another lulling doze as the faintest sound of footsteps returned from the direction Jim had gone. He emerged like a loping tiger out of the trees. "There is a cove," the pirate said, without waiting to be admonished for his sudden disappearance. "You have to climb, but if you go now we can't be seen from up here."

"The boys are dead tired," Thomas said doubtfully, his own voice coming out slightly mumbling, as though his cheeks had been stuffed with cotton. "I don't know if they can go any further tonight."

"We will manage, sir." It was Cole, who had somehow managed to manoeuvre himself into a sitting position. His face was still swollen and unrecognisable in the dark, but Thomas felt his heart lift a little to see him properly aware at last.

"I can help," Jim said, after a moment. "It isn't far."

Thomas roused Pasco with some difficulty from his sleep, but once they were on their feet the boy swayed alarmingly and almost fell. "Sorry sir," he said, almost in tears as he tried to steady himself. "I can't see anything at all."

"Here." In the dark, Thomas half-saw, half-felt Jim reach for Pasco's wrist, and place the boy's small hand on the rope at his own waist. "Hold here and follow." Then he went to Pasco's place on Cole's other side and assisted Thomas in lifting him to his feet. Cole shuddered, but did not protest, too weak and too exhausted to refuse the help.

In this fashion the four of them stumbled blindly through the forest, taking a slightly different path to the one Jim had taken at first — a more direct route, Thomas could only hope. He had no idea how Jim knew where he was going, but he did not ask and he tried not to dwell on it, focusing instead on keeping Cole upright, though at one point he and Jim were mostly carrying him where the ground became momentarily uneven underfoot. He could hear Pasco's ragged, sobbing breathing from behind them, and tried not to notice it for the boy's sake.

Eventually they came to the top of a steep slope. Here the moon lit their way a little better as the trees thinned out around them, and Thomas was able to see where to put his feet as they half-climbed, half-slid down the sandy ridge. He could hear it too now, the sound of slowly running water below. They had indeed reached a cove of some kind where the sea formed a narrow creek, dotted with dark rocks. That was about all he could make out, and he had to rely on Jim going ahead, leading them down, and down, with Cole almost lying prostrate on his back as Thomas dragged him along by the shoulders, every footstep seeming to take an age. By the time the rocky sand gave way to smoother, eroded rock underfoot, he was not surprised to see the first glint of orange rays coming around from the eastern horizon. Pasco was shivering, and Cole wasn't in much better case, but Thomas held his tongue and let Jim lead. The boy had somehow found a small cave at the back of the cove, too shallow for any creature to have taken up residence, little more than an indentation in the rock face. But it was shelter, and they all but collapsed into it as one, falling into an undignified panting heap on the ground.

Thomas groaned and pulled himself up, forcing himself to move at least so long as it took to make Cole at least a little comfortable. There were no blankets to cover him with and nothing to cushion his head, lest they all took off their clothes to make a pillow, but he found the smoothest, dryest corner and settled him into it. Cole mumbled his thanks, his hand going limp across his chest. Pasco had already curled up on his other side, sniffling in his sleep.

Thomas looked at Jim's slumped outline in the near pitch-blackness. He was breathing very hard, almost the first sign he had shown that he was as human as the rest of them. Thomas knew they should take watches, but he also knew he was incapable of it himself at the moment, and even if he thought it was a good idea to ask a pirate to keep watch for them, he could not. "Get some rest," he said, quietly, and then, with some awkwardness — "thank you for your service today. We should never have made it so far, without your help."

Jim hesitated a moment, half-sitting, and Thomas thought he might be about to say something. But he only nodded, and turned over on his side, a little apart from the rest of them. And went still.

Thomas lay beside Cole, thinking that keeping him between Pasco and himself would keep him warmest. As he closed his eyes, finally, he heard at the edge of his awareness a familiar rushing sound, oddly echoed, and realised it had just started to rain.

*

The fresh storm lasted well into the morning, not that they knew much of it. The sun was well-risen by the time Thomas opened his eyes again, and by then it had even begun to peek its way through the clouds. At first it seemed that it was still raining outside the cave mouth, but it was only dripping slowly from some vegetation that must have been growing over the edge of the cliff above.

Cole was lying still beside him, and as he shifted carefully he could see Pasco on his other side, eyes shut tight. He sat up slowly, not wanting to wake the boys. Where Jim had lain there was now only a coil of rope.

He stopped just long enough to check that poor Cole was still breathing before getting up, biting back a gasp at the ache in his legs. He realised that in the last two days he must have walked several miles, much further than he would have done in a week strolling about the deck of a ship. His knees threatened to buckle underneath him, but he grit his teeth and staggered to the entrance, stooping a little under the low ceiling of the cave.

Blinking in the light, he took a moment to take in their surroundings. The storm was hanging out to sea now, leaving behind it a cloudy grey sky fading to blue. The rocky inlet was at low tide, but the water was running into the creek quite fast, buoyed on by the storm waters. The creek twisted and curved around the rocks, splitting up in several places around large formations, oddly beautiful. Some of the rock looked as though it might have fallen from the cliff; Thomas eyed the steep slope warily, but it seemed sturdy enough.

It was only a moment before he saw Jim, crouching on an isolated stone in the middle of the creek where it ran past the cave. He was holding a sharpened branch and staring into the water, until he seemed to sense the eyes on him and looked around, unbending from his knee to stand upright. He stared back at Thomas. In daylight, with his matted hair, scarred chest and torn breeches, he looked quite wild, like a startled animal.

On the other hand, Thomas thought, he himself was not much better put together, with his own breeches ripped in a dozen places and unbuttoned shirt hanging open. He ran a hand experimentally through his hair; there were small leaves caught in it. For a moment they simply looked at each other as a rabbit and a fox.

"Good morning," said Thomas finally, with all the stiff politeness of his old governess, who had used to whack his fingers with a wooden ruler whenever she caught him drawing in the margins of his work. Thinking of her, he found himself automatically fixing the image of Jim in his mind the way he always did when he wanted to remember something to sketch it later. *Foolishness*, he chided himself with an inner chuckle at this fine piece of optimism. It seemed perfectly unlikely that he would ever have the chance to commit any such images to paper ever again.

Jim seemed to relax after a moment and made his way back to the edge of the creek, hopping off his stone and simply stepping across; the water was only waist-height. He pulled himself out, trousers dripping, the makeshift spear still in his hand. Thomas found himself staring a little at the sleek line of his body, his movements as graceful as if he really were some kind of jungle creature. Despite the stitches, the filthy hair… he was oddly beautiful. Just like the island.

"You look like you were fishing," Thomas said, clearing his throat and trying to clear his mind of such inappropriate thoughts. "Is there much chance of that?"

"I've seen some," Jim said, in his succinct sort of way. "It's a long time since I last fished, and this is not very good." He held up the sharpened stick he was holding for demonstration. Its point was freshly cut. Froggie's knife, which Thomas took to be the instrument behind this ingenuity, was just visible near the edge of the fissure, not hidden but put carefully aside. "But I think I can catch some, with a little practice," Jim added dubiously.

"Your talents appear to be countless," Thomas said. He felt quite strangely lightheaded all of a sudden, and his tone must have carried this across because Jim gave him a rather doubtful look. "How on earth did you find this place last night?" he asked, to cover himself.

The boy hesitated. "I followed the sound of the water," he said simply after a moment. "All…" He stopped, blinking, eyes a little wide as though he thought he had spoken wrongly.

"Go on," Thomas prompted.

Jim looked uncertain, but he continued. "All… all islands have secret places like this one," he said, low. "If you know where to look."

"But it was pitch dark."

Jim shrugged, one-shouldered. "I used my ears instead, and my hands. The rock around here is soft. There was bound to be a cave." He stopped again, his fingers tightening around his stick.

"What's the matter?" Thomas asked, frowning. "Is the wound paining you?"

"No." Jim looked down at the row of stitches across his chest. If anything Thomas thought it looked a little better; still gruesome, but the flesh around the wound was not quite so red. "It stung a bit in the water, but it isn't so bad. Your… your surgeon is very good. I've never seen one as good."

Was, Thomas thought, darkly. He *was* very good.

His giddy mood subsided. The mention of food had made his stomach ache with hunger all of a sudden, and the fresh memory of the deaths of his crew was more than sobering. "I have to ask," he said, into the silence that had fallen once again between them. "Why are you so willing to help us? You could have made your escape at any point last night, and made your way back to your crew…"

Jim's bright blue eyes flickered with something strange; he looked away. "To have a crew you have to have a ship," he pointed out, with inarguable but cold logic. "They aren't any crew of mine. And Briggs…" he swallowed, grimacing.

"Ah," Thomas could not help but sympathise on that point, particularly after what he had seen back at the camp. Briggs was certainly not the captain anyone could have wanted. But it still seemed like an unlikely choice, to abandon one's entire crew in favour of the enemy. "But you must realise your chances… that is, our circumstances are hardly optimistic. Your men seem to have all the supplies from the boats, and pistols, and the better numbers, and we have some rope and a knife and little else, not to mention a wounded man." He kept his voice low unless Cole or Pasco should wake and hear him. "If it comes to a fight we are hardly at an advantage, if we even survive so long."

Jim did not argue. He surely could see the hopelessness of their situation as well as Thomas himself. "What will you do?" he asked instead, his blue eyes shining in the sun.

Thomas took a deep breath. He had not yet had a chance to think. "We might make a smoke signal of some kind, when the skies are clearer, and eventually some ship or other may see us. But so will *they*. The only other course is to find a way of getting away ourselves." But the pirates had the only boats. Short of getting them back, they might be able to build something out of wreckage and forest debris, but he doubted extremely that they could manage something bigger than a one-man raft. His greatest hope was finding a ship within hailing range, and that seemed highly unlikely.

Jim nodded his understanding. "If I can help…" he said, hesitantly, as though forming the words one at a time, "will you… that is, will you be going…"

"Back to England," Thomas confirmed. "If I dared to think so far ahead, which I do not."

"Will you take me with you?" Jim asked then, all in a rush. His expression was hard to read. It was not hopeful.

Thomas frowned, hesitated. "You understand they are likely to prosecute you for piracy." Jim's hardened expression said that he did know. "But," Thomas added, after a moment's struggle with himself. "If you do continue to help us, I expect I can put in a good word for you with the magistrates. Though I fail to see why you should want to take such a risk." Certainly a simple man might have done so, such as Thomas had originally believed Jim to be, but it was becoming increasingly clear that Jim was not simple, in the least. Somehow Thomas had little doubt that he understood the fate that most likely awaited him in England.

Jim shrugged. Apparently he had said all he had wanted to say, and was satisfied.

What Thomas did not say was that his own word was unlikely to hold much weight with anyone, once word got around of his failure. One of the finest ships in the royal fleet had been sunk on his watch, to say nothing of all the men killed, including the admiral, and so many fine and promising officers hand-picked by Wickerham for the most prestigious of postings on the *Courage*. He guessed he was more than likely to be court-martialed, and the worst-case scenario that followed was hanging. He could do Jim no good under those circumstances. It was a hard thing to have to do, to give hope where there was none. The very thought made him feel ill. But for Pasco and Cole's sake he would do it. He knew very well that none of them would survive long without Jim's help.

"Very well," he said, his mouth dry. "But if you are to join us, you must follow my orders, and do nothing without my permission. We shall have no more of this running off into the dark with no warning. I know you are unused to discipline, but we have a little more of it in the navy. Understood?"

Jim's lips parted as though to speak, but he pressed them together again and nodded stiff agreement.

"'Yes, sir'," Thomas prompted.

A twitch in Jim's cheek that might have been a grimace. "Yes," he repeated dutifully. "Sir."

"Oh." Little Pasco had appeared at the cave mouth, yawning and trying to hide it behind his hand as he looked around in surprise at their surroundings.

"Mr Pasco, take care of Mr Cole while I scout our location." Thomas shook himself back into the command. "You know what to do?"

"I… helped Mr Smythe in the sickbay sometimes, sir," Pasco said, sounding rather uncertain. "I can wash the wounds, but there is nothing to dress them with."

"Do what you can, and keep him still." Thomas looked back at Jim. "You may resume your fishing. We shall all be glad of something to eat. I will just wash my arm, and then let us see if I can find anything else edible."

— 11 —

He did not find anything edible, at least not anything he knew he could trust. The island's vegetation was too foreign to him, except for the palm trees, and there were less of these on the northern side where the terrain was rougher. Fresh rainwater had collected on some leaves and in puddles on the ground in places, and he drank gratefully, taking note of the best places to come back to, later.

When he returned after perhaps a couple of hours, there was a small pile of middling-sized fish set out to dry on the edge of the creek. What he was surprised to see was Jim, sitting cross-legged with a deep grimace on his face while Pasco, sitting behind him on a rock for the added height, was doing something with Froggie's long knife in his hand. Thomas hurried over, concerned, but then he saw the scattering of clumped dirt-black strands around Jim's knees, and realised that Pasco was sawing off Jim's overgrown hair close to the skull. He made the last cut as Thomas came near, and Jim stood up quickly, scratching at his head furiously with both his hands.

Thomas' confusion must have shown in his expression, because when Pasco looked up and saw him, he grinned rather nervously, as though not sure what his officer's reaction would be. "I told him it will help with the lice," he said, wiping stray hairs off his hands onto his trousers. "Less hair means less places for them to live in." He turned to Jim. "Now you must scrub it in seawater," he said, with all the authority of a naval surgeon in his young voice. "It is a pity we don't have any vinegar," he added, wistfully. "I had lice when I was a boy, and mother soaked my head in vinegar."

When you were a boy, thought Thomas, with amusement at a child of twelve giving orders in such a fashion. He watched as Jim went, silently and rather reluctantly, to bathe in the running water of the creek. He did not, Thomas noticed, take off his breeches.

"Will it really help the lice?" he asked, giving Pasco a rather incredulous look.

"I think so," Pasco said, though he looked a little doubtful. "At least, I think that is what Doctor Smythe does for them. And in any case," he added, shrugging, "if he bathes, he will *smell* a lot less."

*

When Jim emerged, there was indeed a better odour to the wound across his chest, and he looked quite different without the lumps of matted hair falling constantly into his eyes. It seemed to startle him that it was gone, causing him to twitch suddenly every time he turned his head. He looked somehow more human, despite his scarred, rake-thin torso.

Pasco had made good work of cleaning Cole's face, and the wounds did not look so bad now that they were no longer obscured by blood. There was bruising and swelling on his head, down one cheek and across his jaw, and more bruising down one side of his ribs, perfectly visible as he was now sitting naked on the ground save for a thick bandage around his thigh, gone brown with blood. Pasco had also done his best with the bloodstained shirt and underthings, which were laid out on a rock to dry.

As thunder started to roll again above the cave, the four of them sat together and ate the fish raw with their fingers. Thomas was nervous, having never previously been so desperate as to try it in the 'Eastern style', but would not show it in front of the younger officers, and after a bit of grimacing and biting of lips, their grumbling stomachs overcame their hesitation, and they were soon eating as much as they could take. Unsurprisingly, Jim showed no such reluctance to eating his food raw, and Thomas couldn't help but wonder how he had learned to fish in such a primitive way. He held himself back from asking. Even if he expected Jim to answer, which he did not, he felt he had forgone any right he might have had to ask such personal questions now that he had all but sworn the boy into service under such deception.

Cole fell asleep again after they had eaten. Jim went to find some more coconuts, and once each of them had had a drink, he used the knife to cut out as much of the meat as he could without splitting the things apart. Then Thomas took the shells out into the rain and filled them, and they dug little hollows in a sandy spot to keep them cool. Then they all slept once more.

When Thomas woke, Jim was fishing again and Pasco had found a stone to sharpen the knife. He was sitting by the edge of the creek, wetting the stone occasionally in the water and drawing it slowly and carefully along the blade. The knife, which must have come at some point from the galley on the *Courage*, had gone quite dull from being used on the fishing stick and on the coconuts. Thomas praised the boy for his initiative, and he beamed. "I can do your sword too, sir," he said, and Thomas handed it to him, and also the other that he had taken from Bob's body. Then he stripped out of all his bloody, sweat-soaked clothes, and slipped with relief into the creek.

Bathing in saltwater wasn't as refreshing, but it was enough to strip the sticky layer of sweat from his skin, to soothe his sunburn, and to wash clean the healing wound on his forearm. It felt good. He let the buoyancy of the water hold him, floating on his back in the slow current and looking up at the sun coming out once again from behind the clouds.

"It is strange," Pasco observed, when Thomas had dragged himself out of the water, dressed, and sat beside him on the edge. He had made good work of Thomas' own sword and had just started on the other.

"It is?" Thomas blinked, nonplussed.

"Jim, sir." Pasco kept his voice low, so it wouldn't carry over the water to where Jim was waiting patiently for his next catch to pass into his range. "He doesn't act like the rest of them. The ones who… who took us…" he shook his head quickly, as though to rid it of a dark thought, "well, he isn't like them."

"Not all men who turn to crime out of desperation are evil," Thomas said, remembering what poor Father Murray had said about the pirates' immortal souls. "There are stories of even rich men taking to piracy out of some kind of wanderlust. I heard them saying that their own former captain was a merchant."

"That's another thing," Pasco agreed, dipping his sharpening stone once again into the water. "He doesn't talk like a pirate, either. Isn't that strange? He talks like a gentleman."

With a jolt, Thomas realised that Pasco had just hit on the very thing he had been trying to grasp about Jim's voice since he had heard it first. It wasn't the voice itself but the way he spoke; in short, common sentences, to be sure, but with none of the atrocious accents or spitting colloquialisms common to the rest of the pirate crew. He spoke like any of the navy's young officers, like Cole or like Pasco himself.

"Only whenever he says more than just a little, he goes quiet, like he thinks he said too much," Pasco continued, in innocent observation. "Have you noticed?"

"Yes," Thomas said, solemnly. He didn't know what to make of it. It was just more questions.

"He isn't some rich merchant though." Paco turned the sword over and began to draw the stone over the other side of the blade, resuming the rhythmic scraping noise. "No merchant has hair like *that*."

Thomas managed to stop himself from laughing, just in time. "Manners, Mr Pasco," he said, with as much sternness as he could manage. "Why don't you go and ask if he can teach you what he is doing? It can only be a useful skill. Here, I'll take that." He took the sword and the stone out of the boy's hands and watched him go over to Jim's position. He was too far away to hear more than the murmur of Pasco's voice, but he was soon joining Jim on the little rock island in the middle of the creek, taking the stick in his small hand while Jim pointed into the water, showing him where to strike.

Thomas went back inside the cave. Cole was dressed, sitting up and leaning against the wall of the shallow fissure, nibbling at some of the fish they had not yet finished. "Go on," Thomas told him softly when he hesitated on seeing him. "There won't be any shortage for now. You should eat."

He had only meant to check on the boy, but since he was awake he sat beside him and resumed the sharpening of the sword, as though that had been his intention all along. "Yessir," the boy muttered, and finished the rest of his mouthful.

"How are you feeling?" Thomas asked, watching him out of the corner of his eye.

"Much better sir, thank you," Cole nodded without quite meeting Thomas' eyes. "My head pains me a little, but I'm sure it won't last."

"Are there any other adverse effects? Any weakness in the limbs?"

Cole made a show of stretching out and flexing his arms and legs. "I don't think so, sir."

Thomas breathed in inner sigh of relief, though he tried not to let show the real depth of his concern. He had seen a few men ruined by blows to the head, and heard stories of many more, and there seemed to be no way to tell what the result if any would be of such an injury. Some men went blind, some lost all feeling in their legs, others simply went mad. "They certainly made a good job of it," he said, keeping most of his focus on the blade in his hands with only half an eye on Cole, who went still. "Pasco said you fought them off."

Cole swallowed hard. "I had to, sir. They tried... they tried to..."

"I know what they tried to do," Thomas said. He hadn't let himself think it until now, but he hadn't had to. He'd known the kind of men these pirates were since he had rescued Jim from the brig. He hesitated a moment and took a deep breath before asking. "Did they try it with Pasco?"

Cole sniffed and shook his head. "I don't think so sir, not after I kicked the really skinny one in the face, but I know they would have eventually if you hadn't come. I'm sure that's the only reason they left us alive."

Thomas' blood ran cold. Perhaps Bill was right, he thought as he tried not to watch Cole shift uncomfortably in his torn and stained things. He had been naive. He had thought the two youngest and smallest had been spared as less of a threat, perhaps even out of some kind of compassion, to use as hostages or for labour. He hadn't even considered something so intentional, so vile, until Jim had confirmed it to his face. "Tell me what happened," he said aloud, his heart beating hard and fast as though he had been running.

Cole was quiet for a minute. "We were guarding them, Rogers and I," he said finally, in a quiet but clear voice. "I was just thinking it should be time for another shift, and Rogers had turned to me and said he was going to call up for something to eat if they didn't relieve us soon. And then... I don't know... Briggs just came up out of nowhere. He'd been quiet, we almost forgot he was there, but he must have slipped the chain because he was standing up and swinging before we knew what was happening.

He hit Rogers on the side of the head, and while he was turning to see what hit him, Briggs got to his sword..." He swallowed breathily, fighting back the natural emotion of a boy who had seen a fellow seaman, a friend, cut down before him. "I couldn't fight him sir, Rogers was between us. I heard him gasp and then he was on the floor, and Briggs was grinning at me with this horrible look in his eye, and all the pirates were yelling and some of them were cheering... I... I ran..."

Thomas wished he couldn't imagine the scene, the young officer alone, faced down across the body of a dead man in a space too small to cross blades, the din of the prisoners throwing themselves against the bars, crushing each other in their sudden manic desperation. A boy against a man who had nothing to lose.

"Go on," he said, low.

"I heard him pull back the bolts below," Cole went on, his eyes a little too wide as he remembered the fear he must have felt. "They all cheered him. I was trying to find help, but most of the crew were in their bunks. I found Blake, the seaman —" Thomas' heart leapt — "he was taking his tot on the lower gun deck, and we both went to look for an officer, but by then they were already coming after us. I told everyone I could find what was happening, but no one knew what to do... and they were cutting down everyone they could find, and then some of them got their hands on pistols. I saw them kill Taft and Mr Featherstone. I know it sounds silly, sir, but it felt like every one of them was coming for me. I could feel their eyes on me. Nearly everyone who fought got cut down. I tried to make my way to the deck..."

"You were injured," Thomas remembered.

"I think it was the one with one eye," Cole swallowed. "He slashed me trying to get past on one of the ladders. I made it as far as the forward stair, but…"

"Babber," Thomas nodded. We found him later, Jim and I. He's dead."

"Good," Cole muttered.

"And I found you on the stair as I came down," Thomas recalled, heavy guilt settling on him as he remembered that he had thought the boy was done for. "That was just before the ship hit the reef."

"I must have missed that," Cole said wryly. "When I came to I was up to my waist in water belowdecks and Mr Gower was there. He carried me up the stairs, and Mr Smythe was helping the wounded into one of the boats — he came to bind my leg and I must… I must have blacked out again." He pushed back the waist of his trouser to show the decent bandage around his thigh, undoubtedly the surgeon's work. "Then I remember Mr Gower directing the men, and the admiral… the admiral was speaking to me, but I don't remember what he said. The storm was all around us, and I couldn't hear anything else, it was so loud. It seemed to go on forever, and I remember thinking, what if we all died already, and this is hell?"

"How long do you think you were on the water?" Thomas asked, mouth dry.

Cole shook his head. "Hours. We must have drifted miles. The sun was rising before the sea calmed enough for us to make land. I was sitting in the bow with the admiral, and Mr Smythe had asked me to make sure and keep him still while he tended to the others.

Pasco was helping too, I remember. We had pulled a few men out of the sea… but not many.”

“But you did make land?” Thomas asked, surprised. “You weren't wrecked?”

Cole shook his head. “No sir. It wasn't a smooth landing, exactly… it was still a heavy tide and it turned us halfway around. I was still holding onto the admiral, so I wasn't much help… but Mr Gower and some of the men jumped clear and we beached her somehow.”

It was painful, very painful, to hear the last stories of men who Thomas knew were dead, had seen dead with his own eyes, but he knew he had to hear them, that it was his duty to know so that if he ever got the chance, he could pass the tales of their skill and bravery to their families. He nodded for Cole to continue.

Cole had gone a little paler in the dim light of the fissure, but he steeled himself and went on. “Mr Gower gave orders for us to take inventory of the supplies and for some men to search the shore for more survivors. They came back after a while with no word. A few other men went to look for fresh water or food, and Mr Smythe and that seaman Dolson took the admiral on a stretcher to where they'd found some better shelter. And then… then…” he took another deep breath.

“The pirates came,” Thomas guessed.

“We outnumbered them,” Cole said, eyes wider than ever as he stared unseeing at the opposite wall. “We outnumbered them two to one, but they took us by surprise from the trees. We were fighting in the sand and some of us in bare feet… we never stood a chance, sir. The sand… the sand was red with blood. I thought

I would die... but I was ready for it. I didn't run sir, I fought, I fought on one knee, I swear."

Thomas reached out and put a shaking hand on the boy's shoulder. "I believe you," he said, his voice catching in his throat despite his best efforts.

"I saw them grab Pasco, and then one of them... I thought he was going to kill me, but he just knocked me down and laughed and took my sword and my boots... Then they tied us up, me and Pasco, and I looked... and I realised..." he gasped, a painful, ragged sound. "I knew all the men were dead. The blood... and the bodies..."

"I know," Thomas said, gripping Cole's shoulder. "I know. I saw them."

Cole's head came up, startled. "You did, sir?"

"Yes. I washed up on the eastern side, but I found my way to the boat. They took the supplies and left nothing behind — but Bill Blake still had a few minutes of life in him. He told me which direction they had taken you."

"But..." Cole stammered, blinking at him. "But sir... sir, did you not find Mr Smythe?"

"What?" Thomas shook his head slowly. "I didn't... I had no time to identify all the bodies. I started east as soon as I knew that you were —"

"No sir," Cole insisted, his voice breaking briefly into a boyish soprano in his insistence. "Sir, Mr Smythe took Admiral Wickerham into the interior. They weren't in the battle. I don't know if the pirates ever found them."

— 12 —

"If we are to know anything for sure, I must travel to the south side of the island," Thomas said, when full explanations had been made to the scanty remainder of their small and ragtag party. At these words both Cole and Pasco sent up a clamour of protest, insisting that they come along.

"I do much better now, sir," Cole said, though Thomas knew the boy would not last an hour if he had to walk. Even if the head wound was not life-changing, his injured leg was still bad and the cuts on his feet cracked and bled; Thomas knew he would be lucky if they did not soon petrify. "You cannot go alone, sir — it's too dangerous."

"I trust you will allow *me* to make that assessment, Midshipman Cole," Thomas said flatly in his most authoritative voice, shaming the boy into silence only to allow the younger of the two to pipe up in his turn.

"If you think you might find the admiral, surely someone must go and make sure you can help bring him back, and Mr Smythe and Mr Dolson too?" Pasco protested. "Besides, what will we do if you leave us behind?"

"You will take care of Mr Cole," Thomas told him firmly. "For he will not be well enough to travel for a few days — no,

Peter, enough, you know perfectly well you can barely stand," he sighed at Cole. "Those are my orders. The two of you will remain here and stay out of sight."

Pasco went a little red in the cheeks but pursed his lips shut. Cole, however, was not going to be so easily cowed into submission. "What about *him?*" he demanded, pointing at Jim with an expression of deep distaste. "You can't mean to leave us behind and take a *pirate* with you!"

Jim had been sitting quietly in his own corner, without taking part in the discussion. Neither did he do so now; he only offered Cole a raised eyebrow and a sartorial expression. Cole glowered back at him. Thomas couldn't help thinking that Jim had more reason to hate the yellow-haired midshipman than the reverse; Cole had after all held Jim down while he had been stitched without sedative, and Thomas doubted he would have forgotten.

Thomas ignored Cole and waited until Jim turned to look at him. "I won't order you to come, Jim," he said, low, keeping his eyes fixed on Jim's blue ones. "There are bound to be more dangers out there than here, and you have already been of material assistance to our cause...." This, he thought, was rather an understatement, but he was reluctant to be more grateful in front of Cole, who was angry enough to start a fight. "I won't ask for more if you aren't willing to give it. But I must admit I would be happy to make use of your skills in navigation and survival, when the terrain is so unknown. Give me your parole — your assurance that you will not turn against us — and I swear in turn that I will consider you as one of my own crew, and under my protection."

Jim stared at him, his face unreadable. The red line on his

cheek was just visible in the dark. The effect of the hack job Pasco had made on his hair was to make him look older, and less like a wild thing. Except for his eyes, which somehow shone even brighter without the shadows falling down around his face. His gaze sent a shiver down Thomas' spine, even as he dared himself to hope that the pirate wouldn't choose to let him venture out into the island wilderness alone.

"Jim?" Thomas prompted, after a long silence. "Do I have your promise?"

Jim blinked, and with that, the spell was broken. "Yes," he said, finally. "I swear."

Thomas nodded, his heart lifting in relief. Of course it was foolish to trust the word of a pirate, one who had no understanding or respect for the law. And yet, he found himself the fool.

The blue eyes flickered between Thomas and Cole, and then to Pasco. "You remember what I told you?" Jim asked the younger boy. "When you wait for the fish, you have to be as still as the rock."

Pasco hesitated, glanced at Thomas, then nodded. "Yes," he said. "I remember."

"Good." Jim stood up. "You will have to keep both of you fed."

*

They set off with another, better-made leaf satchel filled with coconuts, the rest of the rope, and a few fish which they ate as they walked. After the first pangs of real hunger had been sated the raw fish was more difficult for Thomas to stomach, but he forced himself to eat even after he was no longer hungry, knowing the fish was only good while it was fresh and he would regret his squeamishness later. The knife and Bob's sword they had left behind with the boys; this decision left Jim without a weapon, but Pasco and Cole would need the sword for their own defense and the knife for hunting and cutting new spears. Besides, Thomas had to allow himself that he felt more comfortable knowing that the pirate was not armed, parole or no parole.

Jim did not protest being sent into the jungle weaponless, but walked silently at Thomas' side, stopping only on occasion to investigate a rockpool, or a bush, or a burrow, or anywhere some edible creature might be hiding. He found some unlikely-looking barnacle-like shells, the meat of which was unpleasantly salty to the taste, but Thomas swallowed them whole anyway and sipped from a coconut until his mouth no longer felt so painfully dry. At least the knife wound on his arm had closed, and only bothered him when, forgetting, he scratched at it along with the row of insect bites that had appeared there overnight.

They had decided first to follow the shoreline along the north-western coast, since the pirates were known to be camping in the southeast, and by doing so avoid the enemy entirely. This proved difficult, however, as the shoreline was an uneven terrain scattered with boulders, and alternating sandy coves with almost sheer cliffs. By the second time they had been forced to wade through seawater waist-deep to reach the next passable stretch, Thomas had decided it was not worth the risk. Time, he felt in the pit of his stomach, was of the essence, and they had already lost too much of it. He cursed the time he had spent sleeping and eating, when he should have questioned Cole much earlier, or even pressed Pasco on the details of their capture, but it was done now and all he could do was try to make it up by reaching the other side of the island as soon as possible. This way seemed to take even longer than the hacking, stumbling route through the interior which he had taken the last time.

"We must go inland before we reach the western cliffs," he told Jim when they stopped to camp after the sun had set on the first day. "A good length of them are sheer drops, and we won't pass them this way. Unless you prefer to swim around," he added, with grim humour.

Given the boy had said scarcely more than two words since they had left the cove, he was surprised when Jim answered. "I can swim around if you like," he said, "and meet you there."

It was a moment before Thomas recognised this as a joke, if one made with very little humour. "I imagine you are a good swimmer, as well," he said, and dared to probe further. "Where did you learn?"

"Tortuga." It was the second time he had mentioned the place, and Thomas found his curiosity piqued still more.

"Oh? Were you born there?"

Jim stopped eating, a large hunk of lobster meat halfway to his mouth. He had found the lobsters in the shallows by the rocks and picked them out of the water with his bare hands — three small ones, not any impressive catch but perfectly edible. Thomas had managed to get a small fire started out of the wind, where it would not be seen from anywhere except out to sea, which would have been a fine stroke of luck. Rather clumsily they smashed the shells and roasted the meat on sticks over the flames. It was not an elegant meal, and the lobsters had a strangely smoked flavour, but it was still the best Thomas had eaten in days. He could only hope Pasco and Cole were doing so well. Their fate was a terrible nag at the back of his mind, and he was sure he would have nightmares the moment he closed his eyes.

"No," Jim said after a while, very low. "I was born in England."

Thomas nodded. "I see." That went some way to explaining the accent, he thought, though how such a well-spoken lad had ever ended up climbing trees for coconuts in the Caribbean he couldn't hope to guess. "Whereabouts?"

Jim shrugged. "I don't remember. It was a long time ago."

Thomas would have liked to ask more, but Jim very pointedly finished his meal and curled up with his back to the fire, where he had piled some green leaves for a makeshift pillow. Thomas sighed and did the same, letting the fire burn low. Jim had the infuriating habit of creating more questions than he ever answered.

*

If he had nightmares about Cole and Pasco being set upon by pirates, or being swept out to sea in a freak storm, Thomas did not remember them when next he opened his eyes. The sun was only just beginning to rise in the east, and on the far side of the island there was only the faintest glow of light with which to see. He was awake before Jim for once, he realised, looking over the camp without getting up. Jim had turned over during the night and was now facing him from the other side of the fire's ashes.

In sleep he did not have the tensed hold to his body he always seemed to have, like a rabbit ready to spring. He lay on his side with one hand resting on the other arm, the other hand palm up on the ground with the fingers loosely curled. The chest wound was already healing well, Thomas thought, taking the opportunity to peer at it. He wondered how it had happened — in the battle, no doubt, but who had Jim been fighting? It might have been Gower, or Bill Blake, or any of the men he knew by face if not by name. Had Jim been fighting to kill, like the rest of them? There was no reason to think otherwise, and yet it was difficult to believe. Thomas knew he ought not to trust this soft-spoken, mysterious stranger who was after all one of the enemy, and yet there was something about him that continued to draw Thomas in, whenever he caught a glance of him unawares. And that was not even considering that he had saved Thomas' life, multiple times, whether as a means of self-preservation or not. He certainly had not needed to drag Thomas out of the ocean where he would otherwise have certainly drowned, and Thomas was increasingly convinced that he had done just that even if he would not admit to it.

At least the red sword cut on his cheek was fading, Thomas saw, his gut twisting guiltily. Probably it would not leave yet another scar.

Perhaps he felt Thomas' eyes on him, but Jim did not stay asleep for long. He woke and sat up almost as one movement, jerkily, as though shocked to find himself asleep at all.

"All is well," Thomas told him, moving slowly so as not to startle him further. "We're quite safe for the moment."

Jim did not speak; gone quiet again. Instead he got up and set about covering the remains of the fire with sand, and then they were off again without a word exchanged, working their way up a steep rise to the top of the western cliff face. It was hard going in some places, and Thomas took the opportunity to consider his next questions and how to ask them. He did not have to pry at all, of course, but his curiosity was too deep to simply let the mystery go unanswered.

"How old are you?" he asked, the next time they stopped for a moment to catch their breath and sip some coconut water.

He had half-expected the answer to be 'I don't know', or similar, as he privately doubted most pirates could read or write enough to comprehend a proper calendar.

"Twenty," Jim said, easily.

Thomas gaped at him. "You aren't," he accused, almost all decorum and manners forgotten. He had guessed they might be of similar age, but he had not in the least considered that Jim might be *older* than he was. It was a shock, and for some reason he found himself loathe to believe it.

"I am," Jim said, grinning rather childishly. Thomas was even more taken-aback at this startling new expression, quite different from the boy's — no, not a boy, not at *twenty* — usual sullen expression. "How old are you?" Jim asked in return. "Eighteen?"

Thomas felt his freckled face go red, and found himself wishing he had never asked in the first place. "Nineteen," he protested, suddenly feeling every year he lacked and floundering wildly for the dignity becoming of his borrowed rank.

"Well," Jim shrugged, still grinning, and stoppered up his coconut with a kind of plug he had made out of crushed reeds.

"You don't quite look it yet, that's all."

Thomas stared after him, dumbfounded, as the pirate sauntered off ahead up the cliff. *He's comfortable enough to joke with me*, he thought, in the small part of his mind remaining that wasn't occupied with being offended. *That's something.*

*

They made good time that day, picking their way across the cliffs. Thomas itched at the extra time it took to go around the forest, but he had to admit that this path was safer, having better visibility in all directions. It had the added benefit that whenever he liked he could look out west to the sea and imagine he saw a ship on the horizon — and since no one was there to judge his imagination for its optimism, he liked to fantasise about a navy vessel coming to take them all home. Even though he saw no sails, it was comforting to look out at all the wide ocean, all the directions from which help might come. He tried not to remember that the island was a speck in the middle of the same boundless ocean which no one of sense would like to visit. He clung possessively to whatever hope he had.

Dusk was falling before they could reach the point on the southern shore where the lifeboat had landed, though Thomas judged that it could not be far. When asked, Jim confirmed that he had not been anywhere near the slaughter on the southern shore, but on the other side of the island, having just left Thomas behind for the company of the other pirates, Aggie, Gappy and Big Ears — though Jim called him Horace, and laughed at Thomas' chosen name for him. "It suits him," he said. "They don't do him much good though — the ears — he's deaf in one of them."

Thomas, who was trying not to think about how much he had enjoyed the sound of Jim's laugh — *really*, what was wrong with him to be thinking such thoughts at a time like this — went back to deliberating with himself on whether to go on or not after the sun set entirely. The terrain was still dangerous in the dark, and the closer they got to the beach there was surely a greater chance of running into a pirate foraging party. On the other hand he was loathe to lose the time. "What do you think?" he asked Jim, after explaining his dilemma.

Jim looked up, surprised to be asked. He had been watching a flock of gulls hover over a pool on the lower side of the cliff, rather like a lion watching a herd of gazelle. "I haven't been to this side of the island," he said, after a moment's hesitant consideration. "If you think we might not tumble to our deaths off the side of this cliff in the dark…"

Thomas grimaced. "All right. An hour more then, and we shall make camp."

Jim nodded. "If it helps, we aren't going to be any comfort to your men if we're smashed to pieces on the rocks below," he pointed out. It did not much help, but Thomas smiled at him gratefully anyway. He thought, not for the first time, what a relief it was that he was not out here alone.

— 13 —

They went on, as the sun began its graceful and spectacular descent over the western horizon. They had a perfect view of it, the orange and purple hues chasing each other across the starry sky, and Thomas couldn't help feeling that it warmed his heart, a little.

"Your captain..." Jim asked suddenly, seemingly out of nowhere. "Or is he an admiral?"

"An admiral," Thomas clarified, wondering at the question. "But we address him as captain, of course, as the commander of the ship."

"And his name is Wickerham, you said?"

"I did. He introduced himself to your men, if you recall, before Briggs tried to assassinate him."

Jim frowned. "I don't recall," he said, low. "I suppose I was quite ill already." He went quiet again and moved ahead, so Thomas had no chance to ask him why he had wanted to know.

After perhaps half an hour they came to a point where the Western side of the cliff started to slope downwards into the edge of the forest, with no shoreline to follow. Gingerly they picked their way over large roots and dead, rotting branches, the ground pitted and puddled in places where the storm had battered away at the earth and churned it to mud. They were reaching the end of a particularly tricky stretch when Jim suddenly slipped, his bare feet going out from under him, and he tumbled backwards with a gasp. Thomas reached out without thinking and caught him under his arms just as he was about to hit the ground. In doing so he stepped straight onto the same treacherous patch of earth, and in the next moment they both went sliding down together in a slow, ungainly heap, clothes and skin spattered with black earthy mud, until they eventually rolled to a stop.

"Thank you," Jim said, with heavy irony, when they had caught their breath.

Thomas laughed. He couldn't help it. Something about this mad, wild boy had him caught entirely off-guard, and he couldn't think what else to do. Why not, when it seemed like the world was ending? Jim smiled absurdly at him, rubbing mud off of his nose. Thomas felt something twist inside his chest.

Suddenly he heard a click — a mechanical noise, nothing that could be native to the island. The laugh died in his throat as he looked around to see a figure emerging from the surrounding trees, perhaps ten feet away, aiming a rusted pistol at them. Beside Thomas, Jim went suddenly still.

"What's this?" the man demanded, yellowed eyes darting between Jim and Thomas. He was wearing a blue coat, Thomas noticed; a navy man's coat. It even fitted well. "Whatchoo doin' 'ere?" The pirate was holding the gun on Thomas but glaring right at Jim as he approached. "We been lookin' all over for *you*, maggot."

Thomas risked an attempt to get to his knees, but the pirate took a leap forward and cocked the pistol hastily before Thomas could so much as shift one leg. "Move an' get one 'twixt the eyes," the man spat. Up close, he smelled foul and looked fouler, the whites of his eyes gone dark yellow with jaundice, teeth brown-stained and mostly missing, a flabby belly protruding absurdly from his starved frame. There was no sign that the man recognised him whatsoever, but then, Thomas rather doubted his own mother would have known him on first glance given his current state of disarray. There was no real reason any of the pirates would equate this jungle vagabond with the imperious young acting captain of the *Courage* who had ordered them all locked away, if they would even care to make such a distinction. It was unlikely to save him, in any case.

He wondered frantically what the chances were that the pistol would fire. It would require dry gunpowder, which after the storm and the wreck seemed unlikely, but on the other hand he had seen a second boat at the pirate's camp, and he could only assume that at least some of the twenty-odd pirates he had seen had come ashore without having been thrown overboard. It was possible that they had managed to keep some of their weapons dry enough to function. He should have asked Jim about it while he had the chance.

Jim managed to shift away from Thomas by a few feet and struggled up, slipping a little in the mud. The yellow-eyed man made no move to stop him, only kept half an eye on Jim's movements while keeping the pistol trained fully on Thomas' head.

"Captured by the enemy, were you?" the pirate muttered in disgust, though he clearly expected no answer. "Jus' wait til the Cap'n gets 'is hands on ye. 'Ow many of 'em are there still livin'?"

Jim shrugged and pointed right at Thomas, head cocked slightly to one side. He was wearing an expression quite unlike any Thomas had seen on his face since the *Courage*. Not a frown or smile, but a kind of blank puzzlement. It made him look dim, and Thomas realised suddenly that *this* was what the other pirates saw. A simple boy, unspeaking and barely comprehending. Despite his present danger he found himself fascinated by the performance, and felt a strange rush of irrational pride that he knew better.

"I know about *this* one, ye dumb idiot," the pirate muttered, glaring at Jim. "How many more?"

Jim bit his lip and shrugged again, making a show of trying to count on his fingers.

"Why, you useless —" the pirate growled in sheer frustration, and for a moment he took his eyes off Thomas entirely and his aim dipped. Thomas rolled out of the way just in time as Jim bent forward and ran full force at his former crewmate, slamming his head into the man's stomach and sending him stumbling back and gasping. The pistol went off with a bang, so close to Thomas' ear that his head rang with it as though he'd been struck to the face.

"You treach'rous mangy dog!" he heard the pirate cry through the confusion of sound, and then Jim was there, helping him to his feet, and as more shouts went up around them they ran full-tilt together down the slope and into the forest.

It felt as though the very hounds of hell were on their heels. Clearly there had been a small party of pirates separated by no more than hearing distance, and the sound of the shot brought them all running. They could hear the voice of their assailant calling out to the others, a cry going up, and the muffled sounds of running footsteps. "Go, go!" Thomas shouted as a second shot rang out over their heads, sending splinters, leaves and debris falling onto them from above as they ran. Thomas' lungs burned, his legs, arms and chest protesting, but he kept on, leaping over roots and broken branches and natural dips in the earth, barely visible in the dimming light of the sunset behind them. He had the very real fear that one of them would twist an ankle, or fall, and then that man was done for. Could he leave Jim behind, in that case? Save his own life, to make sure he got to Wickerham? He had promised Jim protection, but his first duty was to the *Courage*, to her captain… these terrible thoughts and worse raced through his mind as he ran.

Voices still ringing out behind them, they came to a sudden decline and had to scramble madly down, weaving haphazardly from side to side to avoid the forest's natural obstacles. Near the bottom Thomas almost went sprawling, his heart in his throat, but the next thing he knew he had been grabbed by the sleeve of his shirt and tugged hard to one side. It was all he could do, all he could think to stay on his feet, and he stumbled and was half dragged down and under a kind of deep overhang shrouded by leaves and vines. Jim had scrambled in and pulled him in after, so that he was pressing himself to the rocks and holding Thomas tight against his chest. He slapped his hand against Thomas' mouth, dirty fingers pressed tightly over his lips. Thomas closed his eyes, pulled his feet in as close as possible and tried to calm himself, breathing through his nose and listening to the voices that came distantly from above.

"Where'd they go?"

"Son of a thrupenny whore, 'e can't have just vanished into thin air."

"Are ye sure it was the maggot ye saw?"

"What d'ye take me for, I'm not blind! It were him and one o' those navy cunts —"

"Together? What's 'e doing with one o' them?"

"Who cares? The liddle shit dealt me one to the bread basket. I'll kill him meself when I get at him."

"Oh aye, we'll see what the Cap'n has to say about that. He wants 'im alive."

"Fuck the Cap'n."

"Oooh, I'd like to see you try." Raucous laughter, and some curses.

Opening his eyes, Thomas stared through the vines into the darkening forest beyond. If he could see through, surely someone standing on the other side could also, or at least, so it felt. The tension was enough to make his hands shake. It was a good hiding place, but they would not be invisible if someone were to look straight at them.

"Fuck this. I say ye never saw anythin'."

"Come 'ere and call me a liar, pigface. I'm tellin' ye, I saw 'em."

"Aye, I saw 'em too, but they're well gone now. Ye know that Jim's a slippery one. He could be up any o' these trees for all we know."

"Oh yeah, ye think he dragged t'other man to the top of a tree?

Halfwit."

"I'm jussayin', no good lookin' for 'em in the dark. Better take what we got back to camp and head back in the mornin'…"

As the distant sound of their conversation faded slowly away, Jim's hand came loose from Thomas' mouth. Thomas felt the fingers come away one by one, and the edge of the thumb brush the side of his lips. His heart leapt; he tried not to move. His chest was aching with the adrenaline. They were pressed together so tightly in the tiny space that he could hear Jim's breathing, feel his pulse through the arm that was around his chest. He could even feel the stitches on Jim's chest-wound against his back. For a long time, neither of them moved.

"We should wait until it's all the way dark," Thomas said eventually, in a whispered voice that came out rather hoarse and strained. Jim didn't say anything, but his breathing was laboured and uneven; frightened perhaps by what they had heard. "Are you well?" Thomas asked, awkwardly. It was almost oppressively hot in their chosen hiding place, and he thought he could feel still more heat coming off Jim's chest. "Is your wound paining you?"

Jim swallowed; Thomas heard it, close to his ear. "No," he said, low. "I'm not hurt."

Thomas shifted, trying to move so that they would not have to be crushed together, and Jim took a sharp intake of breath. "Now what is it?" Thomas demanded in a low, irritated hiss. The proximity was not exactly comfortable for him, either; it had been a long time since he had been this close to another man who was not trying to kill him, and the way it made his heart race was alarming. Ridiculous to be so affected after having just run for his life from a gang of murderers...

When he turned to look, Jim's eyes were wide and staring blue in the darkness, shining. Thomas was suddenly beset by an ugly vision of when he had cut the young pirate's face with his sword out of anger and carelessness; perhaps it wasn't only the pirates Jim was afraid of now. He sighed guiltily. "I'm sorry," he said, as gently as he could manage. "I didn't mean..."

Jim reached up with a trembling hand and touched Thomas' jaw with the edge of his thumb. Surprised, Thomas let his head turn away with the very slight pressure, baring his cheek. "You're bleeding," Jim said, low.

Thomas had no memory of being injured, nor was there any pain. Perhaps a low-hanging branch had scratched him as he ran past, or perhaps he hadn't rolled away from the pistol-shot fast enough after all. There was still a slight ringing sound in his ears. "Is it bad?" he asked. He could feel his own pulse pounding in his throat.

"Just a nick. I don't think you'll die." Jim swallowed. They were so close that Thomas could hear it, could see the lump moving down his throat. Jim did not lower his hand either when Thomas turned back to face him with some difficulty. Thomas blinked in the dark, wishing his heart would slow. The touch had gone on for too long. But he did not protest, and Jim did not move away, and they were already so, so close. Thomas didn't think he would die, either. He felt suddenly, vividly alive.

Their lips touched, and Jim still did not pull away.

It was too dark to see much of anything at all; he had to rely on his other senses to orient himself. The hard rock under his knees where he knelt with his shirt hanging open like a dockside beggar. The dampness in the hot air around them, thick and stuffy in the confined space and hardly breathable. The smell of earth and of distant saltwater. The heat of Jim's skin under his hand as he reached instinctively for his waist, and Jim's hand on Thomas' bare stomach, the strange juxtaposition of rough skin and the very lightest, most exploratory of touches. And overwhelmingly the feel of Jim's lips against his, a moment's indecision only in that touch until Jim opened his mouth and let Thomas take it; slow uncertain kisses making way for deeper, quicker, more frenzied ones, and the sound of their breathing as it grew louder and faster.

This was not like kissing Bill Blake. Bill had rarely kissed Thomas on the mouth, but if he did it had been brief and rough. This was the realisation of a shared desire unspoken of until this moment, the necessity of their near-silence somehow adding to their urgency to have more, to do more. Jim smelled like wet dirt and tasted like the sea; of course, he had been bathing twice a day in seawater on little Pasco's orders, so perhaps that had something to do with it. This thought passed fleetingly in less than a second, until Thomas let it go in favour of throwing himself incautiously back into their blind, feverish groping. One of Jim's hands came up to run his fingers through Thomas' muddy hair. Thomas' fingers felt for Jim's bare arms in turn, feeling hard, wiry muscle under the skin. He felt a complete loss of inhibition brought on by fear and adrenaline and the utter impossibility of being alive, and yet he was still careful to avoid Jim's stitches; the last thing he wanted was to cause pain. Jim made a sound, a low grumble like the growl of the wild tiger he sometimes appeared to be; a creature of the jungle. It sent a shiver down Thomas' spine, and he gasped into the pirate's mouth. "Jim…"

Crammed together as they were, he could feel Jim's arousal against his side. It only served to make him tense even more, his whole body thrumming. Jim's other hand moved and landed on his thigh, dangerously close to where Thomas' cock was straining against his breeches. The intensity was suddenly painful.

He reached for the buttons on Jim's borrowed breeches. Jim did not try to stop him, but his own mind served him a memory in that same second that made him falter. Bill Blake, whispering in his ear. *Let me take care of you.* Cold dead hands reached for him out of the dark.

He realised suddenly that he could barely breathe — the stifled air under the overhang had become unbearable. He let go Jim's mouth and scrambled up, Jim's fingers coming loose from his hair just in time to let him stagger out into the blissfully fresh night air. While they were hiding, the sun had gone down.

Jim came out after him, panting shallowly but saying nothing. When Thomas wiped at his cheek, it came away a little bloody on the side of his hand, appearing as little more than a grey stain now that the dark had leached away all colour from their surroundings. Just a scratch, then. No way to clean it, and he would just have to hope it would heal on its own.

They stood for a while in silence, listening to the sounds of the forest. There was no longer any distant murmur of voices. Perhaps they were safe for now.

"We should find shelter," Thomas said finally, looking up at Jim out of the corner of his eye. Jim was staring out into the distance, not looking at him. He nodded. Thomas knew they could not simply stand out here in the open any longer, but he cleared his throat, awkwardly, and said, "you saved my life again, just now. Thank you." Despite the darkness he thought he saw a flush come up on Jim's face. "I suppose I am one in your debt now, by your tradition," Thomas added, thinking with a sudden rush of sickening guilt about his promise to save Jim from the hangman. He'd given a false promise, and followed it with an even worse sin. What was he thinking?

Jim hesitated, eyes shining in the dark. "No," he said finally, and straightened up, running a hand through his dark, cropped hair. "Call it even."

$$— 14 —$$

They lit no fire that night. They found a hollow that was a little drier than the surrounding foliage and covered themselves with large leaves for shelter and camouflage. The air became quickly stifling but they did their best to endure, for it wasn't worth the risk of leaving themselves open to discovery. It was a tight enough space that they were forced once more to lie together, touching at the shoulders and the knee. Thomas considered turning so they would be top and tails, like he had sometimes done when he had had to share bunks as a younger officer on shore, but he decided it would be too obvious what he was trying to do, and instead he shuffled down uncomfortably into the shallow depression his body eventually pressed into the earth. Beside him he could hear Jim's light breathing. He was very still, too still and too tense to be asleep; making pretence again.

Thomas drifted uncomfortably in and out of sleep himself, waking too often with the sharp, vivid memories of the burst of the pistol into his ear, the desperate scramble down the slope. Of Jim's hand on his thigh and the red heat it had invoked all through his body. Twice he woke, gasping, his loins aching in protest of desires unfulfilled. He clenched his fists and grit his teeth, inwardly cursing the demonic spirits that had possessed his body this way. Whether he got off the island or not, he thought grimly as he tried and failed to force the images away from his mind, either way he was eventually going straight to hell.

The fourth or fifth time he woke it was coming on daybreak, and he could tell that Jim was awake, too. They lay there silently for a long time, Thomas still willing his body to finally submit to rest, which it would not do. It was the sheer awkwardness of awareness; each knowing the other was aware of every breath, every tiny movement, every hungry growl of the stomach.

When he wasn't torturing himself with fantasies, Thomas thought about Bill Blake. Thomas had been barely more than Pasco's age when he and Bill had met on Thomas' first ship, the *Queen Mary*. He had been in awe of the big man from early on, and Bill had always been kind and encouraging to him — to all the young officers. He remembered when some of his bunkmates had found his sketches and had laughed derisively at what they considered a girlish hobby. Some of them had even ruined some of the sketches with ink, drawing lewd additions and altering the faces, making them ugly and hellish. Bill had caught him crying and told him not to be ashamed, that some of the best officers in the navy practiced artistry to document their travels, particularly when they did not have much of a way with words. When Thomas asked him how he knew such things, not being an officer himself, Bill had told him stories to make a boy's eyes go wide; men he had known better than had their peers, and not just other officers but captains themselves, men who liked art for its beauty rather than for its practicality, men who loved music and dancing and fine clothes, whom no one thought any the less men for it. Men who loved other men — for all this might be sinful and illegal, it did not make a man any less of a man. Young Thomas took in all this and more, and Bill never seemed to run out of stories. Thomas trusted Bill, who warned him of things a boy's body would do as a boy started to become a man, and this knowledge once shared was enough to make him something of a hero among the other boys, all past sins forgotten. Bill, who showed him how a man should touch a man, and listened to Thomas' fears and doubts about his desires, and assured him that it was only a natural anomaly, despite what the law or the church may say. Bill had always made him feel safe, except when he was mean with drink, and Thomas learned to avoid him during those times. He took the lessons of Bill's easy manner of conversation into all his relationships, so that he became well-known as a charismatic, confident young officer with a lot of promise.

He was recommended to his next post by his captain, and he recommended Bill in turn, and so it went. Bill never had much money; he spent the majority of his sailor's pay on rum. He was always pleased with whatever Thomas could spare him, always thankful. Never subservient, for their relationship had not altered much with the widening difference in rank as Thomas advanced to midshipman, then third Lieutenant of the *Courage*, and Thomas had always looked up to him, though as he grew older he started to realise just how much he had been manipulated. His doubts grew like a cancer. *Don't be like me,* Bill had said, his dying words. Thomas imagined himself doing the same, taking in some young lad, Pasco, perhaps, and teaching him… the thought made him ill. No, he would never take advantage in such a way. That, along with the fear of discovery, was what had given him the courage to finally tell Bill no.

But this… with Jim. What had happened with Jim. This was different. He had not forced himself on Jim; Jim had reached for him. They had moved together, in unspoken, desperate understanding, rejoicing in the thrill of being alive and despairing all at once. It was different.

Wasn't it?

He thinks I'm saving him, he thought, sickly, curling his fingers into the damp earth under his hand. He was, in the best possible case scenario, leading Jim to his own death or imprisonment. He had lured his pirate into an alliance on false pretences. Accepted his parole. What more possible advantage could he have taken? He was sure Bill would have been impressed by his deceitfulness.

He sat up suddenly, so disgusted with himself that he could no longer stand to listen to his own thoughts. Jim jerked up in surprise. "What is it?" he asked in a hushed voice, blue eyes open and blinking with no sign of having slept at all, dark circles under them. "Did you hear something?"

Thomas shuddered and shook his head. "No," he said, low. "We should make our way, that's all."

*

They crawled with some difficulty out of their hiding place. As usual, Jim started off in the lead, and together they scrambled up to where they could begin walking again without having to use their hands to drag themselves up the slope. As they reached the top, Jim slipped again; Thomas put out a hand and caught him by the pocket of his breeches, which tore. Something flashed in the rays of the rising sun as it fell out onto the earth between them.

Belatedly Thomas recognised the grubby trinket the young pirate had made such an effort to retrieve from Babber's body, back on the ship. He reached instinctively for it, his fingers tangling in the salt-sodden, broken cord it hung from.

"Wait —" Jim reached for it, trying to snatch it back. Thomas put out an arm to stop him. He had realised what he was holding.

It was a navy-issue medal, the design issued to veterans of the Battle of St Laurence. It was recognisable to any officer who had attended any kind of naval dinner over the last decade; many of the older lieutenants and midshipmen wore them, and wore them with pride, on any formal occasion. The ribbon was stained and frayed, almost blackened with grime, and the metal was so dirty it looked like brass, but Thomas knew that it was gold. Not much, about two buttons-worth, but enough to make it a captain's medal. This medal had been personally awarded by a member of the royal family to a captain of the navy.

"Where did your thieving friend get this?" he demanded, turning to glare at Jim, who glared back, uncowed.

"He took it from me — it's mine," he protested, in a voice that shook with anger or anxiety, it was hard to tell. "Give it back."

"It is *not* yours," Thomas replied, appalled. "Unless you were fighting the French at the age of — what? Four? Don't be absurd," he added, as though that were the only argument for such foolishness — no pirate could own a medal like this for any other reason than theft.

Jim grimaced and stepped back, pulling himself out of Thomas' grip so roughly that he almost went tumbling back down the slope once more. "It's mine," he repeated, practically growling.

"Stealing does not make something yours," Thomas snapped. "This belongs to a captain in the navy, or a former captain." He tucked the medal into his own breeches, thinking that in the miracle event that he got off this damn island, he would make an effort to return it; even if they sent him to prison he could do that much, if his correspondence wasn't stopped altogether.

Jim still glared at him, helpless fury shining in his eyes. When Thomas took a step forward to continue, Jim moved into his way, looking as though he were squaring up to a fight he knew he could not win. "Stop that," Thomas said, taken aback. "We don't have time for this."

"Please," Jim said, fists clenching at his sides and teeth grit hard together, as though it cost him more than mere dignity to beg in such a manner. "Please. I… I only just got it back."

Thomas opened his mouth to reply, once again, that a pirate should never have had his hands on such a thing in the first place, but found himself stopped by something in Jim's eyes, a genuine desperation that had nothing to do with less than a handful of gold. He raised an eyebrow, questioning. "Well?"

Jim swallowed, and stared at him for a moment, as though searching for any other way. Thomas stared back, unrelenting. Jim's shoulders sagged. "It… belonged to my father," he said, very low, reluctant.

Thomas almost laughed. He knew he *ought* to laugh, that it was a lie, and a ridiculous one at that. But he did not laugh, and looking into Jim's eyes he could not help but hesitate even in his mind. So far as he knew, Jim had never lied to him.

"Who was your father?" he asked, suspicion edging his voice despite all his best intentions.

Another long pause. Jim dropped his eyes to the sand, defeated. "Oliver," he said, low. "His name was James Oliver."

James Oliver. Thomas knew the name. As a boy he had devoured the lists in the newspaper; the accolades, the postings, the reports of battles especially. *James Oliver.* It was even more of an absurd claim than he could have imagined, out of any excuses he could have invented. It was impossible. "Captain James Oliver," he said, slowly, a simmering anger on the edge of his voice at this unexpected and unprovoked insult, "was a naval officer who died at sea years ago, along with every man who was aboard his ship, when it went down somewhere in the Caribbean. I imagine you heard the name, and invented some fantasy — "

Jim had been standing still with his arms fisted by his sides, but his head shot up at this, his face a mask of anger, his fair cheeks blotched red. "No," he insisted, in little more than a whisper.

"This is not to be credited," Thomas snapped, "you expect me to believe —"

"*No,*" Jim said again, more intensely. He opened his mouth as though trying to speak, but nothing more came out. He held out his hand again instead, the lines dirty and black across his palm.

Thomas hesitated. They were wasting daylight, and neither of them were going anywhere. "Very well," he said, through gritted teeth, trying not to think of where that hand had been, last night — where his own hands had been. "When we have time, you will tell me the truth, all of the truth. And you may have the medal back only if I am satisfied, which I very much doubt."

Jim glowered, but his hand dropped, slowly and reluctantly. He turned and started back up the slope without another word.

*

The sun was not quite yet risen, but they made their way by the dim dawn light anyway. They walked on empty stomachs, sipping from the last of the coconuts and stopping only to smash them properly open to get to the meat inside. It wasn't much to stave off hunger, but Thomas didn't dare stop even so long as to allow Jim to hunt. He felt constantly as though they were being watched, a nagging tickle on the back of his neck. It was so physical a sensation he kept slapping his own skin, expecting to come away with the crushed remains of some giant tropical bug.

The silence between them was almost as oppressive as the thick heat. This seemed to only get more intense as the day wore on, until Thomas was almost wishing for the clouds to open again; just a little relief would have been welcome. They were getting close, he thought, by the way the ground started to give way to sand, and when they reached a sheltered grove of coconut trees around midday, he called for a halt. Without waiting to be asked, or asking for permission, Jim shimmied easily up one of the trees and dropped a sizable bunch of ripe yellow fruits onto the ground, and borrowed Thomas' sword to open them. All this he did without a word. "Why do you do that?" Thomas asked suddenly, unable to bear it a moment longer.

Jim didn't look at him. "What?" he asked.

"Go quiet like that. You haven't said a word in the last three hours. It's infuriating."

After a moment that seemed to last an age, Jim went back to his coconut. "Nothing to say," he muttered.

Thomas was starting to understand the frustration that had given them the advantage over the yellow-eyed pirate the night before, and it gave him an idea. "May I at least postulate a theory?" he said, narrowing his eyes.

Jim snorted. "Be my guest, Lieutenant."

Thomas flinched, but he realised he had never told Jim to call him anything else. It reminded him of Bill being mocking, and set his teeth on edge. "I think," he said, tapping his fingernails somewhat aggressively against the flesh of the coconut, "that you have been playing the mute for so long that you forget that you *can* speak. Or least, you forget that you have given yourself permission to do so." Jim flinched, and seeing he had hit a nerve, Thomas went on. "None of your crew think you anything more than a simpleton, so it must be a very good act. One you've been doing for years, I suspect, until it became more than second nature; it must be an effort to speak, even when you know you can do so without fear."

Jim glared at him. "What I... it's not..." he stumbled for words, rather proving Thomas' point, he thought triumphantly. "It's no mind of yours," Jim muttered finally.

Thomas frowned. "After last night, I rather think it is."

"You —" Jim snapped, and stopped, remembering to keep his voice low. "Last night..."

"Yes?" Thomas' heart was racing again; he ignored it as best he could, trying to look and sound as calm as he wished he felt inside.

Jim was flushed and uncomfortable, shifting on the rock he had chosen to make his seat. "It's not... I didn't think, you..." He swallowed. "I... did not know it could be... like that."

That was not what Thomas had been expecting. He sat very still, as though any sudden movements might startle his pirate out of saying what little he had chosen to share. "Neither did I," he said, softly. Truthfully.

Jim's head shot up, blue eyes staring. For a moment they just looked at each other, no sound but the rustling of the leaves and the distant call of gulls, the soft rushing sound of the sea. "They don't just think I'm mute," Jim said, eventually, very low. "They think I'm mad."

"Why? Why pretend?"

He shrugged, thin shoulders bobbing quickly. "I've known some of them for years. Babber. Gappy. Briggs." He spat, as though trying to rid himself of a bad taste. "With men like them it's safer to be mad than clever, so long as you're useful. But I talk to Aggie sometimes. He's not like the others. He's my friend."

Thomas watched him pick the last bits of flesh from the coconut and toss it aside, stripped bare to the shell. He waited for him to say something else, anything else, now that he had finally found his voice. "You can talk to me," he said, finally, when the silence had gone on so long that it was deafening.

Jim looked up at him, blue eyes narrowed. "I tried," he said, low. He stood up.

"Jim —" Thomas started. It felt bizarrely as though he had

been punched in the stomach again.

"We must be near the shore now," Jim insisted, not looking at him, and headed off southward. "We should start looking for your captain."

Thomas knew he had to follow or he would simply be left behind. He stood up and sheathed his sword. His questions would have to wait. "How close do you think we are?" he asked, adjusting the leaf basket onto his back where it would not get in the way if it came to fighting.

"Not far from the shore; a few minutes," Jim muttered. "But we won't find them wandering along the tideline." He stopped and scratched the back of his neck as he looked around in each direction. "They're bound to have been warned by the noise we made last night. If they have any sense they would have taken deep cover."

Thomas credited Smythe with a great deal of good sense. He would have done all he could to keep Wickerham safely hidden, especially after the rest of the survivors had been slaughtered on the beach. "They couldn't have gone far," he reasoned aloud. "The admiral was badly wounded."

Jim nodded. "We can start on the shoreline and search for tracks," he said.

"I imagine Smythe would have covered the tracks, if there were any," Thomas said doubtfully. "Or had Dolson do it." Dolson was an ordinary seaman, no great intelligence as far as he recalled but a loyal man who took care of his work. Not one to shirk under such circumstances.

"Have you some other suggestion?" Jim shot back, and

Thomas was forced to admit that he had not.

It was indeed only a few more minutes' hike through the forest to the shore. They came out perhaps a mile west of where Thomas had emerged the last time, far enough away from the bloody massacre that the smell did not reach them. Thomas was loathe to go near the place again, especially now that several days had passed; days in which bodies would have putrefied and rotted, and hungry insects would have done their work upon the soft flesh of eyes and mouths. He steeled himself.

"We should cover more ground by taking two paths," Jim said, watching him out of the corner of one eye. Thomas looked up. "I'll go East," the pirate said, nodding in the direction of the landing site.

Thomas was no fool; he knew what was being offered, and that it was offered in spite of Jim's current animosity towards him. "Thank you," he said, low. "Do you need —" he put a hand to the hilt of his sword, not entirely sure himself of what he intended, but Jim shook his head anyway.

"Meet back here in an hour. Try to stay out of sight," he said simply, and started to jog eastward in his bare feet along the sand.

— 15 —

Thomas wasn't sure what he was looking for, but he kept close to the tree line and kept an eye out for footprints in the sand or any sign of disturbance in the driftwood and weed-like plants that grew along the edge of the beach. It all seemed rather pointless, considering that the tide and the storm would surely have washed away any such traces by now. It didn't even take him half an hour of walking to reach the edge of the western cliffs, and he turned around to look back the way he had come. Under other circumstances, he thought, he might have been struck by the beauty of the place. The sky cleared of storm-clouds, the morning shining brightly, the beach was almost pure white and pristinely smooth, save for the shallow depressions that were the prints of his own boots, stretching out into the distance until they faded from sight. The sea was a bright, azure blue, the near-still surface glittering in the sun. He could have been quite content to sit on a fallen tree here and watch the tide go out for hours, with only his thoughts and the sound of the waves.

On the way back to their meeting point, paying more attention to the beach itself, he caught sight of something on the sand that looked too bright and smooth to be of nature. When he drew closer, he saw polished wood and brass, and with a bit of effort he managed to clear a small sea-chest from the sand. It was not old or worn by time, so he guessed it must have washed ashore from the wreck of the *Courage*. The whole east and southern shore must have been being littered with debris as the waves pounded the ship to pieces, he thought sadly, and even the pirates raiding up and down the shoreline could not have picked up every treasure.

A poor treasure this one — some poor soul's simple chest. It was a good solid make, not expensive; he expected it must have belonged to one of the seaman who did not spend all his money on drink or women. It was not engraved, so there was no way to tell.

He found a large rock and battered open the lock. The thing was lined with oilskin; a sensible purchase for a sailor, and the contents were well preserved. Some clothing, folded a little haphazardly but clean and in good repair, and a small package of biscuit. Some small keepsakes also, which did nothing more to identify their owner. He dug a shallow hole in the sand with his hands and buried the things solemnly in the unknown man's honour; a small silver-backed mirror, perhaps a gift from a loved one, a few coins, some sticks of tobacco, and a handful of shells, no doubt collected for no more reason than appreciation for their unique shapes and colours.

He took the clothes and the biscuit, packing them carefully into the leaf basket, and tossed the empty chest into the vegetation among the trees where it would not be easily seen. Of course there was no value in any of those treasured things now, except perhaps the tobacco, but he could not simply leave them lying about where pirates would disturb them. He could only hope the man would look down from above and forgive him his own theft as a necessarily evil.

Jim was waiting where they had parted, looking tense and impatient at being first to arrive despite the longer stretch of beach he had had to search. "Anything?" Thomas asked, as soon as he could be sure that his words wouldn't carry too far.

"I'm not sure," Jim said, eyeing the suddenly bulging leaf basket. "There might be something; there's a place where it looks like people have foraged, but no way to tell if we'd be tracking your men or theirs." Thomas noted that he said *theirs* not *mine*, as though he had somehow arrived on the island independently of all the rest of them. There was no sense in arguing the point, however.

"It's a risk we will have to take," he said, flatly. "Show me."

What Jim had found was an area of vegetation near the shoreline that seemed to have been stepped on in places; there were leaves flattened into the earth and a few scattered buds that might have fallen before their time. Looking at it, Thomas didn't think he would have seen anything out of the ordinary if it hadn't been pointed out to him, even looking carefully as he had been. "Are you sure about this?" he muttered, crouching to inspect the indented earth with his fingers.

Jim shrugged. "Someone was there," he said simply. "I can't tell you who they were."

"Could it not have been an animal?" Thomas stood and brushed rather pointlessly at his trousers.

Jim looked back at him with an upraised eyebrow. "I told you it could be nothing. I can see signs, but I'm no expert tracker."

He looked up and around, glancing up and down the length of the beach. "We should get out of the open, either way."

Thomas sighed. He didn't like to waste yet more time on a false search, but he didn't see that he had much choice in the matter. "Very well."

Jim led the way back into the interior. After the full sun and the fresh sea air of the beach, it didn't take long for Thomas to start to feel the itchy closeness of the forest like a rash on his skin, and it made him still more irritable. Once again Jim seemed to be following an invisible trail, moving light-footed and unconcerned through one seemingly identical patch of natural debris after another. "Do you have any idea where you're going?" Thomas demanded, when it seemed like they had been stalking through the forest for an hour.

Jim stopped and stood up, glaring, from where he'd been examining an apparently insignificant branch across the space through the trees that hardly passed for a path. "There *is* a trail," he muttered, low. "Keep your voice —"

Suddenly a figure burst out of the trees between them and was on Jim in a swift movement, a thick tattooed arm wrapped around his throat. Thomas exclaimed and reached for his sword — but his arm was caught by the leaf basket rope and the draw was clumsy. Time slowed to a crawl, and he felt as though he was fighting through air as thick as mud. Jim must have somehow grown in his mind over the last few days, because he looked tiny against the bulk of the man holding him. His feet were lifted off the ground while he struggled and tugged uselessly at the arm around his neck.

"Stop!" Thomas yelled, forgetting entirely that he was supposed to be quiet, and gave up on the sword belt. "Dolson, it's me!"

For a moment the big man looked only blankly terrified, and Thomas was sickeningly sure that he was going to strangle Jim out of pure panic. Then his eyes widened a little in recognition, and his grip loosened — just a little.

"Let him go, Dolson," Thomas ordered, coming forward to pull the man's unresisting arms aside. Jim fell to his knees, gasping, as Thomas separated them to arm's length.

"Lieutenant?" Dolson exclaimed, baffled. "I thought — but he's a — "

"He's with me," Thomas said, low. They were being much too loud. "Tell me man, does Admiral Wickerham still live? Is he still with you?"

Dolson nodded, dumbstruck. "Yes sir, but —"

Thomas' heart leapt. "Thank God," he said, squeezing Dolson's arm tightly with one hand. The poor man's tattered and dirty clothing was in little better condition than Thomas' own, and there were deep scratches across his face, hidden only by several days' growth of beard across his jaw. He was at least six inches taller than Thomas, and much broader in the shoulders. Thomas did not know him as well as some of the other men; he made a point of making at least a little conversation with all the men in his crew, but their numbers made it quite impossible to be on good terms with them all. Still, he thought they had played cards together once or twice. The man had a family in England, he recalled, a wife and children. "Will you take us to him?" Thomas asked. "We must be quick now, in case we have roused any of the enemy nearby."

"I..." Dolson stammered.

"That's an order, Mr Dolson." There was no more time for explanations. Thomas went to Jim, who was still coughing violently, and helped him to his feet. His neck was sadly bruised, but he shook Thomas off and nodded stiffly when asked if he could go on.

"I don't think I'll die," he said, quietly enough that only Thomas could hear. Despite his confused feelings — the joy of knowing the admiral still lived, the heart-stopping fear he had felt at seeing Jim throttled, lingering anger over the medal and yes, still, the shame of what he had done under the underhang — those words sent a shudder right down to the base of Thomas' spine. Jim gave him a triumphant look, as though he could tell.

It took perhaps another hour, though it was difficult to be sure. The area of the forest they were now in was denser and thicker than any they had experienced so far, making it difficult to see the position of the sun. Thomas kept himself close behind Dolson, trying to take care of where he put his feet. He let Jim bring up the rear, reasoning that it would be best to keep some distance between the pirate and the seaman, though Dolson did keep looking at him nervously over his shoulder. He led them to a place where the forest dipped into a low valley. The bottom was full of rocks, some the width of a man's height, piled together to form a treacherous river of jagged stone. The walls were scattered with tall, thin trees with frond-like leaves. Through these they made a staggered, difficult descent until even Jim was panting with the effort.

"How in heaven's name did you get the admiral down here?" Thomas asked as they finally neared the floor.

"We didn't," Dolson said, muttering. "We came down further south — there's an easier place there. I've been taking a different route in and out each time."

Thomas looked back and caught Jim's eyes. "Clever," Jim shrugged. Thomas wasn't so sure, however. Were multiple small trails any better than one obvious one?

Eyeing Jim suspiciously, Dolson turned and hauled himself over the nearest rock. They followed. It was hard going, and Thomas had to concede that it would take a very determined and enterprising pirate to come all the way down here, for any reason — qualities that as far as he could tell, very few of them possessed. It could well be the perfect hiding place.

Dolson paused, hesitating, at a gap between two boulders. He glanced back between Thomas and Jim, clearly unsure.

"Dolson," Thomas warned.

"Who goes there?" a voice called from somewhere ahead. It was a little shaky perhaps, but recognisable.

"Mr Smythe!" Thomas called back, in hushed excitement.

The man emerged from some dark recess between the stones. Thomas expected him to look much the worse for wear, as they all did, but somehow the surgeon had managed to hold on even to his coat and spectacles, a little spattered perhaps with mud, but otherwise intact. Aside from the beginnings of a ragged beard, it was as though he had simply stepped off a boat onto the beach, and had not been shipwrecked or spent the last week stranded on a desert island. He looked quite out of place, and yet Thomas thought he had never been quite so happy to see anyone in his life.

"Lieutenant Thomas?" Smythe exclaimed, and adjusted his spectacles on his nose, staring wide-eyed from Dolson, to Thomas, to Jim, blinking furiously. "How on *earth...* that is, well met, come in, come in, all of you."

They followed Smythe into the recesses of the stones, where Thomas looked around to discover a kind of deep crevice in the side of the valley formed of earth and rock. It was not what anyone would call excellent shelter, but the walls and parts of the ceiling had been lined with large leaves and bits of deadwood, to keep out the worst of the elements, and enough light came in through what was left to see by.

Admiral Wickerham was sitting upright on a makeshift pallet of the same kind of large boat-shaped leaves that formed Thomas' coconut-basket. Far apart from the lasting vision Thomas had of him — breathless, wan and near death, he too looked much improved, with the colour returned to his cheeks, his wound freshly bandaged. He had been alert and tense at their approach, but as they all came in, making somewhat of a mockery of the small space by their numbers, he put down the sword he had been holding in one hand and his eyes brightened with joy. "Charles," he breathed, in disbelief, and Thomas went straight to him, falling on his knees in the dirt. He felt as though all the air had been driven out of his body.

"Captain," he gasped. He was ashamed to find himself almost in tears.

"How in God's name did you find us down here?" Wickerham

demanded. He too sported the result of several days without shaving, and his beard was white.

"Dolson found us, sir," Thomas admitted, swallowing hard to try and rid himself of the thick emotions that made his voice so high and shaky. "But we have been looking for you for three days now. Captain, I found Peter Cole and Diego Pasco," he added, stumbling over his words a little in his haste to deliver the news.

"You did?" Wickerham exclaimed. "Are they well?"

"They are, sir," Thomas nodded, taking Wickerham's hand when the man held it up to him, and holding it tightly. "Cole was injured, but I believe he will recover. I left them in a safe place, once Cole told me that you and Mr Smythe might be out here, somewhere."

"Good," Wickerham beamed. "That is very good. I have never heard such good news." He let go Thomas' hand and put both of his own to each side of Thomas' face, holding him there for a moment as if to take in the sight. "I had thought us the only survivors," he said, hoarsely. " I think I would have rather committed the ultimate dreadful sin myself than be the last survivor of my own ship. But here you are, and the boys also. And who is…" He finally looked over Thomas' shoulder and frowned in confusion to see Jim there, crouching awkwardly by the entrance which was not quite tall enough for him to stand up straight all the way.

"This is Jim," Thomas said, glancing around to make sure all was well. Jim's face was strangely pale.

"Ah yes, my former patient," Smythe said, business-like, coming forward and peering intently at the slash wound across Jim's chest. "Yes, this is coming along nicely. Those stitches will need to come out sooner than later, however."

Thomas might have expected Jim to protest, given what he endured when the stitches were going in, but he seemed to ignore Smythe entirely in favour of meeting Wickerham's appraising look.

"A prisoner?" the admiral mused.

"Well, sir…" Thomas began awkwardly.

"Admiral Wickerham?" Jim took a step forward, quite uninvited. Dolson made a sharp movement as though he was not sure whether or not to drag him back.

"Aye, lad?" Wickerham raised one bushy grey eyebrow.

"Sir." Jim took a breath, and, while Thomas stared, knelt down beside him to be at the old man's eye level. He was shaking. "My name is James Oliver," he said. "I think you knew my father."

— 16 —

"*Jim,*" Thomas snapped in a horrified whisper. "You cannot — this is *not* the time —"

Wickerham's eyes had narrowed still further, but he had not otherwise moved; if he was shocked or offended by being approached in such a manner and with such a ridiculous statement, he did not show it. "I knew James Oliver," he said, in a matter-of-fact tone that did nothing to betray any emotion. "And I knew his son," he added, which brought Thomas' head snapping around in surprise. "They both died at sea, some years ago now."

"Should I take him out and beat him, sir?" Dolson asked.

"I remember you as well, Captain," Jim said, steadfastly ignoring all the rest of them. "I wasn't sure, when I heard the name, but now —"

"That is enough," Thomas hissed. The insult of such a lie to the admiral's face was staggering, and he felt heartily embarrassed for having brought it upon Wickerham at all, let alone in his injured and aggrieved state. "Dolson, take him —"

"I have proof," Jim insisted, as the broad seaman came forward to put a heavy hand on his thin shoulder.

"What is this?" Wickerham demanded. "What proof?"

Jim looked desperately at Thomas as Dolson took him by the

arm and dragged him up. Thomas tried to look away, to shake his head, but those blue eyes caught at him the same way they had the first time, and he was forced to look right back into them. Like ocean maelstroms, dragging him in. "Please," Jim whispered, barely loud enough to hear. A word for him alone.

"Wait," Thomas said, halting Dolson before he could go further. Slowly he reached into his pocket and drew out the medal, handing it over to Wickerham with care. The admiral took it in one hand and examined it closely, turning it over to see the lettering on both sides.

"That proves nothing," Dolson put in, dismissively, and shook Jim hard as though he were a disobedient puppy. "It proves he's a thief, an' all." Jim glowered around at him.

"Let him go, Dolson," Wickerham said, calmly, without taking his eyes off the medal. Thomas turned to stare at him, all his own manners forgotten.

"Sir —" the seaman protested, or tried to protest before Wickerham changed his tone, snapping at him in a clear order.

"Do what I said, man. Good. Now do you go and stand watch. Go on. It is too damn close in here."

Dolson left, rather red-faced and reluctant, past Mr Smythe who was watching with cautious interest from where he stood near the entrance.

Jim had not struggled in Dolson's grip, and now was left standing alone and trembling, breathing hard.

"You claim that this medal belonged to Captain James Oliver?" Wickerham asked him, holding it up to the light.

"I... I do, yes sir," Jim said shakily.

"Charles," Wickerham said, catching Thomas quite off-guard as he turned in his direction again.

"Sir?"

"You were holding the medal. What do you know about this?"

Thomas could not lie, and would not have anyway, not to a man he so respected, even while he could feel Jim's eyes on him. "I saw him take it off a body, sir," he said, and saw the surgeon twitch in horror out of the corner of his eye. Wickerham did not react. "On the *Courage*, when we were making our escape. I killed the man when he tried to get in our way."

"And you looted the body of a crewmate?" Wickerham turned a hard gaze on Jim, who seemed to have gone even paler, though it was hard to tell by the dappled light coming through between the rocks.

"When I found it on him this morning, he told me he was only taking back what was his," Thomas explained. "I suspected it was stolen in any case, so I confiscated it."

"It *is* mine," Jim insisted. "Sir," he added, belatedly. Thomas had never seen his pirate be so deferential to anyone, certainly not to *him*, and none of his fellow pirates either, whether in word or attitude. He was making an effort now, even if he was not fully aware of the proper protocols demanded when addressing a man of Wickerham's rank and stature.

Thomas wondered when he had started thinking of Jim as *his* pirate.

"All right, enough of that," Wickerham sighed. "Come here, boy."

Jim hesitated and actually looked at Thomas — for permission or for reassurance, it was impossible to say. Thomas nodded, and Jim went gingerly back down to his knees. "Closer, boy, my damn eyes aren't what they used to be," Wickerham muttered, and Jim shifted forward. His face was set, but he could not stop his chest rising and falling noticeably with nervous breath. Wickerham frowned deeply as he stared into Jim's face. "You say you remember me."

"I… I think so," Jim said, sounding much less certain than he had a moment ago.

"Be sure, boy," the admiral's voice cracked across the space between them. Thomas jumped, his nerves utterly shot.

"I… it was a long time ago, but… I think it was a party of some kind, at my father's house." Jim swallowed and clenched his fists in his lap, not daring to look away from Wickerham's intense stare. "I was too young to attend but… I remember my father introducing me to some of the guests…" He hesitated again.

"Go on," Wickerham encouraged him in a softer voice. "Do you remember what I said to you?"

"Yes sir. I… now I hear your voice again, I do." Jim swallowed. "You said… that is, you asked me if I should like to be a sailor, like my father. I said… I think I said that I should like it very much, and then… and then you said…" he stopped, gasping a little as he struggled with the emotion of recollection, his face screwed up into a grimace as he tried, desperately, to remember the words. Thomas could feel his heart pounding in what felt like the pit of his stomach. In disbelief. In hope.

Wickerham put out a hand and held it to Jim's face. He was no longer frowning, but his eyes were smiling and kind. "I said that you might as well sail on the next tide," he murmured. "For surely His Majesty's Navy could ask for no finer a boy."

*

Wickerham asked Thomas and Smythe to leave, and Thomas went with a dazed feeling. The ringing in his ears from Yellow-Eyes' shot seemed to have returned, so that when Smythe next spoke to him it sounded muffled and strange.

"No," he replied, the sick feeling in his stomach only worsening at the surgeon's questions. "No, I did not know. That is… he told me, but I did not…"

"Well, one can hardly blame you for scepticism on that score," Smythe admitted. "Are you well? You look quite thin."

Thomas looked down at himself dazedly; 'thin', he thought, was a rather flattering choice of words under the circumstances. "Well enough," he replied. "Jim — that is, James —" he stumbled over his own words, "he is quite skilled at foraging, and we have not done too badly, this last day or two." He straightened, looking up at the walls of the valley. Dolson was sitting not too far away, scarcely visible in his hiding place between two rocks. "And you?" he asked, dragging himself back to the present. "How did you come to find this place?"

"Luck," Smythe scoffed, beckoning him to one side where another opening, not quite as well-maintained, had been stocked with perhaps an armful of scavenged goods; a little food, some coconuts, and the surgeon's medical kit, which he had by some miracle managed to carry onto the island in good order. There were no weapons.

Smythe sat Thomas down and began tending to the shallow graze on his face, while they exchanged tales. "It took perhaps a day of travel," Smythe began. "Going around in circles, most likely. We heard the pirates attack from our first hiding place. The admiral was insensible at the time. Dolson would have liked to go back, but we had only the admiral's sword between the three of us…" he shook his head, his expression very solemn behind the small round spectacles.

"I understand," Thomas nodded. "There was nothing you could do."

From there it seemed they had wandered in short bursts into the forest, whenever Wickerham had the strength to be moved. In some places Smythe and Dolson simply carried him between them. "I thought our game was really up when we came to the edge of this damn valley," Smythe admitted. "But Dolson went around until he found the best way down. Since then we have survived on as little as nature is willing to provide. Not easy in a place like this. Fortunately there is a small spring further down; fresh water, and clean, or I could never have kept the admiral's wound as well as I have. I tell you, I have never been a particularly pious man, but I will pray three times a day henceforth in thanks from now until the day I die, which I suppose cannot be far away," he added, with black humour.

Thomas retold his own journey in only a few words, but then he was forced to repeat it an hour or two later in detail when Jim came to tell him that Wickerham wanted to see him. Jim still looked pale but only nodded briefly when Thomas asked awkwardly if he was well, and then Smythe insisted on taking out the stitches right away. Jim did not look sanguine at being subjected to Smythe's instruments once again, but went with him without complaint.

Wickerham listened to Thomas' tale in silence, sometimes even with his eyes closed so that Thomas wondered a time or two if the man had drifted off. He opened them again however when Thomas had finished, and sighed deeply, one hand resting over the bandaged place behind his shirt. "And so, six of us left, out of seven hundred men," he rumbled, with disgust. "I do not hesitate to call those pirates a damned curse, and that being generous. How many do you think they have?"

"I thought perhaps twenty at their camp, sir," Thomas said, sickly. He did not need to be told how many men they had lost; still, he had expected and felt he deserved much worse than a reminder. "Two in the forest that we killed, and then the ones who chased us last night... but I cannot be sure if they weren't any of the same that I saw before. Jim would know better."

Wickerham paused, then nodded.

"Sir," Thomas said then, unable to hold back his curiosity a moment longer. "Is he... is Jim truly who he says he is? How can it be possible?"

Wickerham sighed again. "I am certain he is," he said, low. "The medal is real; only three for St Laurence were made in gold. I have one, and the other man is retired and living happily in Yorkshire. Add to that, the face, and the eyes, especially, most remarkable... I knew Captain Oliver as a young man. It is like looking into a mirror through time — though of course the James I knew was never so starved — or quite so badly dressed," he added, the very corner of his lips twitching with dark humour. "Go on now, Charles. I shall need all the rest I can get, if we are to retrieve our boys on the morrow."

When Thomas returned to the other shelter, Jim was sitting slumped against the rocks, nibbling on a piece of the biscuit that they had left behind with the rest of Smythe's stores. "The two of you rest here," Smythe said, standing up from where he had been taking notes in a small notebook, and taking his medical kit. "I shall see to the admiral."

And then it was just the two of them again, watching each other across a tiny space that seemed to encompass miles. "Are you well?" Thomas asked, dragging his gaze down to the bare wound across Jim's chest. It looked much better without the ugly black stitching.

Jim made a face and shrugged, then hissed a little. "It... did not hurt as much as I expected," he said, bravely, though his cheeks were somewhat pale, Thomas thought. He offered Thomas the rest of the biscuit, and Thomas took it — their fingers brushed against each other for a fleeting moment, and Thomas felt the air leave his lungs in a short, sharp breath; Jim flinched away.

Slowly Thomas folded himself down until he was sitting beside Jim on the rock. They were alone, for now; outside the shelter it was almost eerily quiet down here in the valley, and they could not even hear the voices of any of the other men. Carefully Thomas reached into his pocket and drew out the medal by its ribbon, holding it out. "I apologise," he said, low. "The admiral gave it back for me to give to you. I should never have taken it.

Your father was a King's man, and so are you. It's yours."

Jim reached out and Thomas let it drop into his hand. Jim looked at it for a moment, then, with a reluctant, jerking movement of his arm, handed it back. "Will you hold it for me?" he asked, to Thomas' surprise. "I have nothing to keep it in," he explained, demonstrating with one hand the flap of his torn breeches. "I know you will keep it safe."

Thomas swallowed. "I will," he promised.

Jim nodded.

"Will you tell me?" Thomas asked, after a long moment. "I know I have no right to demand it, when I dismissed you so before."

Jim hesitated, then shook his head. For a moment Thomas' heart sank with disappointment, but then Jim said: "No, you were right not to believe me. Sometimes I hardly do myself. I almost believed I was as mad as they all think I am." He already sounded different, Thomas thought. More sure of his words.

Thomas settled himself more easily on the uncomfortable surface, and tucked the medal back into his pocket, his breath threatening to catch in his throat with anticipation. "Go on."

Jim took a deep breath and let it out slowly, his eyes rolling up to the top of the rocks as though deciding where to begin. Then he began speaking in a low voice that seemed with each word to be swallowed away into the surrounding silence.

— 17 —

"I went to sea on my father's ship at ten. I remember my mother did not want me to go; she said it was too young to be around so many rough men, and would have had me in the schoolroom another year or two. It's strange, I don't remember much about my mother, but when I think of her I do remember her crying when I insisted I should like to go away. I remember I was scared, really, but it made my father very pleased that I should follow him in his career, and I wanted to please him very badly.

"There were a lot of men on the ship, but there were other boys as well, and my father put me in their charge, so that they all tried to be the best of friends with me to earn his good favour. Some of the older boys were jealous, I think, but if any of them bothered me, my friends and I would put rats in their hammocks, or cut their trouser strings, and that would put paid to it. I cried a little at first, of course, as all young boys do when they leave home for the first time, but once my hands hardened and I got used to the work, I was happy to be at sea and to serve my father, especially since all the men aboard were very respectful of him, even the older seamen. It made me think that I should like to be a captain one day, as well.

"We were sailing in the Caribbean — I don't remember why,

or where we were going. I heard so many stories about pirates, some that I liked and others told by the older boys when they were trying to scare us. I wasn't frightened, at all. I believed my father would be able to fight off any ships, as all the men said, and when my friends admitted to being afraid I would laugh at them and tell them how foolish they were.

"We were attacked. I don't… remember much of that night. Now I think they must have come up on us in the dark without lights, perhaps near some islands where they could lie in wait for a passing ship. That's what they do. It wasn't just one ship, I remember, it was a small fleet, and we only got off one broadside before they were on us." Here Jim brought his knees up to his chest and lowered his head onto his arms for a moment, breathing heavily as he relived the memory. "They took no prisoners from the men. They killed everyone they fought. They… they killed my father on deck, four of them on him at once. There was nothing I could do. I had never even been in an action before and I could hardly hold a sword. When I tried to fight they laughed at me and beat me. Then they took us, me and some of my friends, the youngest ones. They took us onto one of their ships, and stripped our ship of everything she had, and burned her in the water, with the powder from the gun stores. We could hear the screaming from the men who were wounded…" Jim swallowed hard and shuddered.

"They treated us as slaves. They had no way of knowing that I was the captain's son, but I would see one of them — Babber — he would walk around wearing my father's medals. Briggs was on that ship too, and Horace, the one you called Big Ears." He spat. "Their captain was a cruel master, and they would force us to do as much of the work he gave them as we could physically manage, and if we did it badly, or not quickly enough, they would beat us. Two of my friends got sick and died, and they threw them overboard like so much scraps.

"I don't know how long I was on the ship. At least a year, maybe two. I stole food. I learned not to speak after a while, because they would beat me for speaking the only way I knew, and if I tried to talk the way they did they would beat me even more, thinking I was mocking them. Sometimes it really felt like I had forgotten how to speak at all. They all decided I had gone mad, and it amused them. Briggs... Briggs was one of the worst. Him... him and Babber, and their mates. They would beat us bloody in the day and... and at night... well. You know."

Thomas felt frozen in place, a cold chill going down his spine and bile rising in his throat. He knew instinctively that he was hearing a much more detailed version of the account than Wickerham had heard or would ever hear, that this tale was for him and him alone, and he wasn't sure whether his heart could take it.

"They beat some of us to death, and some more got sick, and others they forced to work until they dropped on the deck. I don't know how I survived. There were more battles and more prisoners, and most of them died, too. But not me. I kept living. I used to watch Babber showing off my father's medals to the others, and imagine how I would get them all back. I would come up with a thousand different ways of killing them, for all I was half their size and weak with hunger and exhaustion, but then I thought I would only be trapped on the ship with them, and someone would find out what I did and kill me just as easily. So I did nothing.

"The ship used to put in at an island perhaps once a month or so for supply and to sell their loot. They never let me go ashore unless it was to carry things, and they would always have someone with me, in case I tried to run away. But one day we were put in at Tortuga, and the captain came and took me to a tavern onshore. There was a woman there who wanted to buy a servant, and the captain said I was worth more than she wanted to pay, because I had already lived so long. But she said that she had heard that I was mute and mad, so she made him lower the price. He was very angry about it, I remember, and later I heard some men laughing about how he'd been beaten at haggling by a woman. But I didn't care. I was just glad to be off of that ship.

"The woman — Mrs Grey, she was called, though I never met Mr Grey, so I don't know if she was ever really married or not — she owned one of the best taverns on the island, and she ran a brothel out of it too. I did scut work, and no one tried to hurt me so long as it was done well enough. I didn't even have to steal food. I would see men I knew there sometimes, and they were always moving from ship to ship — and I would stay out of their way until they were gone again. The girls would tease me sometimes, trying to get me to speak, or telling bawdy stories; they thought it was funny to make me blush. Sometimes if there was no more work to do, they would set me free to move about the island. There was nowhere I could go, of course, and I would have rather died than stow away aboard any of the ships that put in there. So I just wandered around. That was how I met Aggie — Agwe, his name is, really. He was working on the island too, in the smithy. He caught me looking around there one day and I thought I was in for a beating, but he only showed me the things he was mending for one of the ships. After that, sometimes he paid Mrs Grey so that I could come and do some work there, as well — just brushing floors and carrying things, nothing difficult. I was nervous, at first… but he was never cruel and he never tried to touch me. He said he only liked women, and if he couldn't get them to fall in love with him then he would pay for them. He came into Mrs Grey's sometimes, too. He starting taking me out into the interior and he showed me how to hunt, how to fish. He introduced me to some of the native men, and they taught me how to swim and how to climb trees. I trusted Agwe enough that I would speak to him, sometimes, once I remembered how to use my voice. I was… not happy, exactly. I had bad dreams every night about the ship, and my father… but I suppose I accepted it. I grew up on the island, and it became my home. I had almost forgotten who I was and where I had come from.

"Then one day, a few years ago, Agwe and I were fishing, and he told me his own story. He had joined a pirate ship to get away from all the fighting in Jamaica. He told me how they were cruel to him because he was black and because of the way he spoke, and he showed me the scars from where he was whipped. I wondered why he was showing me this, because he had never told me anything like that before, but then I realised he wanted me to tell *my* tale, in return. I resisted at first, because it was a time I didn't like to even think about. But eventually I did tell him, at least as much as I could. He was very surprised to find out that I might have a family somewhere out there. It got me to thinking about my father, and my mother, and about England. Things I had not thought about for years, in case it really did send me mad.

"About a month or so after that, Briggs and Babber and some other men came into the tavern. I hid, but I watched, too. They were very loud, and Briggs tried to shame one of the girls in front of everyone, and he was made to leave. Babber drank a lot, and he started boasting about how great of a fighter he was and all the men he had killed. And then he brought out my father's medal. He had only the one left; he must have sold or lost the rest, but he kept that gold one, and he was yelling for anyone to hear that he had killed a navy captain, himself, and me just… there. I was angry, more angry than I had felt in a long time. I picked up a knife, thinking… I don't know what I was thinking, but Agwe was there, and he stopped me. We left the tavern and I explained that the medal was my father's and should belong to me. Agwe said that if I killed Babber in the tavern for all to see, I would only be killed myself, especially as I never learned how to fight with a blade properly. He told me that I never really belonged on the island, that I should try to get back to England somehow. But I didn't want to go back on a ship. I was afraid. Babber went back to sea the next morning. The truth is, I don't even know if he was one of the men who killed my father. He wasn't wearing the medals when he died; anyone could have taken them from his quarters before the ship burned. And Babber was always a coward, so probably that was all he did. But I still felt a coward myself for doing nothing, and I started to dream of my father every night. I started to imagine what it would be like to see my mother again. I even practiced what I would say to her when we met." Jim sighed at himself. There was a long silence in which Thomas hardly dared to breathe.

"The trade on the island had been doing poorly for some time, with so many of the pirate ships captured and many men executed or turned to other professions, there were only a few ships that still put in there. I knew all of them and most of the men on them too, and I knew it was more than my life's worth to take up with any of them, though I got plenty of offers. By then I was eighteen or so and pretty strong from carrying barrels around for years. I imagine they thought I would make a good deckhand and double as entertainment also," he muttered. "But they all knew better than to steal from Mrs Grey, as she had influence over all the merchants and dealers on the island. So I was not in too much danger of being Shanghai'd, though I made sure to stay nearby the tavern or the smithy whenever a ship was in.

"There was a ship that had been in drydock there for some time: The *Black Gull,* I think. It wasn't much of a ship, and no one had taken the time or money to get her out to sea. Then one day, about a year ago, we heard that someone had been making enquiries. This merchantman who was down on his luck through having committed forgery, or some such thing, and fancied the idea of himself as a pirate captain. Anyway he bought the ship, or took it, I don't know, and fixed her up right and renamed her *Queen of Heaven.* Anyway, word got out that this merchant wanted to sail up the African coast looking for slaves, where the real money was. Agwe said to me, this is your chance. This landlubber might be a loose corkscrew who knows nothing about sailing, but he is going the way you want to go. So he came with me and explained to the man that I should like to take up with him as far as Africa, and I would work for my passage. The idea was then that I should find a ship on the horn heading for Europe, and beg for work there also. And then Agwe surprised me, he offered to come as well. On a *slave ship*. He said that it had been a while since he had been on an adventure at sea, and he should like to see more of the world, but I knew he was doing it for me. I asked if he would come all the way to England, but he said he was too old to start a new life in such a cold country. He would do one voyage for pay, and then use the money to try and get home to Jamaica.

"I thought Mrs Grey might try to stop me leaving, but she had never treated me badly, and she was getting quite old and thinking about retirement. She even gave me a few coins… less than she could spare, but more than I expected. The girls all kissed me goodbye. I should have known it was all going too well. Of course when I came aboard the ship, I realised I would have to spend several months at least at sea with Briggs, and Babber, and some other of the worst men I knew. But it was too late to change my mind, so I steeled myself to it. After all, I wasn't a little boy any longer. And I had Agwe; I stayed close to him and he kept anyone from putting their hands on me.

"Of course, things went badly after we left Tortuga. This captain hadn't thought to hire a decent navigator, and he wasn't good enough to get us clear through several bad storms. We never made it to Africa, or anywhere else offering anything like good supply, and we all started to starve. The captain had kept all the knowledge of our destination and our cargo to himself, which was about the only smart thing he did; it kept him alive. People were knifing each other for a scrap of food, and after nearly a year, I was getting very thin and starting to feel weaker by the day, and I wasn't the only one, either. It felt like mutiny would happen any day, slaves or no slaves. The cargo wasn't any use to us if we were all starved to death in the middle of the ocean.

"And then we saw a ship on the horizon. The captain didn't stop the men when they put around orders to keep distance until dark; then we doused the lights and put on all sail. The plan was simply to get away with as much food and plunder as they could carry. Even when we were close enough to see the size of the ship — a ship of the navy — they would not back down. They even convinced the captain to lead the charge, and of course he was killed in the first minutes of boarding. I would have stayed on board, but they made Aggie go, and I didn't dare stay back without him. I was sure we would all die, especially after the *Queen* went down. I tried to fight, but... well. You know the rest."

"But..." Thomas managed, after letting go of the breath he hadn't realised he had been holding. "But why on earth did you never tell me — I mean, anyone — who you are? That you are... one of us?"

Jim blinked and looked up at him, his face suddenly looking very drawn, drained from the effort of using his voice more than he had done in perhaps years. "Because I'm not," he said, shortly.

"But —"

"Just as I forgot that I... could speak, that I wasn't truly mad... I forgot so much of... who I was. That part of myself. England, my childhood... it's almost like a dream, now, like it never really happened… even up until today, I still had moments when I thought I must have imagined it all. It's not who I am now. On the ship, in the hospital, I could have said something. I didn't think of it, even if someone might have believed me. Those men might not be my crew — anymore — but I am still one of them. I'm a pirate."

Thomas flinched inwardly. "How many people have you killed?" he asked, almost forgetting to keep his voice low.

"What?"

"How many people have you killed? Innocent people?"

Jim stared at him for a moment. "I've never killed anyone," he said, nonplussed, his blue eyes very wide. "Innocent or otherwise, but that means nothing. One of your men cut me down when the *Queen* boarded, but I would have killed him first if I had the chance. To survive. That's what pirates do. Some of them are evil, like Briggs, and some of them are just greedy, like that merchant captain. Some of us are just unlucky. But we all just want to survive, in the end."

Thomas didn't know what to say to that. He sat back, his mind whirling. Jim yawned, exhausted, and slumped a little further down the rock. Thomas knew he ought to say he was sorry, to express some kind of shock or dismay at a story so full of horror and pain, but he felt strangely empty of all of that. "I have a confession to make to you," he said finally. "I… when I said that I could speak for you, in England, I had no… that is, my word is unlikely to be taken seriously in any court. But you have the admiral to speak for you, now, so…"

Blue eyes shone in the dim light. "So you lied to me, to get me to help you."

Thomas swallowed the anguish that rose in his throat, and could not look Jim direct in the eyes. "About that, yes. I am sorry. But I still meant… I do still mean to take you home, of course, if it can be done."

"Do you think it can?"

To that Thomas had no answer. "We may have to fight," he said, low. "Will you…"

"Have hesitations about killing pirates?"

Thomas forced himself to look up. "Yes."

Jim bit his lip for a moment. "I should like to save Aggie, if I can," he said, low. "He is a good man."

"He fought with them. He may have killed some of our men."

"He had no choice," Jim shot back, a little viciously, "No more than I ever did. I know he wasn't on the southern shore; he was up where we landed on the eastern side."

Thomas remembered. "I will make no more promises which I cannot keep," he said finally.

Jim nodded, slowly, and was silent again, shifting down and curling up on the uncomfortably hard ground, trying to find a less awkward position. Thomas knew he was tired and that he should simply let him sleep. *James,* he thought, silently. *James Oliver.* It seemed wrong somehow. *Jim. My pirate.*

He couldn't help himself. "One more question."

Jim made a low, grunting noise of acknowledgement, his eyes already closed.

"The girls you mentioned, on the island…"

The eyes shot open, looking up at him. "In the whorehouse?"

Thomas grimaced at the ugly word, but kept on. "Yes. Did you... well, did you ever..."

"No. Never had any money."

"But would you have, if you did?"

"I... no, I don't think so," Jim said, curiously. "Why?"

"You know why."

There was silence between them again for a long moment, then Thomas said, "Last night... when we..."

"Last night was different."

"Why?"

"This is a lot more than just one question."

"Jim — I mean, James — "

"Yes?"

"I just... I don't understand, why you would... I hope that you don't think that I..." Thomas knew he wasn't making a great deal of sense, and his own confusion rather than just his gentleman's manners prevented him from coming out directly and expressing his precise concerns. "Someone... took the advantage of me, once," he said finally, and he saw Jim's eyes widen again in surprise — perhaps even a little anger. "Not the way that you were," Thomas added quickly, "not like Briggs, nothing as bad as that. But still... I don't like to think that I might have become the sort of man... the sort who would..."

Jim stared up at him. Thomas could feel his heart pounding very hard, suddenly; he was aware of every small noise outside of their shelter. But they were still alone.

"It wasn't that," Jim said, low. "Not... no. I... that was because I wanted to. I... felt safe, with you there. I still feel safe with you, ever since you killed Babber. You could have left me there and got to the boats in time, but you stayed and you saved me. No one ever did anything like that for me."

Thomas thought he might have stopped breathing altogether. "I make you feel safe? Even though I lied to you?" he managed, the words trying to catch in his throat. "Even though I cut you?"

Jim rubbed his marked cheek. "You didn't know anything about me, then."

"That is no excuse." Thomas couldn't help a strain in his voice; he did not deserve to be forgiven so readily by one who had been so wronged by so many. By him.

"You weren't trying to hurt me." Jim glanced up at him. "Anyway, we're matching now."

Thomas put a hand to his own face, tracing the wound he had gained in the struggle before the overhang. It was in almost the exact same place as the mark his swordblade had left under Jim's eye. Smythe had cleaned it, but it still stung. "It's not the same," he said, helplessly.

Jim was silent again for a while with his face turned slightly away, for so long that Thomas wondered if he might actually have fallen asleep. "You feel badly about it," the boy said eventually, very soft. "That's more than anyone ever has before."

Thomas sat and listened to Jim's breathing even out, emotional, mental and physical exhaustion finally overcoming him as the pirate slid into sleep. Somehow forgiveness from someone whose life was so akin to a dog being kicked every day by his master, but still wagged its tail in gratitude when it was fed, felt undeserved. Perhaps he had not truly understood what Thomas had done.

Uneasy, Thomas settled himself with his sword across his knees. It was not yet dark, and he was too shaken by the events of the day to sleep. Instead he stayed alert, thinking quietly to himself and watching over his sleeping pirate, as the nocturnal sounds of the forest began to rise up around them.

$$— 18 —$$

Wickerham was all for making their way northward as soon as the sun rose, but Mr Smythe was not in favour of, as he called it, *'haring off wildly across the interior'*, with Wickerham still so weak from his injuries. Wickerham, frustrated, made the point that he now had four men to aid him through the difficult stretches, and insisted on leaving at once in order to get back to the rest of their crew with the least loss of precious time.

Thomas had to agree, for all he was reluctant to expose the admiral to the rigour and danger of the journey. He was concerned that the longer they stayed in the valley, the more chance there was of being trailed to their position. As good a hiding place as it was, it was not at all the place he wanted to be when the enemy started down on them from either side of the steep slopes. Besides, if anything happened to Cole and Pasco while they were fending for themselves, he would never forgive himself. He already had more than enough to feel guilty about for the rest of his life.

No one asked Jim or Dolson for their opinion, but there were no objections. Thomas exchanged glances with Jim, but they spoke only about their planned route. They both agreed it would be best to avoid the western slope where they had almost been caught before, which left a significant part of their journey an unfortunate unknown. Between the two of them, Thomas and Jim sketched out a very rough map of the island in the dirt. Thomas was a much better cartographer, having had an officer's training in the subject over seven years at sea, while Jim's memory of the territory was far superior to his own. Thomas felt as though he had been turned about a dozen times since he had landed on the miserable spit of rock, and his frustration started to show as they haggled over the exact distance between the valley and the western cliffs.

"It will have to do," Wickerham said finally, scanning over the map. Like all of them but Smythe he had no coat, but Thomas had given him one of the clean shirts he had found inside the sea chest, which gave him at the very least some of the appearance of command. After some consideration Thomas had offered the other shirt to Jim, who had accepted it only a little reluctantly. It looked rather odd once he had put it on, coupled with his poorly-barbered hair and filthy, torn britches, but at least it hid the terrible red scar across his chest and some of the purpling bruises on his neck which had faded only slightly since Dolson had almost strangled him. He looked, Thomas thought, rather aristocratic from the waist up, if more than a bit windswept and starved.

He had to stop thinking about what Jim looked like.

They set off as soon as they had gathered their few supplies into Thomas' leaf bundle, and fuelled themselves with a few bites each of biscuit. Thomas took one of the pistols, and Dolson the other. The sun was well risen, and they were in full view as they began scaling the wall out of the valley, but doing so in the dark was out of the question. It was difficult enough when they were able to see where to put their feet, and in the steepest places, their hands and knees. Wickerham had to be half dragged up the slope, and they stopped several times so that he could catch his breath. Smythe, who while he looked perhaps the healthiest of all of them, was not a young or fit man, and Thomas was obliged to brace him from below on a number of occasions when he was unable to haul his own bodyweight over near-vertical ledges. What had taken Thomas and Jim perhaps half an hour to come down took the five of them nearly half a day to ascend, even in the place Dolson said was the most passable.

Jim, of course, seemed to manage the climb with relative ease, so that when they finally came to the top of the ridge he was hardly breathing more heavily than usual, while the rest of them were gasping from the effort. As Smythe and Dolson settled Wickerham to rest with his back against a tree in the shade, Jim sidled over to Thomas. "We might not get much farther today," he said, in an undertone.

"No," Thomas muttered, his hands on his knees. He was already regretting the decision to move. Now they were out in the open and exhausted, in no condition to fight off an attack. Even as he stood there trying to gain control over his heaving chest, every tiny sound from the surrounding forest set his heart pounding afresh. He stood upright, still panting, and met Jim's eyes. "Will you —" he started, and caught himself. Jim raised an eyebrow at him, querying. Thomas still hesitated. It seemed wrong somehow to order Jim about, now that he knew the truth. Technically he supposed nothing had changed, but he felt loathe to send him off into the wilderness, alone. "Stay here with the admiral," he said finally, settling on the option that seemed least contrary to his conscience, "and I will scout ahead."

Jim's eyebrow raised even higher, and his mouth twisted with wry amusement. "You?"

Thomas looked back, helplessly. "Well…"

"No offence meant, Lieutenant, but those boots and that hair of yours aren't exactly suited to moving invisibly."

Thomas felt his face redden, and tried not to get indignant. "I suppose I should thank you for insulting my appearance rather than my abilities," he muttered, glaring. Despite his annoyance at this disrespect it was difficult not to feel pride at how easily Jim spoke now; a vast contrast from his first few words back on the beach where they had washed ashore. It seemed like weeks ago.

"Well." Jim smirked. "That would be rude."

"Very well," Thomas managed, when he had choked back his irritation. "Go on with you. Be back in an hour or I shall come after you."

Jim flipped him a loose salute, obviously mocking, and took off silently into the trees. Privately and with some heat, Thomas thought that the pirate should have to be schooled in manners for a year before he was allowed back into decent society. And yet why did the insolence send a shiver of elation down Thomas' spine?

"We must not rest long," Wickerham gasped, when he had air in his lungs to speak. He had gone quite pale, and Smythe's face was equally grim as he knelt by his captain's side.

"I agree sir," Thomas said. "But trust Jim to find us the right way." Behind him Dolson snorted, not very subtly. Thomas had to assume that Smythe had informed the seaman of Jim's claims to good society, but it was unlikely he had been given all the details; judicious perhaps to be doubtful. "I know it seems outlandish," Thomas went on, eyeing Dolson defensively. "But he has brought me through so far, and not once been wrong about our direction. I would likely never have found the boys, or you, without his help."

As much as Wickerham would have liked to move on straightaway, there was very little choice in the matter. They ate a little, Smythe rationing out their meagre supply, and Thomas and Dolson stood watch to east and west, eyes and ears over-sensitive to every whistle of wind, every bird call, every rustling in the trees. It was indeed less than an hour before Jim returned, so silently that Thomas only noticed him when he stepped out into full view. He nodded to Thomas from his position without coming into hearing range, which by now was all the communication he needed.

Between them, he and Dolson managed to get the admiral to his feet. "I can manage," the old man wheezed, and when they let him take his own weight he was just about able to limp over to where Jim was waiting for them, Thomas hurrying along behind. "Well?" Wickerham barked when they drew near. "Report, boy."

Jim looked somewhat taken aback, but he set his shoulders and replied. "The way west is steep and out of our way. The northern path seems better, only very dense in places. I can't promise it won't get worse further up, but I don't think it's worth going the other way only to reach the cliffs…"

"I asked for your report, not your opinion," Wickerham muttered, not unkindly but with a growl born out of pain and frustra-tion. Jim flinched, a little, but Thomas thought he was the only one who had noticed.

"Thomas?" the admiral barked.

"Sir?"

"What say you? Did you not say the cliffs were the most passable?"

"Yes sir," Thomas said, with some hesitation. "They are easier than the forest once you get up there, but the terrain is rocky. I agree with Jim; it seems nonsensical to climb up there only to avoid the forest, if the way north is significantly shorter."

Wickerham considered for a minute before nodding with a heavy sigh. "Very well. The two of you take the lead and Dolson will bring up the rear. You are responsible for our direction, Lieutenant," he added, looking right at Thomas, who had to steel himself not to squirm under that suddenly hard gaze. "So do not hand over judgement entirely to your navigator."

"Yes sir," Thomas replied, suitably chastened. He looked to Smythe. "Will you manage?" he asked, in an undertone.

"Oh, I expect we shall muddle along without falling down a ravine," Smythe said airily, though his expression was still stiff and solemn. "I shall let you know if your assistance is required, Lieutenant."

Thomas nodded, and beckoned Jim towards him; together they set off into the forest. "Don't take it to heart," Thomas said, low, when Jim had been silent for a while. Of course, silence was not unusual for him, but it seemed different somehow; an oppres-sive sort of silence. They had moved ahead far enough that they could no longer hear Wickerham wheezing as Smythe helped him along. "He wasn't chiding you."

Jim shot him a look that said just how much he thought of that blatant untruth.

"Well, not intentionally," Thomas amended. "He's in a lot of pain, and he isn't used to... he was born to command. It doesn't suit him to have to rely on secondary advice in this way."

They had to stop to move some fallen branches aside, clearing the path as much as possible to make it easier for the others to follow. It would leave a rather significant trail, but they could only hope none of the pirates would recognise what they had found if they stumbled across it.

"You love him," Jim said quietly, when they had set off again, making Thomas snap his head around to stare at him. "I can tell."

"I... well, as a captain, yes," Thomas muttered, once he had worked his way through his confusion. Jim hadn't meant it as an accusation, he decided. "He is one of the best commanders in the navy. I am privileged to serve under him. He carries a great deal of respect with all his men." Jim made a low, noncommittal noise, and when Thomas dared a glance over at him, he looked unhappy. "Much like your father did as captain, I imagine," he said finally.

Jim bit his lip, the expression fading. "Yes," he said after a while. "The admiral reminds me of him." They ducked together under a low-hanging branch and over a series of small uneven hillocks, like a wave pattern on a beach. "Is he like a father to you?" Jim asked then, looking over at him.

Thomas frowned. "I suppose I never thought about it in that way," he admitted. "He has been... I have been on his crew since

I was fourteen. He has been a mentor to me, of sorts. But I certainly wouldn't presume anything of a more personal nature."

He couldn't have sworn to it, but for a moment he thought he saw Jim roll his eyes, and he couldn't imagine why. "What about your actual father?" Jim asked, an extremely personal question which Thomas suddenly realised he should have expected, given the lack of proper manners.

"My 'actual' father is dead," he said, shortly. "Both my parents died, three years ago."

"Oh." Jim actually sounded sorry. "Were they…"

"It was an illness," Thomas sighed. "Which I expect they caught from each other. A cousin of mine and half the household servants died also. I wasn't there; I was at sea." And it had been a while since he had thought about it, in more than passing. He rather wished that if Jim had suddenly found his voice and wanted to have a conversation, they could talk about something, anything else.

"But before that," Jim insisted, oblivious to Thomas' inner discomfort. "They were good to you?"

"I'm sure I don't know what you mean," Thomas said dryly. "They were not supportive of me going to sea, I can tell you that much; particularly not my father. They had no other children, you see. Letting me go off on my own at twelve seemed like an insult to him, as though I was throwing away his legacy, but I convinced him it was his duty to allow me to serve England in the navy. Still, he certainly would have preferred I wait and go into the army, if I was so inclined. Of course if I had, I no doubt would have died in the same outbreak."

Jim looked like he might have liked to ask yet another question — privately Thomas wondered if there was a way to make him pretend to be mute, again — but they came at that point to a long but narrow ditch, and had to explore ways to either cross the thing or go around it. Jim could jump it, and Thomas might have tried it himself in dire circumstances, but Wickerham certainly could not. By the time they had started to rig a sort of bridge with some thick branches, the others caught up to them, and Dolson jumped in to help. Once they had made it to the other side after an hour of wasted time, Jim had gone quiet once more. The subject did not come up again, to Thomas' relief.

*

It took two and a half days to return to the northern shore. Thomas estimated that if they had tried to go the western route, it would have taken a week. Certainly the distance was considerably shorter, but their pace was painfully slow. Wickerham was fully aware of how much he was holding them back, and his frustration grew by the hour. There was some relief when they emerged onto the rocks and saw the ocean in the distance, but then they had to navigate back to the cave where they had left the boys. Since Thomas and Jim had walked the northern shore once already, they were able to retrace their steps — in some places literally — until they reached the top of the slope that led to the creek.

Here they rested, as Wickerham was in no condition to make the descent. Besides that, the only way back up other than directly up the slope was to follow the coast around until there was an easier climb. In addition they had now gone through all their supplies, and had had nothing but coconuts to eat for the last day; there was little chance of anything better. Fortunately they had arrived just as night was coming on at the end of the third day, and they felt there was little risk of a chance meeting with the enemy in the dark. "I could go down," Jim offered, drawing close enough to Thomas that they could speak with relative privacy.

Thomas shook his head. As difficult as he knew the descent was to make in the dark, it was his own responsibility to check on the boys. He had left them, and if something had happened to them in the week they had been fending for themselves, he would have to face it. Besides, he could well imagine Cole's reaction if Jim turned up alone. He might well come to all the wrong conclusions. "I will go," he said. "And return in the morning, to discuss our next move." Jim nodded, slowly. Thomas thought he looked reluctant, though perhaps he only imagined what he secretly wanted to see.

"I will help to guard your captain," Jim said, solemnly. "He will be safe."

Thomas smiled, a little. "It would be a weight off my mind," he admitted. "Thank you. Take your orders from Mr Smythe. And do not let Dolson bully you; he isn't that vicious."

Jim nodded. "I understand. Good luck."

"And to you." After a moment's hesitation, Thomas held out his hand. To his surprise, Jim grasped him by the forearm instead of shaking it. It was a gesture utterly foreign to Thomas, but he responded, if somewhat belatedly, by squeezing in return. His fingers crinkled the fresh linen of the borrowed shirt, already rumpled and dirty after days traipsing through the forest. "I will be back by morning," he promised.

It was strange to be suddenly alone again, as he had not been since he had captured Jim by the pirate's camp. That was over a week ago now, though he had rather lost track of the individual days.

Although it was only a short journey down to the bottom of the slope, and it was much easier when he had only to be concerned with himself and not an injured man, he felt the loss surprisingly keenly. With no one to watch his back the forest seemed once again a perilous, treacherous place, and he started to feel a growing sense of heart-pounding, sickening dread that only grew worse as he neared the foot of the slope and came out onto the open rocky flat. By now it was dark enough that he could hear the water rushing through the creek better than he could see it, and all around it was otherwise quiet. Too quiet.

Trying to keep his breathing shallow, he edged his way along the foot of the slope towards the fissure — or at least where he remembered it to be. He found that his memory was less than perfect in the dark, made worse perhaps by fatigue and hunger. As he came nearer the shoreline there were two small boulders set between the slope and the creek which he had not noticed before, but in his haste he thought little of it. He continued on his way between them, only to go sprawling forward onto the rock when his ankle caught on something and twisted. Gasping with pain he sat up to find the sharp edge of a kitchen knife thrust into his face.

"Oh!" its wielder exclaimed, thoroughly abashed, and almost dropped the knife onto Thomas' chin in surprise. "Lieutenant! Cole, it is Lieutenant Thomas!"

"Watch where you point that blade," Thomas hissed as Pasco scrambled to help him up, clumsy in his embarrassment.

"Yes. sir," the boy said, miserably, as a taller figure stepped out of the darkness, the moonlight drifting briefly over his face to reveal midshipman Cole, barefooted, his face and shirt made brown with dirt. His face was back to its regular shape, the swelling having receded, but Thomas thought it must still be badly bruised under its camouflage. Bob's sword glinted in his hand.

"And so it was you, watching me," Thomas sighed, breathing out the dread-filled air that had collected in his lungs. He looked down to see that he had tripped over a length of taut rope. "A very efficient trap, boys, well done — though you could have perhaps checked if I were the enemy before you let me walk right into it."

"Sorry, sir," Cole said as Thomas dusted himself off — pointlessly, as he could not be much more filthy than he already was. "I didn't want to call out, in case there were more of you. Are there?" he asked, hesitantly, looking around as though he might see the rest of the crew trotting up behind Thomas' shoulder. "More of you?"

"Yes, yes." Thomas gripped each of the boys by a shoulder, not even trying to hide the relief on his face. "We have found the admiral and Mr Smythe, and Dolson too. They are at the top of the ridge there. And how glad I am to see both of you. Mr Cole, are you quite well?"

"Yes sir," Cole nodded, excited eyes shining in the dark. "I can walk much better now, and I am not dizzy at all anymore."

"I've been making him eat," Pasco said eagerly, practically bouncing on the balls of his feet. "Though we have both gotten quite tired of raw fish, but I knew you would want us to eat as much as we could."

"Quite right," Thomas nodded, his stomach suddenly rumbling. "Have you put in any supply today?"

"A little sir, but we had most of it for supper already," Pasco replied, suddenly hesitant. "Would you like the rest?"

Thomas shook his head. "No, I do very well. But if you would take them up to the top of the ridge, Mr Smythe will share it amongst the others. Can you manage that, in the dark?"

Pasco nodded confidently. "I will get them now," he said, and scampered off over the rocks.

"He will manage it, sir," Cole said, when Thomas looked after the younger boy with concern. "He has been all over these rocks, exploring, and we have both been up and down the coast a little, in case we should find something else to eat, or anything else useful."

"Oh?" Thomas asked, raising an eyebrow. "And have you found anything?"

Even in the dark, he could see Cole grinning. "Oh, yes sir," he said. "Come and see."

*

Thomas ordered Pasco to stay with Smythe until the morning unless he was told otherwise by Wickerham, and he did not return that night. Thomas and Cole spent the dark hours in the shallow cave, which had been lined with the meagre fruits of the boys' labour; scavenged small items from the shore, mostly useless; items of cutlery and broken plates, ruined clothing, a sodden book — unreadable, and pieces of wreckage small enough for a young boy to lift, chunks of wood and iron. And of course, the box, covered carefully with leaves for a makeshift disguise and set aside at the very far corner. Thomas slept fitfully, despite the relative comfort in the cave compared with the very rough berths they had managed in the forest the past several nights; despite the oppressively small space and the sound of Cole's regular breathing in his right ear, he felt oddly vulnerable and adrift, as though he were floating on a narrow plank of wood in the middle of the great wide ocean. Twice he woke with a start having been shaken from sleep by a sudden, heart-stopping falling sensation that left him gasping. It was a relief when the sun finally rose, and he could give up all attempts at restfulness.

It was Jim who came down the slope, nimble as ever, with his rope slung over his shoulder. The relief Thomas felt on seeing him was both extremely consolatory and troubling; he had done his best not to think about the night under the overhang since he had learned Jim's real name, but his mind kept trying to return to it, dragging on his thoughts, distracting him from his purpose. "Oh good," Cole muttered with irony, coming out of the cave to see Jim approaching. "*He's* here."

Thomas hadn't thought to repeat Jim's story for Cole's

benefit, and he had no intention of doing so now, even if it might have softened the boy's attitude. He thought he understood now why Jim had been so careful around Cole — so affable, despite the young midshipman's obvious animosity towards him. And why he was so friendly to Pasco, as well; surely he saw himself in both the boys, or the boy he could have been. "You are here on orders, I hope," he said to Jim, raising an eyebrow, holding back the instincts which would have let him make a warmer, more affectionate greeting.

"I am," Jim shot back, impudently. "Captain Wickerham says to come up if you can, and if you cannot then I will go and fetch Mr Smythe to help Cole," he acknowledged the boy with a nod, "but Diego says he thinks he can manage it."

Thomas looked at Cole, who was a little tight-lipped, but nodded. "I can manage it sir," he said, his voice only slightly hoarse. "But I don't know if I can carry the box, as well."

"Jim and I will take it," Thomas said, giving Jim a quick glance that said to hold his questions. "But we eat first."

Jim spent perhaps an hour fishing, while Thomas and Cole worked on rigging the box so that it could be easier carried. Then they ate their fill of the raw fish, and bundled up the remainder in Thomas' leaf basket, using a number of bowls the boys had fashioned from leftover coconut shells pressed together, to keep them from being too badly crushed. It was not a very pretty meal, but it was much more plentiful than any of Wickerham's men had eaten in nearly two weeks. Thomas would have waited to catch more, if he had been any more sanguine of leaving Dolson on the ridge to guard Smythe and Wickerham alone. He slung the bundle onto his back, and together he and Jim lifted the box with the aid of the ropes lashed around it and fashioned into makeshift handles. Jim did not, despite an expression of mild curiosity, ask what was inside.

Cole went on ahead of them, and Thomas kept an eye out for the boy's footing, ready to stop him rolling all the way back down the slope if he were to slip and fall. Cole moved slowly but deliberately, with determination and the resilience of youth. It was more difficult going for Thomas and Jim, as balancing the heavy box between them proved to be a near impossibility on the uneven terrain. More than once Thomas lost his own footing and had to use his free hand to help himself upright again, his heart pounding.

Pasco was waiting for them when they finally reached the top of the climb, bouncing again from foot to foot with anxiety and not doing a very thorough job of hiding himself. "I was about to come down again after you!" he exclaimed with relief, coming to give Cole his hand for the last difficult stretch; a vertical ledge only a few inches shorter than Cole himself. Jim helped Thomas haul the box onto the ledge before scrambling up and helping him in turn. They did not stop to catch their breath, but followed Cole into the forest where Jim had helped Smythe put up a shelter with the use of living trees and fallen branches, camouflaged with a strategic covering of boat leaves. "There you are," Smythe said as they gathered all together at last. "We were starting to be concerned."

"The Lieutenant made us stop for fishing," Jim put in before Thomas could even answer.

"Oh good," Pasco said — he was perhaps the best-fed of all of them, but there was little anyone could do to satiate a twelve-year-old boy's appetite even under normal circumstances. Jim was unwrapping the leaf bundle from Thomas' back and distributing the fish without waiting to be ordered, and they were all too tired and hungry to object. As they ate, Smythe drew Cole aside to look at his wounds, and after a short examination told Pasco that he had done well, and that his care for the injuries had perhaps even saved Cole's life. The boy's face lit up with so much pride that he had to turn away from them all, and made excuses of going to fetch water in one of the coconut bowls.

Once he had eaten, Thomas sat with Jim while Wickerham had private words with Cole, or as private as was possible, which was not very. Thomas did his best to observe the unwritten sailor's rule of pretending not to hear what was by necessity quite audible from a short distance, but it was difficult not to see the shining of tears in Cole's eyes and the redness of grief in his face as the admiral held him by the shoulder.

"What are we going to do now, sir?" Cole asked at last, his voice a little husky with emotion.

Thomas met Wickerham's eyes, and for perhaps the first time in his memory he thought he saw uncertainty there. What could he say? They were outnumbered and undersupplied, and any attempt to make contact with ships that just happened to be passing nearby, such as fire or smoke signals, would absolutely bring the pirates down on them before any help could reach them. They needed a miracle.

"Sir?" Thomas got up and pulled over the box they had painstakingly dragged up the ridge. "You should see this."

It was a long narrow case, the kind that was sometimes strapped down in an out-of-the-way place aboard ship, for men to store tools and whatever else might occasionally be needed. It was not lined to protect against water damage, but it was well-made, the lid stuck closed and the panels joined together so tightly that it had not so much as leaked before it had been tossed up on shore. They all gathered around it, and Thomas prompted Cole to pry it open, since it had been his find.

Good god," Smythe muttered as the lid was cracked open and pushed back — with some difficulty, as before it had been thrown from the wreck, it might not have been opened for years. The box had clearly been an old storage for weapons, closed and forgotten about; on top were a half dozen swords, mostly old but serviceable, only a couple of them broken. And under these, when they were moved carefully aside, were a number of pistols, either packed in carelessly or tossed about by their journey. Three of them were dry and loaded.

"Well." Wickerham sat back after inspecting the weapons, a grim smile growing on his face. "This may well be the answer to some of our prayers."

Armed with his sword and one of the unloaded pistols — a small but not insignificant comfort — Thomas waited with baited breath in the dubious shelter of a short, squat tree with a wide trunk that curved strangely inward at its base, providing him with a small niche within which to hide himself. He wished there was some better way of telling time than by watching the arduous passage of the moon overhead through the trees. An hour, perhaps, since sunset. Likely less, when he took into account the way time always seemed to drag so much slower when one was tense with anticipation. Every sound was a startlement, every breath of air across his face a reminder that he could not rest even for a moment. His legs burned from the awkward half-crouching position. He could not even turn his head far enough to see Cole, crouching similarly behind another tree on the other side of the open space between the trees which made a natural path. It was wide enough that anyone going to and from the pirate camp would find it eventually, and there were indeed signs that it had already been found and, more vitally, used.

As they expected, it was only a matter of time before someone came along the path; a small foraging party, two men only. They made no attempt at stealth, and Thomas heard their footsteps and their voices long before they came into view.

"I swear, that black'earted swabber just *looks* at me wrong one more time…" one was complaining in a reedy voice as they kicked along the ground.

"Yew need te go duck yer hot head in t'ocean, Denman," the other muttered in reply. "'Afore yew gets us both skewered on a spike an' eaten."

"'E can't afford to kill all of us," the one called Denman sneered. "Even for a hot dinner. Wouldn't be anyone around to do 'is dirty work then, would it?"

As the two men approached their position, Thomas reached with baited breath into the covering of leaves by his feet. His fingers found the end of the rope. He could not see Cole but he was sure that the boy was doing the same with his end.

"I've given up guessin' what e'd do," opined the second pirate. It was impossible to tell by their voices if they were walking side by side or one behind the other, and Thomas regretted not choosing a position better suited to reconnaissance, but there was little to be done for it now. As the footsteps drew level with his tree, he grasped the rope and tugged swiftly upwards. He felt it go taught as, with only a half-second delay, Cole pulled his end up and out. In much the same way as it had worked on Thomas before, both pirates were tripped as the rope scooped their legs out from under them.

One of the men was a little further ahead, however, and the second one only staggered rather than sprawling to the floor. Thomas only caught a glimpse of Cole springing out of his hiding place to leap on the first man, pinning him to the ground, before he had to put all of his own attentions onto disabling the other pirate. This one he could not recognise by face, but there was no time to exchange pleasantries before the man, still off balance, came staggering towards him with a drawn sword. "I'm comin', Denman!" the pirate bellowed, swinging wildly.

Fortunately Thomas' attacker was not a good swordsman, and though the stolen blade he fought with was of good make, it skidded off the edge of Thomas' sword and away, with the effect that he very nearly cut into his own face by the manoeuvre. Thomas sent him careening backwards with a stroke.

"I have him sir!" Cole called out, and Thomas hardened his grip on his sword. They only needed one prisoner.

The man in front of him seemed to realise his danger, looking into Thomas' eyes and seeing his own death looming. Giving his comrade up as lost, he turned and started to run back the way he had come, a yell forming on his lips. It was cut off, strangled, as Dolson stepped casually out of the trees and knocked him down with a blow that made an audible crunching noise.

"Good work, Dolson," Thomas said, swallowing bile, and then his mouth went suddenly dry as an enormous dark figure came looming out of the darkness behind the seaman.

Warned by Thomas' face, Dolson turned, lifting his blade.

"Wait!" Thomas exclaimed, hurrying forward. "Dolson, put down your sword."

Dolson stared at him incredulously as Thomas put himself between him and the newcomer.

It was the man called Aggie, looming above all of them. He had stopped dead and was staring down at his dead crewmate, the whites of his eyes very bright indeed in his dark face. Thomas swallowed; he had forgotten quite how large the man was. He even towered over Dolson. Even unarmed, it would not be difficult for him to kill a man with his huge hands alone.

"Agwe," Thomas said, low; the man looked over at him sharply, surprised to hear the name. "My name is Charles Thomas. I am… a friend, of Jim's. He has told me that I can trust you."

"Jim?" Aggie looked sharply over at Dolson and then Cole, who was still standing over his captive with a sword in one hand and a pistol in the other. The Jamaican searched their faces, perhaps looking for any deception. "Where is he?" he rumbled.

"Back at our camp," Thomas said, forcing himself to keep his own sword lowered. Slowly he reached into the pocket of his trousers and brought out the circle of gold, dangling by its broken cord. Aggie stared at it for a moment and then his gaze flicked back up to Thomas' face, a deep frown creasing his brow. There was no real reason for him to trust them, at all, Thomas thought, since he likely had no idea that Jim had taken the medal from Babber, and certainly not the circumstances by which Thomas now came to be in possession of it; he might after all have simply taken it off the dead pirate himself. But after a moment the man jerked his head in a barely perceptible nod, and settled his shoulders in a more relaxed posture. "I will come wit' ye," he said.

"Sir?" Cole muttered as Thomas approached him and his prisoner. Denman was groaning, his wrists tied, face-down in the dirt with Cole's bare foot pressing into the small of his back. Cole looked up at Thomas, silently questioning. They had only wanted one prisoner, but now, with Aggie, they didn't even need so many.

Thomas hesitated. Objectively he knew that their plan ended with all the pirates who were not aiding them dead in the sand. He had already made the same mistake too many times to consider leaving any of them alive when they might return to attack yet again; no court would judge him for it now, at least no court on earth, in this life. But it still felt sickeningly wrong to slay a man in cold blood where he lay helpless and unresisting, no threat to anyone in that moment. He wasn't sure he could bring himself to it, but he certainly could not pass the duty onto a fifteen year old boy barely risen from his sickbed. He swallowed hard and tightened his grip on his sword, steadying his resolve.

"I'll do it, sir," Dolson said low, coming up behind him with his own blade drawn. Thomas looked up at him helplessly; he wanted badly to accept the offer, though somehow the notion of ordering a subordinate, not even an officer, to do what he did not like to do himself, he was sure could only be called cowardice of the weakest kind. And yet when he opened his mouth to protest he could not quite manage to form the words.

"Go on, sir," Dolson urged, solemnly. "I'll take care of things right enough. Go you on back and I'll catch up as soon as I may."

Without looking at any of them, Thomas nodded with thickness in his throat.

Aggie followed him and Cole into the forest to where they had left the other four; not too far away, but far enough that they would not have been discovered in a narrow search of the area, should something have gone awry with their plans. Thomas still felt nervous with the enormous bulk of the man hovering over his shoulder, but the look of relief on Jim's face when he came out to meet them and saw his old friend was enough to do away with almost all his fears.

After a hasty explanation, after which Wickerham with only a moment's pause promised him safe passage to England and a good word to the magistrate in exchange for his cooperation, Aggie seemed only too willing to provide details of the pirate camp in his lilting, musical accent which Thomas did not altogether follow, but he understood the words 'guns' and 'flares', the second of which made his heart race with excitement.

"We need those flares," he said, looking to Wickerham, whose face had a trace of the old warrior's determination in it now, seeing at last a better way out of their predicament.

"Why have they not yet used them?" Smythe wondered aloud. He was sitting on the other side of the small pit Jim had dug for a small cooking fire, the flames hidden by the depth of the pit and the smoke invisible against the darkness and the trees, so that only the sound of it was a potential danger. Still, Thomas thought it was worth it when he tasted the deliciously roasted seabirds which had been cooked in his absence.

Jim and Pasco between them had brought the birds down with stones and slings made out of scraps of their own clothes — the new shirt Jim had been wearing was sadly cut about, but Thomas could hardly call it wasted. The food was certainly enough to put heart into any man who had lived the last two weeks on coconuts and barnacles.

Aggie was also eating with enthusiasm, though he did not look at all starved. Thomas guessed that his own hunting skills were nothing to be taken lightly, if he had had any hand in teaching Jim what he knew, and he had no doubt been instrumental in feeding not only himself but the other pirates, all this time. "Dey waiting for some sign of a ship, so not te waste da flares," he said easily now, spitting out a wing bone into the pit. "Cap'n Briggs' orders."

"That makes sense, doesn't it?" Pasco blinked, looking around at Wickerham. The boy looked even smaller and younger next to the huge Jamaican, the skin around his lips still greasy from his meal.

"You could be waiting half a century on this rock before a ship came into sight," Wickerham muttered, dismissively. "And that only if you had a watch set every hour of the day, and what if they were passing at night? A flare in the dead of night might be seen for hundreds of miles around. It would be foolish not to use them."

"Briggs doesn't want to be rescued," Jim said then, surprising them all. Thomas looked around at him, frowning at what seemed a rather absurd claim.

"What do you mean, Jim?" Pasco's over-excited eyes widened even further, staring across the fire.

"Well, if it's unlikely that they might find a ship passing," Jim went on, glancing a moment towards Thomas before continuing, "think how unlikely it is that that ship would be inimical to rescuing a score of pirates. Surely any merchant or private sailor would pass them on, and any military vessel would either press them into service or shoot them all on the spot. I expect Briggs has made very pretty excuses for waiting, in the hope that he might somehow become king of his own little island here. It's about the best he could ever hope for. Except for the lack of women," he added, grimly.

"What about the boats?" Thomas asked, incredulously. "They have two dry boats waiting in their camp. Surely some attempt might be made —"

"None of them are any great sailors," Jim replied before he could go further, and Aggie nodded silent agreement as he finished the last of his bird. "Not without a good navigator, and they haven't one, nor any maps, and remember that they are most of them used to sailing only around the Caribbean and the American coasts. If they tried to row to the continent from here... well, if they did not all drown in the first day or starve by the end of a week, Briggs knows they will turn on him. He's a mean fighter, but he can't fight all of them."

"He be hurt," Aggie put in, shooting Jim a look which Thomas interpreted as curious, or perhaps impressed. "Must 'ave broke 'is wrist gettin' out da chain; can't use dat arm at all, now."

"So you see, it suits him to keep them all here on shore," Jim finished, biting his lip. "If anyone suggests taking a boat out to sea, he will just say 'go on you then, and bring us back news of what you find', which will scare most of them out of it, and if they *do* go, likely they will never come back, and he will tell the others that they must have died in the attempt, and so it is better to wait for a ship that might never come."

"But surely he cannot keep up such a charade forever," Smythe exclaimed. "Some of the men must surely see through it already."

"I am sure they do." Jim reached behind his head to tug at locks of hair that were no longer there in an anxious gesture. "But he has saved them once already, or at least they see it that way.

He has followers. If there is a mutiny it won't be more than half the men, and he will make sure those who are the most loyal to him have all the best weapons. And then, well..." he trailed off, uncomfortably.

"Less men dere are, more food dere is," Aggie finished his thought for him, shrugging unemotionally. "Dat is how he t'inks. And, he is not wrong," he admitted, cocking his head to one side while Cole and Pasco stared openly at him at this barbarous suggestion. For a moment, all was quiet as they looked around at each other.

"We had planned to liberate one of the boats," Wickerham announced, for Aggie's benefit. "Since they are kept in the camp, we expected to have to wage all-out battle with the men guarding it to even have a chance of success. But if we could only get our hands on the flares..."

"It will still be a battle," Thomas pointed out, grimly. "As soon as we set off a flare they will be on us." He realised too late that he had spoken out of turn; such concerns should not have been voiced in front of an audience.

"Still better to await rescue here, where we might be sure of fresh water and at least a little food," Wickerham countered stiffly, while Thomas flinched at the silent reproach. "Better that than floundering in the middle of the ocean; even if we might hope to get further than a dozen incompetent pirates, we should scarcely have a better chance of making it to the African coast before we starve."

Thomas privately had a little better opinion of their party. With Jim's help they could put in a decent supply, and Dolson, Cole,

Pasco and himself should be able to pilot a small lifeboat quite easily, he thought, with Jim, Aggie and even Smythe perhaps, as hands. Wickerham was a legendary navigator, and Thomas knew his own skills were not lacking, at least not at sea. But he dared not argue any further with the admiral's assessment, though it made a significant change to their plans. After all, he had to call himself in favour of any alternative that stood less chance of getting them all killed.

"Well, Jim has been made," he said instead, thoughtfully. "He cannot simply go walking into their camp. Perhaps…?' he looked up at Aggie, half-hopeful.

Aggie shook his head. "Dem lot don't trust me," he said. "Cos I ain't one o' dem, an' dey know I came along for da boy dere." He nodded in Jim's direction, and the blue-eyed pirate ducked his head. "No chance dey let me near dem boats alone. Dat where dey keep da flares, in da boats," he added.

Thomas understood. The lifeboats were fitted with small cases of emergency flares, water-protected for just the very situation they found themselves in now. If Briggs didn't want the flares used, it made sense to keep them out of the way in the very boats they had been stowed. "In that case, sir," he turned back to the admiral. "We might return to the original plan, with some alterations."

"Perhaps, but it will require a lot more thought. I will not for the sake of desperation go blindly into a pirate camp. A sound strategy, that is the thing." Wickerham turned to Aggie and, with forced politeness said, "Mr Agwe, if you could assist us perhaps in ascertaining a better grasp of the geography of the eastern shore..."

"Sir," Thomas put in again, flinching inwardly once more at the look Wickerham gave him for the interruption. He would not have dreamed of arguing so with his superior officer, two weeks ago, and he wasn't sure what gave him the wherewithal now. "Sir, I must remind you that the pirates are now missing three of their number, and a short search in the right direction is all it will take from them to realise we are in the area. Can we afford the time?"

"Our strategy requires a defensible position on the eastern shore from which to fire the flares," Wickerham said shortly. "Which we do not yet have."

"Then take Jim." Thomas saw Jim's head come up sharply out of the corner of his eye, but barrelled on. "He has been along the shore, and I have full confidence that if such a position is to be found, he will find it."

Wickerham still looked doubtful. "Then who will undertake to steal them?" he asked, his eyes narrowed. "Unless you had planned on a new career as a burglar yourself, Charles."

Thomas flushed.

"I can do it sir," Pasco piped up, drawing all of their eyes. "Please, sir," he added, as Thomas and Wickerham both opened their mouths to refuse him. His voice shook only a little, his expression determined. "Jim has been showing me how to move quietly. And I am the smallest and the quickest," he added, straightening his shoulders. "I can do it."

Thomas' instincts railed against allowing a twelve-year-old boy to take on such a dangerous and vital role, and he was sure that Wickerham felt the same. But if Jim couldn't do it there was very little other choice. Thomas was too tall and his hair too bright, even if he hadn't been so unused to stealing silently through a jungle. Cole was not altogether recovered and was not fast enough on his injured leg, and Dolson would be needed for the distraction which was the lynchpin of the plan.

Cole cleared his throat into the silence. "Perhaps," he offered, looking over at Wickerham rather dejectedly. "I could try…"

"No," Wickerham waved him off. "It is not to be risked. Diego stands the best chance."

Pasco bit his lip. Solemnly, Jim reached over the fire and handed the boy the rest of his roasted bird.

— 21 —

"Are you quite sure about this, Dolson?" Thomas asked, crouching painfully yet again behind a tree as they prepared to part ways.

Dolson nodded and reached up to touch a non-existent hat before blinking in momentary confusion. They were all tired, and in poor condition to carry out their mission; Thomas wished they could have waited an extra night, but the risk of being discovered by the enemy in the meantime was too great. "Aye, sir," Dolson said, finally, grave-faced.

Thomas looked up at Aggie, crouching on one knee beside them, who grinned a yellowing grin. It was gone midnight now, the moon glowing white overhead amid a scattering of perfectly clear stars. A good night for sailing, Thomas thought, with all the hope he could gather in his heart. "Very well," he said, shaking both men by the hand. "Godspeed." The big Jamaican and the broad-shouldered seaman slipped away together into the forest, a most unlikely pair.

Pasco was by Thomas' side, and together they crept around to the south. They were so close to the camp that Thomas could hear voices, jeering, laughing and even a snatch of song, quickly silenced. Pasco did move remarkably silently, Thomas thought, more than he would have given him credit for, a week ago. Jim had walked along with him as they had travelled with Wickerham and the others, demonstrating where to land his feet and how to place them noiselessly. When they had parted about a half-mile from the camp, Jim had muttered private words in the boy's ear and Thomas had seen Pasco smile back, nervously. Then Jim had looked straight at Thomas. The bruising on his neck had faded to mottled yellow. There had been no words, no time for any more conversation, but Thomas wished there could have been. Somehow a look was not enough. Those eyes were burned into his mind now as they picked their way around to the shore, tensed and prepared at any moment to be leapt out upon.

This time Thomas had one of the loaded pistols, Dolson having taken another and Wickerham bestowing the last one on Cole, whose task would have to be to protect the admiral and Smythe while Jim fortified their position as best he could. Everyone else had at least one of the swords, except Pasco, as a long sword would only hamper him, small as he was. Instead he had the knife they had taken from Froggie tucked into the belt of his trousers.

Thomas was very aware of every sound that he made, every footstep, every broken twig, every leaf rustled by his passing. When they reached the shoreline it was a relief to step onto the sand, though it felt painfully exposed on all sides. At least here he felt better-oriented, having travelled along this stretch of beach once before. There were signs of men having gone to and fro, impressions in the sand, and there was even evidence of attempts at fishing; sharpened sticks and squares of net made of frayed canvas. "I can't hear anything," Pasco said, low, his face scrunched up as though he was straining. Thomas realised he was right; they had travelled too far from the camp.

He beckoned Pasco to follow him and they headed back into the forest, until they could see a fire burning up ahead, yellow flames flickering between the trees. The noise had died down, in favour of sleep, perhaps, but Aggie had assured them that there would still be men on watch. They had approached from an advantageous direction, anyway — they could see the stern end of both boats where they lay haphazardly with the keel sunk into the earth. Thomas realised sinkingly that Wickerham was right — they would never have been able to get one of the boats out through the trees without being caught and killed, even if they could have managed to move it with their limited number of hands. This did not however make him feel better about the current plan; they had chosen to approach during the night without counting on the size of the fire. The pirates it seemed were not altogether without skills of survival on land.

Together they ducked down behind a fallen tree. Thomas kept his head down, allowing Pasco with his dark hair and sharp eyes to look out while he focused on staying still and quiet, waiting for the signal.

It was not long in coming. Thomas' heart jumped out of his chest as Aggie roared into camp, waving his arms wildly and rousing all the sleeping men from where they lay on the ground around the blaze of warmth. "Where the fuck have ye been, Aggie?" Thomas heard one of them yell amid the chaos — whether it was Briggs or not he couldn't be sure.

"I been runnin'," Aggie panted, very convincingly. The pirates were all up and moving about; Thomas tugged Pasco down beside him until they were both practically flat on the ground, out of sight of any stray glance into the forest. "Dey still after me, dem navy men."

"Ye led them here?" There was a scramble as the men reached for their weapons and gathered. "Idiot!"

"Dere's not many of dem. Hurry, hurry, we can catch 'em."

"Steady," Thomas whispered in Pasco's ear, and the boy shifted his position, ready to rise, as the pirates streamed out of the camp brandishing swords and pistols. The ruse had worked. They could only hope Dolson would be able to outrun them. "Go," he hissed, and Pasco sprung up like a frog. "Watch your shadow in the fire," he added, using the din of the pirates' movements to mask his own voice. Pasco hopped easily over the tree and began creeping quickly towards the boat. Thomas could do nothing but wait with baited breath and his hand on the pistol in his belt. He wanted desperately to look, to watch the boy's progress, but he could not; there was no way to tell if men had been left to guard the supplies, and he could not risk increasing Pasco's danger. He could hear the boy moving across the forest floor, but then he was listening for it, and he could only hope any remaining pirates would be watching in the other direction, the way Aggie had come from.

He waited, heart pounding, listening to the yells and whoops of the men retreating to the north. Dolson should lead them as far as he could before circling his way back around and heading for the rendezvous — Aggie also, they hoped, would be able to get away from the main group when the pirates eventually split up to widen their search. Then it all depended on Thomas and

Pasco getting the flares safely away to be fired into the night, the eastern shore being the best place for a ship to land and the most likely way any legitimate vessel would be travelling, according to Wickerham. And that was if everything went according to plan. So far so good, but that didn't stop Thomas imagining the hundreds of things that could go wrong. A ship might not come. Or the pirates could simply find them and slaughter them all first. Or worse, if Briggs had anything to say about it.

After waiting for what seemed like an age he could no longer stand it, and he lifted his head just enough to see clear to the boats. A dark shape was picking its way back towards him, staying low, and when it got closer he could just make out the oblong box clutched to Pasco's chest. The boy's face, just visible in the distant firelight, was flush with triumph. Thomas helped him over the tree and they hurried back through the remaining vegetation to the shoreline. "Well done," he whispered, and they balanced the box between them by the rope handles. It wasn't heavy, but it was long and unwieldy for a child to carry alone. They set off, weaving a little side to side as they tried to avoid the shifting areas of dry sand. No sign yet of any of the others.

Pasco started to lag a little, his short legs unable to keep up with Thomas' stride. Thomas took the box from him and balanced it on his shoulder as they kept on. "Not far now," he panted, ushering the boy to go ahead. "Keep an eye for Jim."

Somewhere behind them a shot rang out. Pasco gasped and stumbled, and Thomas found himself trying to duck instinctively, swaying under the weight of the flares. Shouts were being raised in the forest not far away. And suddenly Jim was there, waving them towards him, recognisable in the dark only by his lean stature. "What happened?" he asked, breathless and wide-eyed, looking over their shoulders as though he might be able to see.

"I don't know." Thomas' heart twisted in his chest. He thought of Dolson and his mouth went dry. "Take Pasco and the flares to the rendezvous. If I don't join you in time, tell the admiral to go without me." He lifted the box off his shoulder and passed it bodily to Jim, who just managed to adjust to its weight before it hit the ground.

"You can't go back there alone," Jim hissed. "You'll be killed."

"If Dolson is hurt, I can't leave him," Thomas insisted. "I've already lost enough men. I won't lose more, on my life."

"Sir —" Pasco gasped, protesting, and Jim looked likely to argue also.

"I have a responsibility, damn you," Thomas hissed at him, practically shoving Pasco forward. "Take the boy and go. Go!"

Jim's face was hard, but he grabbed Pasco by the shirt sleeve and dragged him onward in the night. Thomas turned and dove into the interior, without looking back.

$$— 22 —$$

He didn't know where he was going, but he headed in the direction he thought he had heard the shot. He drew his own pistol and held it loosely in one hand, its loaded weight the barest comfort. Shapes were converging around him as he ran, men yelling as they gathered, but he just kept running; hiding now would be more conspicuous than another faceless figure moving quickly in the dark.

One of the rushing pirates all but crashed into him as they converged; acting purely on instinct Thomas lashed out with the pistol butt and tried to tackle the man to the ground. The resulting return blow sent his head snapping back and left his ears ringing, but he managed to keep his grip with one hand as he hammered away with the other, bashing his opponent about the head until he went still. Gasping, his hand bloody with spray, he stripped the pirate of his ragged shirt and tugged it over his own head, swallowing hard to keep from gagging at the smell; he also tore off the headscarf that was so filthy it was practically black and swiftly covered his hair before scrambling onwards.

"You see any others, Aggie?" he heard a voice call up ahead. Perhaps a dozen men were gathered around as Thomas approached, keeping his head down. Fortunately their attention was all directed elsewhere, and as he crept up between them he saw their target. Ice ran down his spine. Dolson was kneeling at Briggs' feet, looking dazed, with blood flowing from a deep wound above his eye, and Briggs' had his pistol to the seaman's head.

"Keep 'im alive," Aggie was saying, from Briggs' other side. "Maybe 'e lead us to de others."

Keeping back and out of Briggs' direct line of sight, Thomas tried to assess the group. These he judged were perhaps all of the pirates remaining; he could see Yellow-Eyes, Big-Ears, and Gappy among them, Gappy still sporting Thomas' ruined coat. The numbers seemed about right, particularly when Yellow-Eyes called out, "Nah, 'e just killed Willy, an' Lawson an' Smithy too, most likely. I on'y seen one other one. Kill 'im now and there's on'y that one left."

"Don't forget the two liddle ones what killed Bob an' Froggie," one of the others protested in a high, nervous voice. "They must'a had help, we dunno how many more is out there. They could be tryin' to pick us off one by one."

"Fah," Gappy spat thickly onto the earth. "Kill 'im now and we'll go after the rest, all of 'em. They can't be far. We must outnumber 'em or they would've attacked us in force, right Briggsy?"

Thomas realised now how truly mad his gambit had been. There was little he could do now without simply ensuring his own death right alongside of Dolson, even if he could send one or optimistically two right to hell right ahead of him. He stepped back into the shadows, hoping he would not be seen until he could formulate a plan that might go some way to giving Jim and the others more time.

Briggs seemed hesitant, perhaps unwilling to make a decision that went against the majority of his ever-dwindling force. Mutters of approval and disagreement alike were going around the group, generally unsatisfied.

"I can take care of it," Aggie put in, stepping forward and gripping Dolson by the shoulder with his large hand. "I take 'im out to da sea an' drown 'im, no point in wastin' da shot, eh? Den we all go back to camp, look for 'em in da mornin'.'"

Thomas let out a breath. Briggs, frowning a little, half-lowered the pistol.

"I say we go after 'em, now." Big Ears, the one Jim had called Horace, stepped forward. He was armed only with a knife — not one of Briggs' allies, perhaps, but one of the alternative faction that Jim had guessed would be the architect of any mutiny. "Wassa matter, Aggie? You were all for chasin' after 'em a minute ago. Now you want us all to go back? Whose side are you on?"

"Aye, we can't trust 'im no more," Yellow-Eyes put in, snarling. "E's not one o' us, anyway — he's friends wit' the boy, the traitor —"

"Aye, so you keep tellin' us," Gappy said dismissively, rolling his eyes. "Dat one's too stoopid to be a traitor, 'e dunno who's friend or foe."

"'E's a traitor, and *this* one's in league widdim," argued Yellow-Eyes, levelling his stolen sword in Aggie's direction. "I say we do away widdim an' all. One less giant mouth to feed."

Aggie drew himself up, hugely, as though daring him to make a move; some of the pirates closest to him stepped rather pointedly back as he dwarfed them all easily.

"Aye!" Thomas' heart leapt into his throat as a familiar voice rang out from somewhere in the forest. Too familiar. "I don't wanna be murdered in the night; I wanna live long enough to get off this damn island. We gotta find all of 'em." Thomas looked about wildly, but saw nothing but trees, darkness, and ragged indiscernible shapes.

"If you think we're ever gettin' off this damn island you're a bloody fool," Horace spat into the darkness. More murmurs went around, louder, discomforted.

"Briggsy'll get us off the island!" called the same voice. "Won't ye, Cap'n?" Thomas could see Briggs looking around too, put on guard by a voice he didn't recognise. The pistol rose again to press against Dolson's temples, and the seaman closed his eyes as though in prayer.

"Who is that?" Yellow-Eyes demanded, one jaundiced hand raising a sword towards the dark forest ahead of him. "Who goes there?"

"Tell 'em, Cap'n." The voice seemed to come from a new direction, causing all the men to whirl round with weapons raised. "Tell 'em how you're gonna save us."

"Show yerself!" Briggs barked, the muzzle of his pistol forcing Dolson's head to one side. "Come out, or I'll 'ave 'im eatin' 'is own brains!"

Don't, Thomas begged silently. *They'll kill poor Dolson either way. Go now, get free. Don't be a fool.*

There was the shifting of leaves, and Jim stepped openly out of the shadows and into the circle of men. The ruined shirt hung off his shoulders, the red scar across his chest showing through. He had no sword and no gun. Thomas, despairing, reached for his pistol, but he only had one shot and there were too many men. "Horace is right," Jim said, into the stunned silence.

"You!" Yellow-Eyes exclaimed, recovering long enough to wheel around, waving his sword in Jim's direction "There, didn' I tell ye all?"

"The blighter can talk!" Gappy gasped, and pointed as though admiring a particularly exotic creature in a menagerie. "Did ye 'ear 'im? Briggsy, did you 'ear?"

Briggs had not moved; he stood still and staring grimly over Dolson's kneeling form, his bad arm still strapped against his chest. Thomas remembered what Aggie had said about him breaking his wrist to get out of the chains in the brig. A man who would do something like that... what else would he do? "Been lookin' for ye, maggot," Briggs snarled, keeping the gun steady. "Thought ye knew better than to 'ide from me." He made a slight motion with his head, and Yellow-Eyes stepped forward. Thomas' body lurched of its own accord — what he thought he would do he had no notion — but before he could move any further, Horace leapt across the sand and brought his own blade to lie against Briggs' neck, halting Yellow-Eyes in his tracks. "One more move and the Cap'n dies," he snapped, glaring around at the rest of the pirates as weapons bristled all around. "Let the boy tell ye all how I'm right. I wanna hear this."

When Jim looked at Briggs, Thomas saw in his expression something he had not yet seen in his pirate's face. He wondered if he imagined it, or the starlight was playing tricks on him, or if the pure hatred in Jim's eyes had turned them so much darker blue. Multiple pistols and swords were pointed at him, but he took no notice, showed no fear, except perhaps for a slight trembling in his fisted hands. "I've known your Captain here since I was a boy," he announced in a loud voice, without breaking Briggs' gaze. "I know him well. He has no intention of getting any of you off the island."

"Lying cunt!!" Yellow-Eyes roared, knuckles whitening on his sword hilt.

"How do you think he'll do it?" Jim asked, still glaring past him into Briggs' face. "He knows any ship that chances past will either leave you marooned or carry you all to execution. All the bodies are still rotting on the southern shore. King's men."

The pirates looked around at each other. One or two of them lowered their swords by just a fraction.

"Ah, ye ain't listenin' to this lyin' shitstain?" Briggs' lips curled up into a sneer and he hawked up spit, but could not let it fly with Horace's blade so dangerously close to his throat. "Listen' to 'im. Talkin' like a King's man isself, playin' mad. Spyin' on us."

"All the better to know you, Osham." Jim smirked, eyes burning, and Thomas felt a wild rush of pride caught up in fear for him all at once.

"The boy's right!" one of the other pirates called out, dropping his sword away from Jim and turning on Briggs. "No ship's ever comin' for us. I knew we should'a taken the boats. I druther die at sea than wastin 'away on this rock."

"Ye won't last a day," Briggs said sharply, turning his head heedlessly of the sharp blade at his throat, so that it left a thin red line just under his bristling chin. The sight of him scowling blackly at his own men with blood trickling down his throat was enough to send a shiver of horror down Thomas' spine.

"Then what's the plan?" Yellow-Eyes suddenly demanded, his resolve faltering. "Ye promised us a ship, Cap'n."

Briggs snarled. "What good's a ship ever done any o' you?" he demanded, glaring around at what remained of his crew. "More fuckin' blue coats. More fuckin' merchantman thinkin' they own the waters. Stick wiv me and we'll live like kings."

"Eatin' coconuts, drinkin' seawater and fuckin' whores made of sand?" Yellow-Eyes howled. "Kings of one big rock and a pile o' bones?"

"He's no Cap'n of ours," Horace crowed. "He killed one o' our own for no more'n givin' 'im lip. Podunk was a good'n, but Briggs is an evil son of a whore."

"No better'n any o' you fuckin' flotsam!" Briggs roared. Without warning he ripped his bad arm out of its binding and elbowed Horace in the face, knocking him back. Freed, he rounded back on Jim, the pistol whirling around to point directly between the boy's eyes. Behind him, Dolson sagged to the ground. "You can talk now, eh, ye blue-eyed cockroach." Briggs held steady as the men surrounding him began to eye each other with fear and suspicion. "You'll talk a lot more afore I'm done wit' ye."

"I'm not afraid of you," Jim said, low.

"Not afraid of me, eh?" Briggs leered. "Ye should be. Oh, ye should be. Ye'll die slow. I'll cut off yer fancy mouth and pluck out yer eyes an' eat 'em, an' I'll keep ye on a leash like a fuckin' dog. Then I'll fuck ye to death. Hear me, *maggot?*" The pirate's hand was dangerously still, but the rest of him practically shook with mad rage. "I'll rip ye in 'alf wiv my cock if it takes me *years*."

Thomas howled and ran. Possessed by the devil, with a terrible noise roaring in both his ears, he was suddenly on Briggs, shoving the pistol aside and knocking him down. The man cried out in pain as his broken wrist hit the ground, trying to bring the gun back around to bear. Thomas slammed the butt of his own pistol into the pirate's face, slamming him back, but before he could so much as take aim, a solid grip had him around the arm, dragging him away.

Around him it was sudden chaos in the dark. Even Briggs' men had hesitated to go to their Captain's rescue, and that moment's doubt had been enough for the mutinous faction to make their move. Swords clashed and men yelled, swore and screamed all around as all-out battle broke out among the pirates. "Jim!" Thomas gasped, looking around, but it was Aggie who had pulled him back, sweat dripping down his face. Dolson was struggling nearby to get to his feet, clutching the egg-sized lump on his head. Thomas looked around one more time for Jim, but through the darkness and the tumult it was impossible to make out any faces. Aggie ran into the fray without another word, and Thomas could only hope he was gone to find his young friend.

"I'm sorry sir," Dolson murmured in a dazed voice as Thomas helped him up. He only had a second to steady the seaman before he was forced to draw his sword and turn towards a skinny bearded pirate who was charging towards him with blade raised. As he fought the man back, his weary arms straining with the effort, he considered his chances of surviving the next ten minutes were slim indeed.

"For the King!" he bellowed, and cut the pirate down, blood spurting across his face. "Run man, if you can," he ordered Dolson over his shoulder. "We can't be far away from the rendezvous — run east and yell to Cole to set off the damn flares. We'll hold them off as long as we can."

He looked back to where he had left Briggs, but the man had scrambled up and was facing Horace and Yellow-Eyes together, the jaundiced pirate apparently having changed his allegiance. The two men came at Briggs from either side with Horace already squinting badly out of one black eye. Briggs levelled his pistol, but it was either a bluff or he was unwilling to waste his only shot. Thomas lost sight of him then as the melee shifted, and suddenly Gappy came launching himself directly at Thomas, sword raised, blue coat flapping. Thomas ducked the first blow and staggered back, trying to make room for his own pass while struggling to draw his pistol one-handed. The filthy cap fell off his head, revealing his mop of mud-stained golden hair.

Gappy's eyes widened in recognition. "It's you," he snarled, waving the sword so wildly that it was quite impossible to predict its trajectory. "Call yerself a Cap'n? Die, ye pompous navy cunt!" Thomas twisted his body away from the onslaught, but he was unable to avoid the tip of the blade as it cut across his shoulder.

"That coat doesn't fit you well at all," he shot back, gritting his teeth against the pain and catching the next blow on the guard of his sword where it met the hilt. "You could sell those silver buttons, though, if you liked, but I should expect a commission, since I paid for them."

Gappy glowered, leaning all his weight onto the sword so that Thomas' hand was forced back onto his own chest. There was a large black space in the front of the pirate's row of teeth where one or even two had been knocked out, and his breath at this range was abominable. Thomas knew he was stronger but the angle was bad, and it was all he could do to keep the crossed blades from cutting his throat. "Finders keepers," the man leered at him, lips twisting into a terrible grin.

Thomas saw his opportunity in a split second. He kicked out sharply and his boot contacted hard and painfully with the bone on the inside of Gappy's ankle. The pirate howled in pain and lost his grip; Thomas thrust his head forward into the man's temple. It felt as though his forehead had been split open, and he saw stars, but the pressure on his chest eased enough that he could shove the man back with his elbows, giving him enough room to stab the pirate in the heart. The blow was not quite good — he felt the blade glance off the edge of a rib — but Gappy gasped and went slowly to his knees, blood pouring from the wound and staining the blue coat brown. "You can keep it," Thomas panted, before struggling back to his feet and staggering away, leaving the man to die in his own time. His shoulder ached badly, feeling more like a fracture than a flesh wound. Blood ran down his arm through the sleeve of his shirt; he could feel it oozing between his fingers.

He almost tripped over another thick root, dizzy from the self-inflicted blow to his head, but suddenly Jim was there, hauling him back up by his good arm. "How are you not dead?" Thomas muttered, furiously relieved, as he was drawn away from the fight and into the forest.

"I'm fast," Jim said shortly. "You should go while they're all killing each other."

"What about you?"

"Aggie," was all Jim said. Looking over his shoulder, Thomas saw the big black man still in the midst of the battle, bleeding from a dozen wounds as he fought off blades with his bare hands. There were at least three men on him, and the only way through to him was past a half-dozen men with swords.

"You can't —"

Suddenly there was an explosion of light and sound overhead — bright red sparks hot against the blackness of the sky. The pirates ducked and yelled, forgetting their murderous urges long enough to look up at the lights dissipating into a red glow.

"You!"

Thomas twisted his head around so fast it was painful. Briggs was tugging his sword out of Horace's limp body, dripping blood, and coming straight for them — which of them he wanted to kill first, it was hard to tell. Yellow-Eyes was already lying in an ugly heap.

"Go," Thomas told Jim, low. "Go… I'll catch up to you." There was no way he could run at any kind of speed, but Jim might have a chance — *would* have a chance, if Thomas could slow Briggs down… But Jim did not go, like a fool, he curled his fingers into Thomas' shirt sleeve with a vice-like grip and tugged at him, trying to make him run.

Aggie had seen what was happening; he pushed his way through the crowd, still bleeding, and launched himself at Briggs with a roar. Briggs whirled, saw his danger just in time. He hoisted his pistol and fired. Aggie's head snapped back and he collapsed in a dead heap on the sand.

"No!" The strangled shout ripped from Jim's throat, and he let go of Thomas' sleeve. His eyes were bright with tears. Briggs was still coming, his face a mask of fury.

"C'mere you play-actin' liddle *maggot*," Briggs roared. He dropped the useless pistol and swapped his sword back to his good hand.

"Jim, go," Thomas breathed, trying once again to pull out his own pistol in a hand slippery with blood. "Go!" The gun came suddenly out of his belt unexpectedly sharply, and slipped out of his fingers onto the ground. Before he could reach for it Jim lunged into Briggs' path as he came within striking distance. Without thinking, Thomas gathered all his remaining strength and thrust him aside, sending him sprawling.

Briggs collided with Thomas instead. The pirate's sword went in under Thomas' ribcage, and he was sure he felt every inch of it as it sliced all the way through and came out through the back of his shirt. Briggs was so close that he could see every pore on the man's furious, hideous face, every speck of dirt. There was strangely no pain. Briggs smiled hideously.

Then there was a sound like a cannon, so close that Thomas felt the force of it in his head, and he wondered vaguely whether he had been bludgeoned. Briggs' eyes bulged, and blood spurted from between his lips. His hand dropped away from the sword and he fell to one side, spluttering and choking. Behind him, Jim was standing and holding Thomas' pistol, the barrel still smoking.

Jim threw the gun aside. He tried to catch Thomas before he could fall, but the dead weight was too much for him and they both went down in a pile together. Overhead came another explosion, high, high above them, another shower of sparks going up. Thomas felt very cold, all of a sudden. The hilt of the sword still emerged from his chest, and he wondered in confusion if it was the same sword Briggs had stolen from Rogers and used to kill the poor man in turn.

Jim was holding him, heedless of the danger to his hands from the blade and looking around wildly for something to stop the bleeding. "Don't worry," Thomas managed. Was he imagining it or did his own voice sound somehow thick, laboured?

"Look at me," Jim demanded, and reached to lift up Thomas' chin. His blue eyes were bright and wet with tears. "Just keep looking at me, Thomas."

"Charlie," Thomas muttered, looking up at him. "You can call me Charlie." Another shot rang out then, right over their heads — close, too close. He lifted a shaking hand and tried to push Jim away, but he seemed to have no strength in any of his limbs. He reached instead for his pocket, pulling out the gold St Laurence medal. "Go. Get out of here. Go home. Jim."

But Jim was ignoring him, staring away, and then he yelled and waved with one bloody hand. Footsteps were hurrying towards them from the forest, not from the battle at all. Was that young Cole's voice, shouting? "Fetch Mr Smythe," Jim yelled, and Thomas tried to tell him no, that they should save themselves, but all he seemed to be able to do was cough blood.

"God almighty." That was Dolson's voice. And that was all their pistols gone now, Thomas thought absurdly. All three shots. He couldn't tell if Cole's shot had hit its mark. He hoped so, for the boy's sake.

"Charlie, look at me," Jim said again, and Thomas forced his eyes back onto his pirate's face. He would be quite happy, he thought, if those bright blue eyes were the last thing he ever saw. And there would be no prison, he realised. No court-martial, no answering to the admiralty. No more guilt for any of the things he had done. "Diego's gone for the surgeon," Jim was saying. "Just keep on looking at me."

"You... should run," Thomas managed. He tried to press the medal into Jim's stubbornly resisting hand. His chest felt heavy, and he was bone-achingly tired. He just wanted to close his eyes. "Before they..."

"They're all gone, Charlie," Jim said, low, his voice breaking a little. "All of them. They fought each other to the death."

Oh, Thomas thought, realising that the echoing silence all around was not just in his head. *That's all right then.*

Jim touched his lips with bloody fingers, and one of his tears landed on Thomas' face. "Don't go," he whispered. "Please. I can't leave you here."

Sparks flew across the sky for a third time, and for a moment Thomas imagined he was no longer looking up, but staring down into the depths of the deep, black sea, lit by the reflections of swirling red stars. He closed his eyes. "Go home, Jim," he whispered back. "Go home."

— 23 —

It was a modest house on a small country estate, at the end of a long and winding gravel road; three stories with an outhouse and a small stables. A groom appeared almost as soon as Thomas had ridden into view, and took his horse politely in hand, leaving him to ascend the steps alone and lift the knocker.

A fresh-faced footman opened the door and, after taking his name, ushered him inside. The hallway was only dimly lit, the windows having been covered with gauze curtains to keep out the summer sun, and despite the surfaces being well-dusted and the floor well-swept, there was an eerie, un-lived-in feel to the place that reminded Thomas rather unhealthily of his own house.

"Mr Thomas?"

He turned and bowed politely to the woman descending the main stair. She was quite small, and frail-looking, but she descended in a rush towards him nevertheless and took his face in both her hands. "Oh, and I have never been so pleased to meet anyone all my life," she exclaimed, quite overcome, and he was forced to endure her folding him in her thin arms in a most intimate way, so that even the footman looked rather shocked at it.

"Very pleased to meet you as well, Mrs Oliver," he said, without knowing what else to do, and she brushed his formality aside with a wave of her hand.

"No, no, none of that. You shall call me Isabelle. Carlson, do go and fetch James, will you?" she told the footman, taking Thomas' arm and leading him most enthusiastically into the dining room. "I hope you won't mind a private dinner with no ladies to make up the numbers," she said. "I would have invited some guests, but we have had so many visitors all at once, I am afraid my cook and all the maids have been overwhelmed, and I may very well lose some of them to better employment if I press them further."

"Oh, quite all right," Thomas said, with private relief. He had been dreading having to spend the evening entertaining whichever young lady was seated with him, knowing full well that she would be evaluating him for his prospects. "But I am rather dusty after my journey; perhaps I should change."

"Not at all," Isabelle said, once again waving aside his protests as they came to stand at the head of the table, where three simple places had been laid. "No, I am far too eager to sit with you and give you my thanks — all my thanks," she added, tears actually beading in her eyes as she looked at him. "James has told me so little, but he has made it quite clear that it was you who finally saved him from those monsters. After ten years… sir, I can never thank you enough even if I gave you all that is mine to give."

"There is no need for that, Madam, I assure you," Thomas muttered. "I only —" He stopped, suddenly, distracted by movement in the corner of his eye, and looked up over her shoulder.

The young man standing in the doorway had dark hair cut short, too short for a gentleman, though it had already started to grow again into natural waves around his ears. His skin was still faintly tanned, and he wore a formal dress coat and neckcloth, stockings, breeches with buckles around the knees, and buckled shoes. Even disguised by all the clothing he looked better fleshed, the picture of a healthy country lad. Fed properly, he was even broader than Thomas himself. Thomas might not have recognised him at all if it weren't for the eyes, which were made even brighter by a dark bruising of tiredness around them, and the very faint hint of a thin scar across one cheek.

He realised too late that his own mouth was hanging open, and shut it quickly. "Mr Oliver," he said, the name coming strange and unwelcome to his lips.

The young man nodded, without taking his eyes away from him. "Lieutenant Thomas."

Thomas coughed to clear his throat. "Mr Thomas," he corrected, heat colouring his face. "That is — Charles. Please."

"Ah." Jim gazed at him, and Thomas found himself wishing he would look away, to give him a chance to catch his breath. "Yes... we heard you had been dismissed from the service. I am sorry."

"Ridiculous goings-on," Isabelle exclaimed. "I have read all about the investigation in the paper, but I cannot imagine what their lordships must be thinking. They should have given you a medal and an admiral's flag before they made such an outlandish decision!"

Thomas couldn't help smiling at this piece of absurdity, for all Mrs Oliver seemed to take the notion quite seriously.

"I don't take it to heart, I promise you," he said. And found oddly that he meant it, though it had been a difficult blow to bear, at the time. Admiral Wickerham had done what was in his power, though the rest of the admiralty would have blamed the man's own injuries on Thomas too, if they could. The old man would certainly never set sail on a navy ship again, and his loss to them was felt almost as keenly as all the lives of the rest of the crew, and the *HMS Courage* herself — these losses they had done their best to heap at Thomas' door, since no one else was left to blame. Still, no one could say what he should have done differently.

Thomas knew that he was lucky to have been spared the noose, and he had Wickerham to thank, at least, for his life. Even Mr Smythe had stood up and spoken on his behalf, though Thomas suspected that this favour had more to do with the surgeon not wanting to waste the six months he had spent nursing his patient back to health, aboard ship.

They had been picked up that self-same morning of the pirates' battle by a passing merchantman. Fortunate for Thomas, for he almost certainly would have died otherwise, and the ship had — even more fortunately — an experienced surgeon of its own with a well-equipped hospital. The ship had waited only long enough for the crew to bury the bodies of Gower, Bill Blake, and the rest of the men of the HMS *Courage* who had been left on the southern shore, and also poor Agwe, at Wickerham's insistence. Then, they started a course back to England.

That time seemed to Thomas little more than a blur of pain and illness and infection, drugged into insensibility on a daily basis by so much cheap brandy he could no longer look at the stuff without his stomach turning on him. Dolson had to be treated for his injuries also, but had risen from his bed after only a week or two, while Thomas had been resigned to it for almost the entire stretch of their journey home. He had not even had the pleasure of much company, since Wickerham, given a seperate cabin for his own recovery, had made sure to give Pasco and Cole and even Jim so much work to do that they had little time to spare. Jim had also been sequestered with the admiral for several days writing letters of introduction and explanation to be sent upon their arrival. Thomas had been agitated by this news, but Wickerham, on one of his sparing visits, had assured him that no one would make any charge against his young pirate. The admiral planned to present him as a former prisoner aboard the *Queen of Heaven* who had been of invaluable assistance to the navy. Only then had Thomas dared to rest.

He had seen next to nothing of Jim himself, and they had been separated almost as soon as they had arrived in London — Thomas ushered along to Whitehall with Wickerham, and Jim to lodgings where he would await answers to his letters. When the admiralty's hearing was over, Thomas went home, only to find his family's estate cold, empty and mostly neglected by its servants.

"It has been some time since I was at leisure to do as I liked, though it will take some getting used to," he said now, dragging himself back into the present. They all took their places at the table as the first course was served, a petite dish of shaved fish accompanied by a fine Riesling. "I have taken up painting, and while I don't consider myself by any means a Michelangelo, I have already received a handful of commissions."

"Oh, you simply must do James," Isabelle insisted immediately, before the wine had even been poured. Thomas was glad he had not yet put food or drink to his mouth, and had to force himself not to meet Jim's eyes. Neither of them could know, of course, that he had already filled one sketchbook with likenesses of her son, from memory, and had started another. "I have been meaning to get it done for weeks," Isabelle went on, "we have only been waiting for him to gain enough weight —"

"Mother," Jim protested in a soft voice, a faint, embarrassed smile on his face. Thomas hid his own smile behind his fork, and after he had assured Mrs Oliver that he would do the portrait, and she had insisted on offering him double what it should really be worth, they managed to turn the conversation back to less emotional subjects, such as the pleasantness of Thomas' ride to the house, the long history of the estate, and Jim's plans for the future.

"James would like to go to London," Isabelle said despairingly. "Though I cannot imagine why, and of course I shall have to go with him or I shall simply die of worry. If only I can get him married as soon as possible, so I can die knowing he is well looked-after."

"Mother," Jim sighed. "You mustn't say such things."

"We will find you a nice young girl to settle down with, and you will thank me," his mother said, ignoring him. "Your father married me at your age, and he felt all the better for knowing his legacy was intact, when he next went off to sea. Why, you must be glad to have the opportunity now yourself, Mr Thomas," she added, rounding on him and forcing him to swallow his last bite of plum duff a little too quickly, so that he had to cough to clear it out of his throat.

"I had not much thought about it," he said, and regretted it immediately when she promised to put together a list of enterprising young women who might suit a young man of his standing and talents, and to put together a proper dinner party so that he might meet some of them.

After the dessert was finished, Jim offered to give Thomas a tour of the grounds. Thomas was afraid for a moment that Mrs Oliver might insist on going with them, but Jim quickly added, "We shall ride, I think — it will be only be light for an hour or so yet, and we can go all the way around the estate, that way," and his mother was forced to beg leave since, Thomas had to assume, her frailty prevented her from riding all but the most sedate of horses on the easiest of terrains.

"You boys will be galloping about all down the banks, I expect," she chided, kissing Jim's cheek and calling for the footman to bring him his riding trousers and boots. "You will stay tonight, Mr Thomas? Of course you will. I refuse to take no for an answer."

Thomas was obliged to accept. He bowed over Mrs Oliver's hand, and waited until they had been left alone to walk the short distance to the stable before turning to Jim and asking, "but can you ride?"

"I'm learning," Jim said flatly. "Or re-learning, I suppose. It's more uncomfortable than I remember."

"The difference between being a boy and a man," Thomas said, without really thinking, and when Jim caught his eyes with a raised eyebrow he flushed and looked away.

"We needn't really ride, anyway," Jim said finally. "I only said that so that mother would stay behind. She means well, you know, but she is rather afraid to let me out of her sight for a minute or two."

"I suppose she cannot be blamed for an abundance of caution," Thomas pointed out.

"No, not entirely, I suppose. But it is… nice, to be alone, sometimes. I am after all a grown man."

"Ah. Ought I leave?" Thomas asked, smiling.

"That isn't what I meant."

"I know." They had stopped by the side of the stable. There was no sound from inside; presumably the groom had gone to his own dinner. "Did you recognise her?" Thomas asked after a moment. "When you first saw her again, I mean."

"Oh, yes." Jim looked over Thomas' shoulder, a far-away look in his startling blue eyes. "I'm remembering a lot more, now. Strange how just being here brings it all back. Sometimes it feels like… like the islands were really the dream, and this is what's real."

"Can't they both be real?" Thomas asked.

Jim didn't say anything for a while, leaning against the brick wall that formed the back and sides of the stable building. If anything it put Thomas more at his ease; silent Jim he was used to, even if he could still not quite equate the wild, rake-thin island boy with this neatly-dressed, well-built country aristocrat. "Your mother said you had seen a lot of visitors," he said finally. "I did see the story about your resurrection in the paper."

"Oh, that was nothing," Jim sighed and reached up to push aside a lock of hair that had fallen into his eyes, as it was not yet long enough to pull back to be tied. "It is all our family come out of the woodwork; some I am sure are not even related by blood. But I suppose they all were counting on being gifted a portion of the estate when my mother died, and they want to make sure I was not…"

"A charlatan?" Thomas suggested.

"Well yes, I suppose," Jim sighed. "Or otherwise so badly damaged that I cannot be trusted with my own inheritance. One of them was of the opinion that I should be committed, on account of having been reduced to *the understanding of an unlettered savage.*"

Thomas' blood boiled in his veins. "He actually said so, to your face?" he exclaimed, appalled.

"I don't think he thought I would understand," Jim shrugged, smirking. "I was playing mad-Jim. It had got him very irritated, for some reason."

"Well," Thomas spluttered, trying to get a hold of the sudden bout of rage. "That *is* infuriating, in my personal experience, but that is still no excuse for such an ignorant insult. He should count himself fortunate I was not there, or he would have found himself twenty paces away from the end of my pistol —"

Jim kissed him.

It was not the desperate, furious crashing of mouths that had been back in the forest, the kiss that he sometimes dreamed about, that woke him up in a sweat even on cold nights. It was soft, uncertain, but it still sent a bolt of lightning down his spine all the same. It was so exposed, so open out here where anyone could see them, and the thrill of it made him shudder.

"Jim," he breathed, his back flush against the stable wall, Jim's weight holding him there. "I mean… James…"

"You can call me Jim." He smiled. "Someone has to remind me who I really am, occasionally."

Thomas found himself shaken by the casual tone. He glanced quickly over Jim's shoulder, but all was quiet between them and the house. "Tell me you understand how dangerous this is," he said, looking back to Jim with his heart in his throat. "It's illegal. You could be put to death."

Jim made a face. "Not you, too. Of course I understand. I don't care."

Thomas swallowed. "But I thought… when you didn't write…"

"I didn't know where to write to. Did you think I'd forgotten? I had to petition Admiral Wickerham for your address in the end."

Thomas flushed. "But… I would understand if you had… doubts, regrets… I would never have even mentioned it again, if you hadn't…"

"Why would I have regrets? You think I want mother to marry me off to some harp-playing socialite?"

Thomas shook his head. "You realise she will do that regardless. You have no excuses for not marrying."

"She can't force me. Could you imagine it? Awful for me, but for the poor girl too. Besides, no one would want me for their daughter, would they? You should read what they say about me in the society magazines."

"Jim..." Thomas stared at him, helplessly. He didn't know why he was so insistent on making arguments for his own damnation, but he had woken with a jolt more than once since the shipwreck with Bill Blake's dying words echoing in his ears. Jim was older than him by several months, but he had been apart from society these last ten years and could not be expected to know what he was entering into by his unspoken suggestion, by that kiss, by the way he was still standing close, too close, with his hand tucked behind the lapel of Thomas' coat. And yet in that moment Thomas could not bring himself to protest as harshly as he knew he ought.

"Come with me," Jim said.

$$— 24 —$$

There was a fence lining the eastern side of the estate, with a gate at the far end and a stile which Jim hopped easily. Thomas grunted a little as he clambered over with very little grace, thinking that he might have preferred to walk a little further and go through the gate instead. He shook his head when Jim offered his hand and stepped down himself, ignoring the twinge of pain down his side. Even with all Mr Smythe and the merchant ship's surgeon could do, he was going to feel the effects of the injury for the rest of his life.

Jim led him perhaps half a mile into the forest, up the side of a gently sloping hill. Here a natural hollow between the trees had been dug out a little more and lined with dead leaves. When Jim ushered him to sit, helping him down despite his protests, Thomas looked out between the trees at the western sun just beginning to lower behind the distant house, orange light tinging around the roofs. The view was no island sunset, but it still caught Thomas' breath in his throat.

"Pretty, isn't it."

"Beautiful," Thomas agreed. There was silence for a while.

"Charlie?"

Thomas smiled, unable to help showing on his face the warmth he felt to hear that name. Now that Bill was gone, no one else was left who knew him enough to call him so. "Yes?"

"May we speak plainly?"

Thomas raised an eyebrow. "I am not altogether sure I can be capable of it, but if you wish, I will try."

He looked over and caught Jim rolling his eyes. "You asked me once about the girls on Tortuga," Jim said after a moment, making Thomas' heart leap. "I wasn't lying when I said I had no interest. I... prefer men. I don't know why," he added, a flicker of consternation going across his face. "Maybe because..."

"No," Thomas shook his head. Plain talking be damned, he knew precisely what Jim was thinking. "It's not that. It wasn't *done* to you. Some men just are, no matter what anyone might say." He tried to remember what Bill had told him, years ago. An unreliable source, perhaps, but Thomas had spent enough time at sea among men of all kinds to know what was true. "Some men are tall, or short, or have red hair," he began. "Some like oysters, and some can't stand the taste. Some men bed other men out of necessity, but some number of them simply have no other affinity. They are just so."

Jim considered this, the golden light of the setting sun bathing his face. "And you are one of them?" he asked finally.

Thomas' freckles flushed, his manners catching on the sharp edge of his truth. "Jim..."

"Tell me."

Thomas blew air from his nostrils, grimacing, and forced it out. "Very well, yes... I am. I have... desire only for other men." It was strange to say so aloud.

Jim nodded. "I thought so," he said, satisfied. "Since that night on the island. You wanted more."

"*Jim* — "

"You still want more. I could feel it when I kissed you."

Thomas buried his face in his hands. "God forgive me."

Jim snorted, very ungentleman-like. "Then what holds you back?"

Thomas' mouth was dry. He didn't dare look up, to meet Jim's eyes. Those damn eyes could see right through him. "It's too late for me," he said instead, low. "I will be content to live off my family's estate for the rest of my life, with no need to save anything for the children I shall never have. There is still a chance for *you*. If not for marriage, then a chance at... some kind of life, at least a proper career..."

"I don't want a *proper career*." Jim's eyes flashed. "I just want you."

All the blood in Thomas' body rushed towards his groin, or at least so it felt. He did not pull away as Jim reached for him, dragged him once more into a kiss. Now he was properly reminded of the moment under the overhang, after their mad dash down the cliff. Jim's mouth was just as hot, just as demanding. Despite the extra layers of clothes they wore, he imagined himself back on the island, his shirt hanging open and his hair gone wild, Jim in nothing but filthy, mud-spattered breeches. His pirate. The son of a Captain, who had walked right up to the gates of hell only to be spat back out again. Without him, who was to say where Thomas would be now, or Wickerham, or little Pasco? A pile of bones left in the sand, most likely. He deserved better.

Jim reached for Thomas' neckcloth and untied it one-handed with a flash of his nimble fingers. Thomas groaned into Jim's mouth as that same hand pushed the collar of his shirt aside and danced along his jaw.

"What do *you* want?" Jim asked, close against his lips.

"Jim," Thomas breathed, bumps rising along both his arms as Jim pushed his coat back from his shoulders. He knew perfectly well what he wanted, *had* wanted since that first night on the island, but couldn't bear to say it aloud. "You… you're certain?"

"I never lied to you," Jim murmured, making Thomas flush again, but this time with guilt. The coat slid off into the leaves. "Why would I start now?" Jim's thumb pressed against the corner of Thomas' lips. "I know you don't want to hurt me," he whispered, their noses lightly touching. "But you won't. No one ever will, again."

"No." Thomas swallowed. "I won't let them."

Jim made the same sound then that he had made the first time they kissed, a low, purring sound, and Thomas gasped shallowly into his mouth as that sound threatened to make him shudder all over. "And I won't be like him either," Jim insisted, his fingers dancing over the buttons of Thomas' shirt. "Like the man who hurt you."

Thomas breathed all the air out of his lungs. He had forgotten that he had ever mentioned Bill, but of course he should have expected Jim to take it to heart. "You're nothing like him," he promised.

"Then tell me what you want. You have to tell me, Charlie. I have to know." Jim sounded almost desperate. The shirt fell open and Jim's fingers — the fingers which could crack open a coconut and scrape it dry, that could clamber up a tree as quick as winking, that could undo a ship's knot one-handed in half a second — hovered over the fastenings to Thomas' trousers. "Say you don't want me and I'll stop," Jim said, very low. "Say it."

"I want… I…"

"Say it. Tell me."

"Jim…"

"*Please.*"

Thomas swallowed hard and closed his eyes. If he refused now… it would not just be tonight that he lost. It could very well be forever. The thought was unbearable. "I want… you," he managed, his voice coming thick and difficult, because never before had he been asked.

Jim kissed him then, hard, leaning into him, and Thomas' back hit the bed of leaves with a soft thump. "I know," Jim breathed, and shifted, his mouth going to taste Thomas' throat. Thomas threw up his arms, his fingers tangling into Jim's hair. It was soft and clean, no longer matted, no lice. It seemed so long since Pasco had hacked most of it off with a blunt kitchen knife.

Jim pulled back then, only long enough to start shedding some of his own clothes. Thomas watched in fascination as Jim's shirt was undone to reveal the old wound across his chest, a thick weal noticeably lighter in colour than the rest of his skin. Thomas traced it with his fingers and leaned up to press his lips to it, feeling the skin ripple under his lips as Jim shuddered. "It healed well," he murmured, and drew Jim's face closer to run his thumb over the other, the much thinner mark that was so dangerously close to his right eye. "I'm sorry it left a scar," he whispered. "I never wanted that."

"I don't mind it," Jim replied, letting the shirt hang open as he touched Thomas' face in turn, tracing a similar mark that ran through his freckles. "Besides, we're still matching. Yours healed slowly for such a small scratch," he noted, with a frown.

"Yes, I had a horrible infection," Thomas admitted, trying not to revisit the ship's hospital in his mind. Even Smythe had thought he was going to die of the fever before anything else. "It was somehow almost worse than the filthy blade that went all the way through me."

Jim hissed between his teeth and pushed Thomas' shirt aside to run his fingers over the deep scar left by Briggs' stolen sword. "I thought he'd killed you," Jim growled. "I thought…"

"Hush." Thomas drew him down into the leaves. "He's gone, and good riddance. God must truly not hate men like us, for here we both are, and that… *cunt* is burning in hell."

Jim laughed, shakily. "Why, Lieutenant Thomas," he said, blue eyes sparkling. "I am surprised you even know such a word."

"I've been keeping bad company." He reached for Jim's riding trousers, and looked back up at him for confirmation. Jim nodded wordlessly. Thomas drew them down. His mouth watered to see Jim's cock at last; long and thick and pink, much more pro-portional to the body he had now than the skinny beast he'd been on the island. But he was only risen halfway, despite all his bold talk, and Thomas thought he knew why. "Have you… ever done this?" Thomas asked, forcing himself to speak. If he could do the deed, he ought to be able to say the words, gentleman or no. "To enjoy it, I mean?"

Jim slowly shook his head. "I watched,' he said, his voice faintly hoarse. "In Mrs Grey's. Women and… men, sometimes. I know how. I know it should be, but I never wanted…" he faltered, his teeth sinking into the soft flesh of his bottom lip.

Thomas reached out with his fingers and pulled the lip free before kissing it, softly, tenderly. "Tell me to stop," he murmured.

"No," Jim said, with fervour. "Please…"

Thomas took Jim's cock in his hand, watched Jim clench his jaw. "Tell me to stop."

"*No*. Don't stop. Charlie…"

Thomas stroked with his hand, slow, careful, until he saw Jim's lips part at last and his head loll slightly forward as he surrendered to his own desire, as the tension left his shoulders. All Thomas needed to see to know that Jim trusted him. He ducked his head, ignoring the insistent strains of his own body singing out for more; it could wait.

"*Charlie*." Jim gasped as Thomas took the tip of his cock into his mouth. God, he loved hearing it. He pulled Jim's trousers even further down, letting his knees fall apart. A leaf fluttered upwards and away in the resulting rush of air, and he let his tongue dart out, tasting Jim, tasting him from the sea-salt tip to the heady place at the apex of his thighs. Jim hardened under Thomas' tongue, and when Thomas looked up at him he was looking right back, mouth open and panting, blue eyes gone dark with lust. Thomas deliberately kept his eyes on Jim's face as he opened his mouth and let Jim's length slide in between his lips. Jim moaned, watching him, feeling him, and Thomas ducked his head and swallowed him properly, coaxing him all the rest of the way until, when he finally let go, Jim's full hardness sprang back against his stomach.

"*Fuck*," Jim exclaimed, dragging Thomas back up to him. The kiss that followed made Thomas' head spin as Jim claimed his mouth, his teeth tugging almost painfully at Thomas' lips.

"Jim," Thomas breathed, when they were forced to stop for air. "Will you... I want..." He swallowed. "I want you inside me," he managed finally, his face flushing.

Jim's red lips parted. "Are you..."

"Yes. I can show you how. It won't hurt me, I promise."

Jim bit his lip for a moment before he nodded, smiling shyly. Thomas dragged him back; another kiss, another promise. "Let me take you to bed," Thomas said finally, throwing all caution to the winds. "We can be quiet, no one will hear —"

"I hate the beds in that house," Jim breathed against his lips, his prick pressed up against Thomas' thigh. "They're too big, too soft... I can't sleep in them."

"Where do you sleep, then?" Thomas asked, incredulously, his hair gone loose with their frantic undressing and fallen around his face like a halo.

Jim smirked. "The stables. In the loft. I get up before the servants so they won't catch me."

Thomas sighed at him despite his pounding heart and aching cock. "That is *not* gentlemanly behaviour," he chided gently.

"And this is?" Jim heaved up, rolling Thomas onto his back and pinning him there with both hands on his biceps. The forest floor was rough under Thomas' back, but not unpleasantly so. "I don't want to stop now," Jim begged, pressing his lips to the underside of Thomas' jaw. Thomas hissed, every touch making him burn all over, his cock straining impatiently against his smallclothes. "I've waited months, and I don't want to have to be quiet."

"Jim —" Thomas swallowed. "I won't say no, but there are things… ways to make it easier, that would be —"

Jim grinned and sat back, and Thomas stared at him as he dug around in the inner pockets of his discarded coat and pulled something out. It was a tiny glass jar, the kind one might use for tobacco, or cloves, but it was half-filled with something yellow and viscous. "Olive oil," Jim confirmed, laughing at the expression on Thomas' face. "Stole it from the kitchen."

"Why you…" Thomas was dumbfounded. "You… *pirate.*"

Jim laughed again, and the sound made Thomas shudder with something quite new and strange. "I told you," Jim said, those deft fingers finally going to tug apart the laces on Thomas' trousers. "Men shared beds sometimes; Mrs Gray never complained, and they left the doors open half the time. I couldn't *help* but watch."

"In a brothel," Thomas growled, his hips arching into Jim's hands despite the very real scandal he felt at the idea that this whole affair had not been nearly so spontaneous as he had imagined. "I warn you now that if you attempt to pay me I shall not be amused."

"I could afford you now, though. Anything you want, if you stay."

"*Jim.*" Thomas smiled faintly, despite himself. "I don't suppose you thought to bring a blanket, as well."

"We have our coats."

"Which may already never be the same again. They need to be hung up, not thrown down and defiled."

Jim hesitated, his face faltering a little. "We don't… if you don't want to… I'm sorry, I didn't think."

Thomas caught his mouth before he could say more. "I don't care," he murmured against Jim's lips. "I want you now. But I intend to get you accustomed to doing this in bed, when we have time."

Jim's eyes flashed, full of hope. "Will we have time?"

Thomas reached up and held his face, gazed into his eyes, the eyes that had caught him from that first moment in the bowels of the *Courage* and never let go. "Yes. We will have time."

They undressed the rest of the way, tossing their boots, trousers and smallclothes aside. They piled the coats and shirts atop the bed of leaves and Thomas lay back as Jim dared to touch him, to explore his nakedness. He kissed the freckles on Thomas' shoulders and caressed his erection with a kind of fascination, brushing his fingertips against the gold-coloured curls that framed Thomas' cock. 'It looks bigger, close up," he said, making Thomas choke and lift on his elbows.

"Explain that."

"I saw you naked before."

"*When*?"

"In the cove, when you were bathing. I was supposed to be catching fish, but I was watching."

Thomas groaned. "Why am I not surprised?"

Jim's smile widened. "Pirate."

"Indeed." Thomas reached for him in turn and Jim flushed, his skin hot to the touch despite the dying rays of the sun over the distant horizon.

"Say it again," Jim breathed, pressing against him, his lips brushing the scar on Thomas' cheek.

"I want you."

"Again."

"Fuck me, Jim." Thomas smiled wickedly, feeling lightheaded and free despite the tugging at his side where the sword wound ached. Jim purred again, his hand going for the bottle. An island tiger in an English forest. Thomas knew he should urge caution, show Jim how to make it last, how to prepare him best, but his own impatience was tantamount. Besides, he couldn't count the number of times he and Bill had made it work aboard ship with nothing but spit and sweat. He could take it. He wanted it more than anything.

He guided Jim's hand, hissing through his teeth at the sensation of those nimble fingers inside him. He hadn't realised how it would feel after so long. Jim was gentle, almost gentler than Thomas could stand. "Jim, please," he moaned, his whole body arching against the ground towards him, their legs tangled together. "*Please.*" In his frenzy he knocked over the bottle so that most of the oil ran into the ground; he took the rest and stroked Jim's cock with it, *once, twice,* making the blue-eyed lordling gasp and groan with pleasure. "Now," Thomas begged, lifting his knees.

Jim shifted, breathing hard. Thomas could feel his hardness brushing up against his own. "Jim," he murmured, sensing hesitation. Jim looked up at him, eyes wide. Thomas opened his mouth to reassure him again, but thought better of it. There had been too many words already, for a man who had barely spoken since the age of ten. Far too many. Instead, he raised his shoulders off the ground and threaded his fingers into Jim's hair, drawing him down, and kissed his mouth; long and slow and deep. He was sure he imagined it, but somehow Jim still tasted like the sea.

Jim's cock slid inside him then, and Thomas was glad at last that he hadn't insisted on going back to the house, because there was no way he could ever have stopped the cry that burst from his lips at that moment. Jim panted silently, shuddering, his oiled fingers digging into Thomas' thighs. There was a long moment where they just hovered for a moment as one, hot breath misting on bare skin.

"Oh my god," Thomas breathed, practically whimpering. It was blasphemy, but that ship had, he reasoned, already sailed a long time ago. Jim moved, shifted inside him, and Thomas' head fell back. He tried to bite the back of his own wrist, to swallow his sounds, but Jim growled with wordless dissatisfaction and tugged his arm free. Jim wanted to hear him, Thomas realised, and there were no cabins, no hammocks swinging feet away, no curious ears trained on them. No reason to hold back.

"Jim," he moaned, as his pirate began pressing into him; slowly, tenderly. Thomas braced one hand against Jim's firm, muscled, scarred shoulder, the other going to dig into the thicker flesh behind his hip, echoing his movement. "Yes... Jim. More. More, please."

Jim shuddered at the words, strands of dark hair sticking to his forehead with sweat despite the sun having quite vanished beyond the horizon by now. His lips parted, and he had to try twice before the words came: "Y-your… your side…"

"Fuck my side," Thomas groaned.

Jim huffed out a breathy kind of laugh, his knees shifting against the bed of coats as he moved. "Now who's talking like a pirate?"

"I can take it. I need… *please*, Jim. I need you. *All of you.* Please."

Jim's eyes darkened to almost black. The next thing Thomas knew, the careful, slow movements had given way to deep, forceful thrusting. Thomas moaned, open-mouthed, every pounding stroke forcing a low cry from his mouth. He could feel Jim's thighs flexing, muscles tightening with every plunge, and hear every smack of flesh as loud as gunshots in his ears. He closed his eyes tight for a moment, and when he opened them again he could see stars coming out through the trees above. This was not just fucking, which he knew of; this was something he had never before experienced. To be truly one with a man he would give his life for. Whom he almost had.

"Charlie." Jim moaned and dug his fingers even harder into Thomas' flesh. "It's… so…"

"Don't stop," Thomas breathed, his heart pounding madly and his cock aching hard against his stomach as Jim sent waves of pleasure crashing over him again and again. He raised his hips further still, his face twisting into an expression of ecstasy despite the growing burning pain in his torso. The pain was just another reminder that he was alive. That *they* were alive. "Harder. *Harder…*"

Jim growled in the back of his throat, wild and animal-like. His palm took hold of Thomas' shoulder and pinned him down to the ground again. Thomas gasped, feeling himself tighten instinctively around Jim's cock in response. The next time Jim slammed into him, Thomas howled and swore aloud, a string of words he had never spoken before and would have blushed to hear under any other circumstances. "*Jim —*"

Jim cried out, no words, just a low, joyous noise, and Thomas felt it as his pirate finally spent himself inside him, shuddering all over. Thomas reached for his own leaking cock; Jim pushed his hand away and took it himself. One jerking stroke was enough to make Thomas gasp and come apart, his whole body trembling with the intensity of it. "Jim —" he gasped, in the split second before their mouths met once more, Jim's sweat dripping onto his face as they kissed, deeply, tenderly.

The cold night crept in as they clung to each other, skin against skin, until Jim had caught his breath enough to roll off of Thomas onto the makeshift pallet beside him. In the fading ecstasy of his release, Thomas thought vaguely that the coats would absolutely be ruined. He hoped they would not be forced to explain their loss to Mrs Oliver. Jim gazed up at the sky, breathing heavily. "Charlie… that was… I never…"

"I know," Thomas murmured. "Nor I. You need not say."

Jim turned his head, beaming. Thomas winced a little, settling into a position that he hoped would ease the aching in his side.

"Are you well?" Jim asked. "Did I hurt you?"

"It'll pass," Thomas said, smiling. "I have never been so well in my life."

For a while they lay there together, gazing out at dusk falling over the countryside, listening to the sounds of the evening forest around them. They had put back on their trousers and shirts, loose, for comfort and warmth. Thomas' heart had slowed back into its natural rhythm; he realised he was quite absurdly happy, despite the inherent danger they put themselves in even now by lying side by side. He had not realised how afraid he had been that he would have to pretend to be a friend — or less than a friend, only a passing influence on Jim's life. He ran his fingers once more over Jim's scar, thinking that he ought to let Mr Smythe know how well it had healed, if there were any way of doing so without inviting uncomfortable questions about how exactly he knew.

"Why do you want to go to London?" he asked eventually, his voice sounding over-loud in the surrounding quiet of the forest.

"I… I'm not sure." Jim frowned up at the stars. "I shan't be a country gentleman for the rest of my life, no matter how much money I have, or I *shall* go mad. I thought… well, when I was in the city waiting for mother to arrive, after they sent her word… I saw little children on the streets. So many of them. So many boys, younger even than I was when I went to sea, and even some girls. No one else seemed to notice them, and they all looked so hungry, and I wanted… I don't know if there is anything I could do, but if there was, I need to do it. I suppose I thought I could work that part out once I got there. I expect I can't just stand in the street and hand out money."

Thomas laughed, though he didn't think he had meant it as a joke. "No, you would be knifed to death within hours, I expect, and your purse stolen."

"Well, I wouldn't mind the purse, really. I have more coin now than I know what to do with, once Mother is taken care of." A sigh. "I don't mean to be foolish, only it's all I can think about."

"Well," Thomas said, speaking his thoughts aloud. "It isn't as though you are talentless. No, don't scoff at me," he chided, when Jim made a dismissive noise and rolled his eyes. "Your skills are those that any city boy would love to have — climbing, swimming, fishing, hunting…"

Jim turned his head to stare at him, incredulous. "You think I should teach them to fish with spears?"

"You taught Pasco, and he kept himself and Cole alive for a week. And you taught him to move silently through a forest in just a matter of hours. That story is sure to inspire any snotty little guttersnipe who hears it. You could establish some kind of boarding house, perhaps, and help them to find employment where they are best suited — in the country, probably," he said, thinking aloud. "Or the navy," he added, smiling ruefully. "For the best ones."

Jim chuckled at this, but did not argue with the merits of the idea. For a while he was quietly thoughtful. He leant against Thomas' shoulder, and instinctively Thomas folded his arm around him. It was warm and surprisingly comfortable in the leaf-lined hollow, though privately Thomas thought he'd rather had enough of sitting on the ground to last him a lifetime.

"I am only glad you aren't in prison," Jim said after a while. "I don't know how they even thought to try it."

"The *Courage* was wrecked under my command," Thomas replied, unable to keep sorrow out of his voice as he recalled that night yet again. He knew in his heart that there was nothing he could have done, save perhaps for killing all the pirates before they could do the same damage, which Wickerham had not ordered and would not have allowed. And besides, then he would have killed Jim, instead, without ever knowing him. That thought made him sick to his stomach. But he would never forget the *Courage,* and if he ever forgave himself for losing her it would be a long time in coming. If they had not stripped him of his rank and struck him from the service, he would have quit it himself, and he had no intention of sailing again, even privately. That part of his life was over forever. Besides, he found that after the island he had quite lost all taste for the military life; he would be quite happy if he never had to see blood again.

"You saved my life," Jim said, soft. "You brought me home."

"You saved mine a dozen times over," Thomas pointed out. "Not that I approve in the least of keeping score, of course."

"Oh yes, I know." Jim shifted his body a little to bring them closer, sighing with contentment.

"There's something I've wanted to ask you," Thomas said, low, after a while.

"I thought there might be."

"When I asked you, on the island, if I owed you my life, you told me that our debts were equally paid. I never understood why. I had treated you rather badly up until that point, I thought, and you were forever keeping me from getting killed, as though you made a pastime out of it."

Jim chuckled at that, and Thomas felt a rush of warmth in his stomach at the sound. He had to wait a long time for the answer, occupying himself by trying to memorise the minute detail of Jim's scar, committing it to memory. Jim still, he thought, took a little extra time when working out what he would say, particularly if it were especially important, and he had to be patient for his sake.

"You saved me from drowning tied to that bed, back on the ship," Jim said, finally, as though he were telling a story he had not really been a part of, detached. "And then again from Babber. I don't even know why he grabbed me; maybe he thought he was going to die and wanted to take me with him."

Thomas shuddered. "And in return you carried me out of the water," he said, low. "And you drew them away, keeping them from finding me on the shore."

"Well… it wasn't just out of thanks, you know," Jim pointed out. "I needed your help. You couldn't help me if you were dead."

"And the third instance?" He couldn't think of another time he had rescued Jim from any situation he could not have saved himself from; instead he had taken him prisoner and used his abilities to his advantage. "The one that paid for you rescuing me from Yellow-Eyes on the cliff?"

"I… it's hard to explain."

"Try. Please."

Another long pause, and Thomas found himself trying to quieten his own breathing to give him space to speak.

"You… reminded me who I am," Jim said finally, soft. "Not my name, or my history, I never really forgot that. You made me remember the part I *had* forgotten. The part that made me James Oliver's son. I think I would have rather died knowing that, than living the rest of my life as just mad Jim."

"You were never really mad Jim," Thomas said, low. "And even if you were…" He trailed off, drifting for a moment in his own thoughts.

Jim turned his face to look up at him, blue eyes shining. "Oh? What were you going to say?"

"Enough," Thomas chuckled. "For someone who spent half his life as a mute, you talk enough now to drive the birds out of the trees."

"Not all the time. Sometimes I still forget, and I can't find any words at all. I know it upsets mother, but… it's difficult. It's easier with you."

Thomas couldn't help it, not when Jim was curled so neatly against him, not when he tilted his chin up so invitingly. He leaned towards him for another kiss, slower, deeper than before. Exploratory. Jim let out a soft, contented sound, and for a while that was all they did, sated and relaxed at last in each other's arms.

"Will I see you again soon?" Jim asked, after a while. "Will you come with me? To London, when I go?"

Thomas thought of his family's house. Half the rooms unused. Servants who barely spoke to him. He thought of Pasco, who had been sent home to his family in Spain; so young, yet so brave, and the way his face had lit up when Jim had only praised him. He imagined seeing that look on the faces of other children, children with no other chances. Seeing it reflected in Jim's eyes. "Yes," he said, breathless with it. "I'll come with you."

"Good." Jim sighed contentedly and returned his head to Thomas' shoulder, as though he might like to go to sleep, out here in the open forest, which probably he would prefer to any civilised accommodation. *My pirate.*

"Ought we go back?" Thomas asked, low. "Before your mother sends someone to search for us? It's getting quite dark."

"Not dark enough," Jim whispered. "A little longer."

Thomas let himself sink into the hollow between the roots of the trees, and his gaze wandered up through the leaves. The moon was high in the sky now, the low rush of wind through the branches sounding almost like the gentle swell of the sea. Jim's breathing evened out before long, and his hand went limp against Thomas' leg. Thomas stroked his hair, thinking what a shame it would be to wake him, and far above he watched the stars come out, their patterns a loving message to any English sailor who could read them. They said: *you have come home.*

CONTENT WARNINGS

This book contains the following themes which may be distressing to some readers:

- References to sexual abuse and grooming of a minor
- References to physical abuse and slavery of a minor in a historical context
- References to slavery, slave ships and the slave trade
- Rape threats
- Systemic and religious homophobia in a historical context
- Some ablist language (such as dumb, idiot, simple, etc.) in a historical context
- Explicit consensual sex
- Violence / fighting in a historical context
- Death or dying
- Gruesome injuries
- Blood

THE AUTHOR

Andy Neville was born in England and travelled around the world for a while as a child before finally settling in Melbourne, Australia where she lives with her Golden Retreiver, Finn. Her ultimate dream is a property in the country where she can write all day and adopt multiple dogs. An avid reader and writer from a young age, *Pirate's Parole* became her debut published novel in 2021. Her next project is *Laneways,* a series of stand-alone but connected modern LGBT Romance novels set in Melbourne.

For updates on future books follow @andy_neville on twitter or visit andynevilleauthor.com.